IRRESISTIBLE

LANDMARK MOUNTAIN
BOOK 3

WILLOW ASTER

Willow Aster
www.willowaster.com

Cover Design by Emily Wittig Designs
Photo: ©Regina Wamba
www.ReginaWamba.com
Map artwork by Kira Sabin
Editing by Christine Estevez

NOTE TO READERS

A list of content warnings are on the next page, so skip that page if you'd rather not see them.

CONTENT WARNINGS

The content warnings for *Irresistible* are a cheating ex, profanity, and a surprise pregnancy.

CHAPTER ONE

FIRST IMPRESSIONS

MARLOW

I've only been here for a few hours, but I already like Landmark Mountain. The mountains surrounding the quaint town are unlike anything I've ever seen, and from what I could tell when we were driving in earlier, everything about this place is cute, from the shops to the restaurants to the little park with an old caboose sitting near the swings.

But the only reason I'm here is Sofie. I have missed that

girl something fierce, and after hearing her talk about this place and Theo Landmark all these years and finally meeting Theo tonight, he proved that he's exactly the kind of person I'd hoped he'd be with my best friend.

And this town might be just as great as Sofie described it too.

After Sofie and I made the grueling drive from Texas to Colorado with Dakota, my four-year-old daughter, the last thing I want to do is get back in my SUV and drive to the little market I saw on the way into town. Dakota and I fell asleep for about an hour after dinner, but then I woke up and realized I was out of medicine for her fever. She's been sick for a few days and the doctor in Texas said it was a virus and to just keep her fever down. Sofie was on her way to bed when I came out of the bedroom and insisted I let her or Theo go to the store, but I didn't want to inter-fere with their time together. Sofie's got to be as tired as I am after making that drive with me, so I asked her to keep the monitor on in case Dakota woke up and said I'd hurry back.

I feel like I got hit by a cyclone, I'm so exhausted, but the night sky is gorgeous, the twinkle lights on the shops are idyllic, and there's something about being 777 miles away from my soon-to-be ex-husband that is downright exhil-arating.

If I'd been told yesterday that I'd be feeling so full of hope and optimism after finding Cash, my *husband*, in *our* bed with Maggie O'Leary, the girl who's been salivating after him for years, I never would've believed it.

It's crazy what distance and a new perspective can do.

I should've left Cash a long time ago. It didn't take distance or a new perspective for me to already know that much, but it's now clearer than ever that I should have never married him. Being away from him is already making me a helluva lot lighter.

My sunglasses fall out of the windshield shade and onto the floor as I turn into the parking lot of Cecil's, startling me. I jerk the wheel when I jump and the next thing I hear is a loud *bang* as the car jolts forward and back. I think I call on Jesus before cursing, but it's all so fast, I can't be sure which comes out first. My hands are shaking as I try to get my bearings and step out of the car.

The first thing I see is a tall guy in scrubs stalking toward me. He runs his hand through his thick hair, sending it into disarray that frankly makes him look even better than he already did.

No one should look this good.

But the rage on his face has me squaring my shoulders and bracing myself.

"What the hell was that?" He doesn't yell. It's more of a seething low growl. "I was *clearly* backing out."

"I'm so sorry. My sunglasses—" I start. But the way he's shaking his head and scowling at me sets me off. "You know what? It happens. You could've honked or something…"

"I could've honked? How could I possibly honk when you're plowing into my rear end?"

My lips twitch with his choice of words. I try to hold back the maniacal laughter that's threatening to burst out of me, but the way his eyes flare even hotter reels it in. I take a deep breath to say something calming, but he's just getting started.

"Of course this is how this day ends. It fucking figures," he mutters.

"Oh relax, it can't be that bad," I snap.

"*Can't be that bad*, she says." He brushes past me, scoffing as he goes.

Okay, now I'm annoyed.

"I'm so fucking done with this day," he says under his breath.

I roll my eyes and turn on the flashlight from my phone, shining it on the damage inflicted on his shiny Lexus.

"Okay." I exhale and try to keep from making a face. It's not great. "Well...it's a little dent and a pretty long scratch, but the good news is...I have insurance."

He waves his hands in front of him, eyebrows lifted, in what I interpret as a sarcastic *big whoop*.

"You know what?" My Southern accent kicks in a little more when I'm angry and tired, so it's turned *way* on right now. "I'm really sorry I hit your car, and as I've said, my insurance will take care of it. I don't see any reason why you have to be so rude about all of it, but you do you."

"You do you," he repeats, this time mimicking my drawl.

"Oh, you are so—" I shake my head.

"Move your car," he says.

"What?"

"Kindly. Move. Your. Car," he repeats slowly, as if speaking to a child.

I growl at him and his eyes widen like he's just daring me to argue.

"Don't we need to—" I start, but he just points at my vehicle.

I grit my teeth, turn around, and get in, carefully backing up before parking a few spaces down from him. When I turn the engine off, I fan my face and take a few deep breaths before getting back out. I'm not going to let this arrogant jerk ruin the little bit of Zen I had going on.

I grab my wallet and step out, and when I turn to walk in his direction, I keep turning because not only is his car no longer where it was—it's not even in the parking lot.

Unbelievable.

I'm in such shock and more than a little wilted from that encounter that I almost forget to go inside the store and grab the medicine, but I do and head back to the house, driving more carefully this time, sunglasses tucked away safely in my purse.

I'm still fuming as I lie next to Dakota, listening to her stuffy nose as she sleeps. I wanted to do right by that guy and get his car fixed, but the last thing I need is for my insurance to go up.

So, I'll take it as a gift that I'm off the hook. It's a relief that I won't have to deal with him again. It's just a shame that those exceptionally good looks are wasted on such a jerk.

CHAPTER TWO

EYES WIDE OPEN

WYATT

"Hey, Dr. Wyatt, how are you today?" Linda asks as I'm passing the nurses' station.

I give her a pained smile. "Okay. How about you? I was hoping you took the day off."

"I can't stop thinking about that little boy," she says. "I'm just coming on now—Amelia needed me to cover her shift."

Linda was with me yesterday when we lost a patient.

A six-year-old boy from Ohio was on a road trip with his family. He fell from seven or eight feet and hit his head on a rock. By the time we were rolling him into the ER, we were losing him, but we kept working on him for almost another half hour. Telling his family that he didn't make it was the saddest thing I've ever done and I've had some hard days since becoming a doctor at Pine Community Hospital.

"Neither one of us should be here today," Linda says.

I nod. "You're right about that. But it's what we do. Yesterday was one of the worst days I've had here," I admit. "And then when I left, I got rear-ended...decided I should get home before anything else went wrong."

"No way," she says, her eyes full of concern. "Ugh, are you okay?"

"I'm fine." I wave her off.

"Is your car okay? Do you need me to have Bill look at it?"

"It's not great. Yeah, I think I'll definitely need Bill to take a look if he can fit me in." I start walking toward the room of my next patient, calling back to Linda. "Tourist girl wasn't paying attention. Dented the rear and left a long scratch. Whole thing was stupid."

She sighs and shakes her head and I lift my shoulder like *what can you do?*

I pause outside the cracked door and quickly take a look at the chart. Four-year-old little girl with an ongoing fever and congestion. Negative strep and flu tests as of a couple days ago. I try to shake my mood and smile before I knock on the door, walking in with a cheerful, "Hello, I'm Dr. Wyatt Landmark, you can call me Dr. Wyatt—"

I quickly close my gaping mouth, looking from the little girl in the room to the angry face of the woman who hit my car last night.

Tourist girl in the flesh.

I was right that she's not from around here. I know everyone in Landmark and a lot of the recurring tourists that come to our small ski town, and I would've remembered seeing this woman.

In the light of day and with some of the trauma of yesterday behind me, I notice a lot more than I did then. Her long blonde hair falls past her slim shoulders and stunning tits, and she has the most expressive—somewhere between venomous and curious at the moment—hazel eyes and full pink lips. The little girl looks like the woman's mini-me but with dark brown eyes and lighter hair. She's wearing a *Beauty and the Beast* nightgown and her cheeks are rosy, her eyes glazed with signs of a fever. Between growing up with a little sister and treating enough little girls, the Disney princesses and I are on a first-name basis.

The two of them look exhausted, dark circles under their eyes and hair going everywhere. I feel a little bad for all that hostility I shot her way last night. I don't care much about my damn car, even though Bill stays so busy with auto repair here in town that it could take a shit-ton of time before it's fixed.

For a brief moment, I want to scoop these two up and tuck them under the covers, let them both rest a while.

But when the woman's eyes narrow on me and she stands up, her petite frame defiant in front of me, I remember how lippy she was and I'm back to being annoyed.

It has been a *rough* twenty-four hours.

"*You're* Dr. Wyatt?" she says. "Great. Just great." She leans her head back and grips the bridge of her nose between two fingers. "You are the last person I want to see right now."

"Excuse me?"

"You heard me," she says, leaning in so only I can hear. "My little girl is sick, and I don't care who you are, I'm not gonna have some rude, egotistical bast—" She pauses and looks back at her daughter, who is sleepily watching us as she clutches her pink blanket. "Can we please see another doctor?"

Her accent really works for her. It's both endearing and maddening.

"Are you hearing me?" She props her hand on her hip and her eyes flash at me.

"Believe me, I'd hand you off to Dr. Langley or Dr. Brady if I could, but it looks like your little girl needs someone to see her right now, not in the hour it'll take for them to get to her."

She blinks, her chest rising and falling. She takes one last deep breath and holds up her hand. "Okay, fine."

She steps back and her next words are louder and injected with a lot more warmth than I know she's feeling. For her daughter's sake, I'm sure. She's *good*.

"Uh, I'm Marlow Hennessy and this is my daughter, Dakota. She's been sick for a couple of days and the fever just won't go away," Marlow says.

Marlow.

I did wonder what her name was as I drove home last night. She looks like a Marlow. Sexy as all hell and tenacious, ready to take on whatever she has to, whether she feels like it or not.

I clear my throat and try to get my wayward thoughts under control. Putting all my focus on the little girl, which is what I should've been doing in the first place, I smile at her and mentally reset.

"Hi, Dakota. I hear you're not feeling so well."

She shakes her head and sniffles. I sit down and face her.

"Would you mind saying *ahh* and I'll take a look at your throat? Are you hiding Belle in there?"

Her eyes light up and she giggles.

"No," she says before opening her mouth wide.

I study her throat and it's red but doesn't look too bad. "You're right. No Belle in your throat." I feel the sides of her neck and grin. "Not here either. Let's see if you swallowed any of her books." I hold up my stethoscope and listen to her heartbeat and it sounds steady, no fluid in the lungs. "Whew, I'm glad you didn't swallow Belle's books. That'd be sad."

"I'd *never* swallow books," she says, laughing.

Marlow smiles at Dakota and squeezes her hand.

I pretend to wipe the sweat off of my brow in relief.

"One more place to check." I pick up the otoscope and show it to Dakota. She studies it carefully. "I'd like to take a look in your ears if you don't mind."

She nods and glances at her mom, smiling. I make the mistake of looking at her mom too, and Marlow's eyes are also lit up, as she smiles the sweetest smile at her little girl. When she looks at me, her eyes are open and vulnerable. I blink and nearly drop the otoscope, and it so fully and completely fucks me up, I nearly leave the room to see if Emma can take over.

Which is exactly what I should've done as soon as I walked in and saw this honey-blonde siren.

Something flashes across the otoscope and I glance up, seeing the wedding ring on Marlow's ring finger.

I'm not sure why I never considered who this woman might be attached to, but fortunately, it's not my problem.

The woman is walking chaos and it's clearly someone else's mess.

Dakota sniffles and fuck me, I'd fire myself right now if I could. I've never been so distracted with a patient.

"I'll just turn you this way and take a look," I tell her.

Once I see the inside of her ear, it's obvious what's going on with her.

"Oh, that's a nasty ear infection."

I can barely make eye contact with Marlow now, but I can tell from the way her breath staggers and her feet shift anxiously that she's alarmed.

"Her ears were just checked a couple days ago," she says.

I look in the other ear and wince. "Both sides. And this side looks like it's been going on for a while."

"Oh God, her doctor looked at her ears and completely missed it," Marlow says, her voice close to tears.

I write a prescription on my tablet and hand it to her. "Start her on this tonight and give her the full course of antibiotics even if she starts feeling better. Once she's done in ten days, it'd be good if you got her in to see her pediatrician."

"I just moved here. We don't have one yet. Can you recommend anyone?"

"Where did you take her a few days ago?" I ask. "*Not* there."

I am striking out on professionalism right and left.

She frowns. "To her doctor in Texas...who *obviously* didn't do a good job."

Guilt stirs in my gut, but I have to do my due diligence when I'm dealing with a patient. She brought her daughter in now and I'm pretty sure I believe her when she says she took Dakota somewhere else a couple days ago. Someone who didn't try to take care of their daughter wouldn't be about to cry right now, and the fact that Dakota is cuddled up to her mom like she's her whole world is another good sign that this little girl isn't being mistreated.

It's sad that we're trained to think this way, but I'd rather be suspicious than let any neglect slide through the cracks on my watch.

"Dr. Langley is great. Dr. Brady is too. If you're not able to get an appointment with either of them and Dakota is still sick, you can always bring her into the ER again and one of us will take a look."

"Are you a pediatrician or an ER doctor only?"

"I'm a family physician and we all rotate shifts in the ER."

"So we might have to see you here again too…"

I resent the way she says that, even though I know it's for the best. We got off to the wrong start and there doesn't seem to be hope of that changing.

But the way she's pushing to get her daughter seen again is another check in the positive column for Marlow. I have no doubt now that despite the state of Dakota's ears, her mom is a good one.

"I'll do my best to make sure you're seen by Dr. Emma Langley," I say abruptly, standing up and putting the otoscope in place on the table. "I'll send Amelia back in to go over the prescription with you and the options for getting it filled. Bye, Dakota." I wave at her and she waves back, leaning into her mom's side.

Emma Langley or James Brady will have to take Dakota as a patient because I'll be staying as far away from this Marlow woman as possible.

"Wait," Marlow calls after me. "What about your car?"

I sigh and she shifts her feet, her cheeks splotchy with anger.

"Leave your number and I'll be in touch," I grumble.

I leave the room feeling like I've been tossed in the dryer on high.

CHAPTER THREE

IMPACT

MARLOW

I feel eyes on me and try not to smile, pretending to be asleep for a few minutes longer.

The exhaustion is bone-deep from the past few days.

It's been a hard week, to put it mildly.

And to top it off, Dr. Wyatt Landmark.

What are the chances that the guy I had that weird and awful interaction over the fender-bender with would be

Theo's brother, Wyatt? And then it just got worse when we saw him in the ER. Before I met Wyatt, I was expecting him to be as charming as his brother.

Theo has been incredibly kind and generous since we invaded his home a couple nights ago. The fact that Sofie has loved Theo and his family all her life made me believe I was in safe hands when I heard Dr. Wyatt would be seeing us at Pine Community.

And he *was* incredible with Dakota.

That's all that matters, I guess.

It was just strange. He diagnosed her with a double ear infection, which made me sick to my stomach because Dr. Johnson, her pediatrician back home, missed it, and my girl's been suffering. But with me, Dr. Wyatt has been nothing but cold and rude, and he acted like he couldn't get out of the room fast enough. He even went so far as to make it clear that I should go to someone else in the future, which is fine by me. I don't want to run into him again.

After the humiliating week I've had, I don't know why his assholery even registered on my hurt scale, but it's been on a continuous loop with the rest of the grievances piled on me right now.

"Mama, are you asleep?" Dakota whispers, her fingers prying one of my eyelids open.

I snort out a laugh and she jumps back, startled but smiling when I open my eyes.

"You *are* awake!" she says happily.

"You must be feeling lots better," I say, laughing.

I pull her close to me and she cuddles in, her arm draping over my stomach.

"I'm all better," she says, her voice still nasally from congestion.

"You're a trooper is what you are. Are you sure we're awake enough to get up yet? We could sleep a little longer..." I run my fingers through her hair the way she likes me to when she's falling asleep.

"Auntie Sof is probably worried about me. I should tell her I'm better."

"You're right. We should get another dose of antibiotics in you too, so you'll feel even *better*."

"Hey, Mama, why did Miss Maggie have her nibbles out?" she asks, her head popping up to look at me.

And I guess we're doing this.

At first I'd hoped that Dakota's fever was too high and she wouldn't remember seeing her dad in bed with another woman, but unfortunately, when Cash jumped up mid-coitus interruptus and Maggie's bare chest and "nibbles" were on display, it made a lasting impression on Dakota. This isn't the first time she's brought up Maggie's nipples, and I doubt it will be the last. Before, I brushed it away because she was sick and told her we would discuss it when she was feeling better.

"And why did he yell at us to get out?" Her voice is tentative and I close my eyes, counting to ten until my rage at her father dims just enough to speak.

It's actually a good thing Cash yelled at us. It jarred me enough to bolt out of that room. I'm not sure how long I was stuck staring at the two of them.

Too long, since Dakota saw them.

I'd been so intent on getting back in bed after a sleepless night with Dakota that I hadn't even registered the clothes in the hallway leading the way into the bedroom. Cash, being the clueless bastard he is, probably had no idea Dakota was even sick since he slept soundly all night long. On a normal day, Dakota would've been at preschool and I would've been at my temp receptionist job already.

"They were doing something they shouldn't be doing... with each other, and Daddy didn't want us to see that," I eventually get out.

What is the right thing to say to your little girl when something like this happens? I'm at a total loss.

Maggie hadn't bothered to cover anything up. She just sat there brazenly, as if daring me...to what, I don't know. But I guess she finally got what she wanted. My husband.

Cash has worked for Maggie's dad for a long time. It's the same ranch where Sofie worked, and I met all three of them when I took riding lessons there. When Sofie and I became friends, she warned me that Cash was a player, but I didn't listen. I don't know when I started compartmentalizing all the times I saw him flirting with other women. He made me feel like I was imagining it or that it was just him being friendly.

That good ol' boy with the Southern charm and the flashy smile worked me over and the next thing I knew, I was a floppin' fish snared with a lure. He caught me and as much as I've struggled, he's been slow to let me go.

By the time I got pregnant with Dakota and we got married right before I had her, I had so many reservations, but I tucked them away, hoping he would realize what a good woman he had right here.

I suspect he was cheating while I was pregnant, but I've never been able to prove it. And for a while now, he's been drinking and staying out with his friends, which has made me wonder all over again, but I've been in survival mode. I work, take care of Dakota, pay the bills, and repeat. I've never known what it's like to be happy in a relationship, so I've just been doing what I have to do to get by.

We haven't had sex in so long that I don't even know when the last time was. A year, maybe longer. I haven't wanted him to touch me when he can't even come home at night to see his daughter, smells like a bar when he does come home, and never makes an effort to know how either one of us is doing, but complains all the time about me not being in the mood.

I've thought about leaving him so many times. But more than wondering if he's cheating, or the way he treats me, it's the way he barely acknowledges Dakota that gets to me.

When we first had her, he'd say he wasn't good with babies, so I kept thinking at some point, he'd get better with her, but she's four now and the two of them still haven't bonded.

"I like it here," Dakota says, bringing me back to the present.

"You do? You've been so sick I haven't been sure if you'd even noticed where we are yet."

"I missed Auntie Sof."

"I did too. So much. I like it here too," I whisper.

Sofie has been telling us stories about Landmark for so long I feel like I've already been here. Despite the horrific things that happened to her when she lived here before, she always dreamed of coming back. And those months without her in Texas just reminded me of how alone I really was without her.

No more.

I'll have to find a job and a place to live and file for divorce, but for the first time in a long time, I feel hopeful. And Cash has been trying to reach me since I left Texas, but not as much as I thought he would.

I think he knows we've reached our expiration date.

My only hope is that I've left in time to keep my little girl from being scarred any further from any of this.

Despite the run-ins (literally and figuratively) with Wyatt, it's only been a positive experience since I got here. If I can just keep my distance from that broody jerk, I'll be fine, but I have a feeling it's hard to avoid anyone in this town...especially Wyatt Landmark.

CHAPTER FOUR

SMELLS AND SWEETS

WYATT

After working on the new stables at Theo's place all morning, I volunteer to check on the horses so Sofie can oversee everything else.

My brother is building new stables for his love and her horses, and the whole town has come out to help at some time or another. At least that's how it feels—it was getting a bit crowded with everyone trying to be helpful. Not to mention, I still haven't recovered from learning that Marlow is the best friend from Texas that Sofie has told us about.

On my way to the pasture, I run into Grinny.

"You heading out?"

"I am. I'm worn out. And I'm missing you, my boy," Grinny says. "You working too hard?"

"Trying not to, but you know...seems like I do anyway."

She leans up to kiss my cheek. "Don't forget you need to rest too." She pats my chest and chuckles. "How do you manage to stay so pristine even while working outside?"

I grin and shrug. "Someone taught me to take care of myself and my things."

"You give me far more credit than I deserve," she says, laughing.

"Not possible," I tell her and I mean it.

Grinny is more than my grandmother; she's the reason I survived my childhood. When our parents died in a car accident, Grinny raised five grandkids while Granddad ran the Landmark Mountain Lodge and Ski Resort, and she never once made it seem like anything but her joy to do so, even during her own grief.

"Well, I'm glad I have you fooled." She grins. "Call me. We can at least fit in one of our Happy Cow runs or something."

"I will. Love you."

"I love you," she says, smiling at me one more time before heading to her car.

I walk the rest of the way to where Sofie's five horses are grazing and am petting Lady when I hear a little voice behind me.

"Is it okay if I pet the horses too?"

I turn and see Dakota standing there. Her eyes wide

and her smile bright enough to compete with the sun. She's so stinking cute.

"It sure is, but it's important that you always check first with an adult just like you did."

She nods. "Sofie says I'm not ready to be with them by myself yet."

I point to Sofie's newest rescue. "Did she tell you to be careful around Fiona? We're giving her a little time, so let's not get too close to her. These guys though—they're greedy for someone to pet them."

"Yep. She said that. But I don't know what's the matter with Fiona," she says as she steps next to me and pets Lady.

"She's shy and afraid. We're not sure what she went through before she came to live with Sofie."

"What do you think she went through?" she asks, eyes widening again.

"I'm not sure. I think maybe her owner didn't know how to take good care of her."

"My daddy takes care of horses. He's with them always," she says. "Every day, every night..."

"He must love horses," I say.

"Mama thought I was sleepin', but I was sneakin' to the kitchen for a cookie." She looks at me, her face solemn, like she's telling me a big secret. "I was 'sposed to be in bed," she whispers.

"Oh." I nod, unsure of where this is going.

"She said, 'You spend more time with those horses than you do your daughter.' And he said, 'Because horses don't talk as much as you and Kota do.'" She looks up at me with those huge brown eyes and I melt. "Do I talk a lot, Dr. Wyatt?"

I'm too busy cursing her dad out in my mind to answer right away. I bend down and get at her eye level.

"You talk just the right amount," I tell her.

She grins and surprises me by wrapping her arms around me in a huge hug. It's over before it can even fully register because Lady snorts and Dakota rears back and stares at the horse and then me before laughing her little head off.

"I think she sprayed snot on me," she says, wiping her arms.

Her nose crinkles, but she's still laughing and now I am too.

"Yuck," she says.

Lady does it again and I feel a little mist on my face.

"Yuck," I agree.

She wipes her arms so hard that she falls down.

"Oh no, wait, hang on a second, you're dangerously close to"—I try to stop her before it's too late—"manure."

Her hands land in a big pile of shit and she lets out a warbled moan and cry before she looks at me in horror.

"I didn't...what do I—" she says, looking like she might cry.

"It's okay, Sweets. Here, let me help you up." I try to school my grossed-out face.

I deal with messes all day long, it's one of the reasons I like my house and car and everything else around me to be meticulous the rest of the time, so what's a little horse shit?

But Dakota looks like she might panic. She's struggling to get up, too stunned by the atrocity on her hands.

I tug her up from her elbows and we're doing good until she almost slips again and she reaches out, clutching me hard, her hands smearing shit all over my sleeves.

If Grinny could see me now.

Dakota gasps when she realizes what she's done and lets out a whimper. Her face wrinkles up as she starts to cry.

"Oh, please don't cry. Look—" I hold my hands up once she's steady on her feet. "You barely even got me." I grin and her lower lip trembles as she tries to keep from wailing.

"But your shirt is so disgusting, like my hands," she says.

"It's all right. Let's get you cleaned up, okay?" I make sure she's still on solid ground before I take a step back and motion for her to follow me.

"Okay," she says, sniffling. "It was nice of you to call me Sweets. I liked that." She shakes her head. "That made me feel a little better because I smell awful and I made you smell awful too."

I laugh and she sighs before giving me a reluctant smile.

"We'll smell good again, I promise," I tell her.

"Dakota," her mom calls.

"Oops, I don't think I told her I was coming out here," Dakota whispers.

Shit. The last thing I need is another altercation with Marlow.

When she's within about twelve feet of us, she calls out, "Dakota, we've been looking everywhere for you." She shoots a glare at me. "Leave Dr. Wyatt alone. You're not supposed to be out here. And he's busy."

"She's not bothering me at all, but she does need to wash her hands...fast." I'm about to apologize for not checking to make sure it was okay for her to be out here when Marlow gets a good look at Dakota's hands.

Her expression is priceless.

"Oh shit," she says.

Dakota looks at me with her eyebrows raised and then to her mom, she says in an almost whisper, "We don't have a swear jar here, but that's okay, Mama. You can put it in the jar when we get home."

Marlow shoots her a look and then follows it with a scathing glare at me too.

I stand there with my mouth gaping and shit on my sleeves as I watch them walk away.

I can't seem to win with that woman.

CHAPTER FIVE

NOT MY DOCTOR

MARLOW

The past three weeks in Landmark have been eventful.

I expected this quaint little town to be sleepier than it actually is, but they know how to have a good time around here. It feels like I haven't stopped going since I arrived. I'm exhausted, but coming here has been the best decision I could make after my marriage fully crashed and burned.

Dakota and I moved into an open condo at Landmark Mountain Lodge a few days after we got into town. Sofie insisted we didn't need to go anywhere, but I never want to be a bother, and infringing on Sofie and Theo's space after they've spent so much time apart just felt all kinds of wrong.

I've gotten to know the Landmark family through helping Sofie with Grinny's birthday party and also helping with the stables project at Sofie's place with Theo. Sutton, the oldest Landmark sibling and a judge, has helped me file divorce papers in the most painless way possible. And Grinny is a hoot. She welcomed Dakota and me with arms wide open the moment we met her. With the exception of Dr. Why You An Ass Landmark, I absolutely adore everyone in the family. Even the grumbly Callum, who has few words to say, is more of a people person than his brother.

What a waste of a beautiful man.

I mean, the entire Landmark family is exceptionally good-looking. Scarlett is like a supermodel with her long dark hair and eyes and curves for days. Theo and Sutton favor each other and are both gorgeous with features similar to Scarlett's. Sofie told me that Jamison, Scarlett's boyfriend, who fits right in with his own hotness, said that Callum looks like a cross between a hipster lumberjack model and a serial killer, and I laughed my head off because it's the perfect description.

But the doctor...he is...well, there are no words.

Since his eyes are drilling through me every time he sees me, it's impossible to miss how green they are. Or how his hair looks like he's attempting to tame it, but it never quite works and ends up looking perfectly messy.

I guess I have more words about him than I thought. But, like I said, what a waste.

I've tried to be at Sofie's when he isn't, but yesterday we happened to be there at the same time, and seriously, the glare on that man. So I dented and scratched his car—that doesn't seem insurmountable to get over. He still hasn't called me to deal with it. I guess I could've gotten his number from Theo or Sofie, but I haven't...so maybe that's his reason for being bitter, but other than that...I have no idea what his problem is with me.

And then we were all looking for Dakota and I was too shaken up to be anything but relieved and then infuriated to find her way out in the pasture with Dr. Wyatt. He must not have heard us calling for her, and Dakota is the one who ran off without telling me where she was going, so I guess I can't really hold it against him.

He's just...under my skin.

I really hope these feelings don't affect the job interview I have this morning.

I just dropped Dakota off at Sofie's, where she is as happy as can be. She loves being over there with Sofie's horses. She's loving being in Landmark, period. With the exception of Wyatt, who I have to admit is better with Dakota, everyone has been so kind and welcoming since we got here. I took Dakota to see Dr. Langley last week—a lovely doctor—and her ears looked great, which is such a relief.

My phone rings as I'm pulling into the parking lot and I groan when I see that it's Cash. I'm thirty minutes early for my interview because I'm anxious and the last thing I should do is talk to Cash, but I answer it. He's been uncharacteristically quiet since I left him.

I grab my bag and folder with my resume and references and get out of the SUV, leaning against the front before I bite the bullet and answer.

"Hello?" I stare at the tree ahead.

"Hey."

He sounds so much more subdued than normal.

"You got the divorce papers?" I say, trying to speed the conversation along.

"Yes, and I won't contest it."

"Great. I'd like to get this over with as soon as possible."

"Listen, I know you're probably expecting an apology for what you saw, but...you and I both know we haven't been a real couple in a long time," he says, pausing to turn down the music in the background.

When he doesn't say anything else right away, I reach in my bag for one of Dakota's squishy balls and squeeze it to ease some of the tension.

"No, I didn't expect an apology from you, Cash. I just wish you'd been honest a long time ago when I asked if you were cheating on me. Or better yet, that you'd left me before you ever started cheating in the first place. That way we could've avoided our daughter seeing what she did...and I wouldn't feel like I wasted years of my life."

"Oh, come on, you don't mean that. I do regret that Dakota saw what she did, but she's too young to—" he says, and I interrupt.

"I don't want to get into that or anything else with you. Sign the papers, and we can both move on."

"I will. I, uh...since you've decided you're moving to Colorado, I don't believe I should have to pay child support," he stammers.

You lying, cheating, manipulative, back-stabbing weasel.

"If you read the papers again, you'll see that I'm requesting full custody since you've never tried to have a relationship with your daughter." I sound rageful through my clenched teeth, but it's the best I can do. "I don't expect you to pay anything and I also won't keep you from seeing her if you ever want to set up a time to visit, but I tried to make the terms as simple as possible."

He didn't even make it to the hospital when Dakota was born. That should have been just one more sign that I should leave.

"Good," he says. "I think that's for the best."

"I'm so glad you agree." The sarcasm is about as thick as it can get, and my grip on the phone is probably going to give me carpal tunnel. "Is that all? I really need to go."

"Yeah. We...had some good times, Marlow," he says.

I'm shaking my head, the anger too thick to say anything.

"Those early days when we couldn't keep our hands off each other—"

"I'm not going down memory lane with you, Cash. And you know what? Our times weren't that good. Sign the papers, preferably as soon as you get off the phone. Okay? Thanks, bye."

I hang up and try to take a few calming breaths, sounding like an asthmatic as I sit and fume. I close my eyes and breathe in the mountain air, and the summer breeze lifts the hair away from my face, calming me. The heat in Texas would be unbearable right now. This feels like my dream weather, and as I think about Pine Community Hospital, I hope that this will also be my dream job.

I open my eyes and Wyatt is standing there.

All I can think of is Sofie's fake-swear that she pulled out of her hat in front of Dakota and it's stuck ever since, *dammi-dalmatian*.

"How long have you been standing there?" I ask.

"Long enough to wonder if you're all right."

I lift a shoulder, surprised by his bordering-on-kind tone. He hasn't used it with me before.

"I will be," I finally say. I shake my head slightly. "No, I *am*. I'm better than all right."

He assesses me carefully and I shiver, rubbing a hand over my arm. His eyes track the movement before he swallows and lifts his hand to adjust the collar of his button-down shirt.

"Good," he says simply. "I'm glad."

He says it like he genuinely cares and for some reason, the kindness brings tears to my eyes.

I look down to my bag and reach inside for the stress ball I'd dropped back in there, anything to keep from crying.

"You play ball?" he asks, his voice almost playful.

I shift my lips to the side as if I'm annoyed, but I'm just biding time because I don't know what to do with myself around an almost nice Wyatt.

"If squeezing the bejeezus out of stress balls counts as playing ball, then yes." I squeeze it as tight as I can and can't hold back the smile when he winces.

He clears his throat and nods. "I'm surprised the ball hasn't exploded by now." His eyes widen and his mouth parts. "That-I..." He points behind him. "I better get to work."

I laugh as he stalks off. That was...interesting. I didn't expect to see that side of Dr. Wiseass today. Or ever. But as embarrassing as that whole exchange was, it got my mind off of Cash before this interview.

Dr. Langley is actually the one who told me about this job opening when I saw her last week for Dakota's follow-up visit. When she found out I planned on staying in Landmark, she offhandedly said, "Well, we have a few openings around here if you need a job," and I jumped on it immediately.

If I don't get the job as the front desk receptionist, I'll

apply for the cafeteria. I'm not picky. I have some savings left from my grandparents' estate, but I don't really want to touch that any more than I have to. I hope I don't have to see Dr. Wyatt much, but I really need the job.

I walk into the hospital, my heels clicking against the floor and I stop at the front desk, smiling at the elderly lady sitting there. I recognize her from Grinny's party, but I didn't meet her that night.

"Hello, I'm Marlow..." I pause before saying my last name. I'd really like to change my name back to Walker, so I don't want everyone here getting used to Hennessy.

She smiles and her curly hair lifts with her smile. "Hello. Sofie told me about you. I'd hoped to meet you at the party, but it was so crowded...crowds aren't really my thing." She laughs. "I'm Helen." She stands up and motions for me to follow her. "I hear you're interviewing for this job. I've been filling in when I can since Naomi left. Before she came, I worked here for thirty years..." She shakes her head and I fall into step beside her. "Looks a lot different now than it did back then."

I admire the tall ceilings and the piano we pass beyond the front desk. It opens into an atrium, couches and small tables set up to enjoy the music and the view out of the floor-to-ceiling windows.

"It's the prettiest hospital I've ever seen," I say.

She nods, pleased. "Isn't it? Dr. Wyatt oversaw the renovations for this place. He really had a vision for what would be a healing environment."

The man is just full of surprises.

Once we're past the atrium, we go down a hallway and she stops at the first door.

"Your interview will be in here. Since you're a few minutes early, would you like to grab a coffee down the hall? Maybe a pastry? They're brought in from Happy Cow," she adds.

"I think I'm too nervous," I admit. "Maybe I'll get something after…"

She smiles sweetly and pats my arm. "You're going to do just fine. Any friend of Sofie's is good people."

I smile back at her. "Thank you, Helen. You're putting my mind at ease and I'm really grateful."

She opens the door and I walk into the room, surprised to see it's bigger than I expected. Windows overlook a courtyard that is just as picturesque as everything else in the hospital. I wonder if Dr. Precious designed this room too.

Helen taps on the door as I sit down and I look back at her. "Let me know if you need anything. I'm sure it'll only be a few minutes before everyone arrives."

"Thank you."

She closes the door and I try to get my nerves under control. My hands are clammy and I wipe them on my black pencil skirt just as the door opens.

Dr. Precious himself walks through the door and looks shocked when he sees me sitting in the room. He turns to look at the door like he's in the wrong place and then turns back to me.

"Did you lose your way to the ER?" I ask through a gritted smile.

Which Dr. Wyatt will I get this time?

"You're the ten o'clock interview?" His voice is like a blade over my skin, cutting and uncomfortable.

"I am." I attempt a cheerful tone, but I feel about as doomed as his face looks.

CHAPTER SIX

BLINK-BLINK

WYATT

I can't believe it when I see Marlow in the conference room.

I didn't want to do this interview to begin with, but I got roped into it since I had a cancellation. It's awkward seeing her after what I just overheard...and the way it's been between us every other time doesn't help.

Her husband sounds like a real dick.

I would've already looked at her differently today without hearing her on the phone because of the conversa-

tion I had with Theo, Sofie, and Grinny about her just last
night.

"I'M SO *glad Marlow and Dakota seem to be settling in,"*
Grinny said.

"She's loving it here," Sofie said, leaning her head on
Theo's shoulder. "And nothing makes me happier. It was the
last thing on my wish list, but I never thought she'd really
make the move."

"What is her story anyway?" I asked. "She's so infuriat-
ing. I feel like she has had it out for me since day one."

Sofie's brow pinched at my sharp tone. "I'm surprised
you don't already know. She's been here a few weeks and it
isn't a secret."

I frowned. "We haven't exactly...hit it off. I don't know if
she told you, but she hit my car a few weeks ago...maybe right
around the time she got here. And it's been downhill from
there."

Sofie's frown deepened. "No, she didn't say anything
about that. Was she hurt? Were you?"

"Neither of us were hurt. My car is—" I waved my
hand. "Bill was able to fix it last week. Stupidly expensive,
but—"

Sofie sucked in a breath. "I bet that hurt for her to pay."
She shook her head. "I can't believe she hasn't said anything
about this."

"I didn't...I took care of it. She gave me her number, but I
haven't..."

"Well, that's really nice of you. What do you mean you
haven't hit it off though?" she asked.

"We just kind of clash. I was in a bad way the night she
hit me. I'd lost a patient—it was awful...a little boy." I ran my

hand through my hair. "Anyway, I might've taken it out on Marlow a little bit."

"Wyatt Henry Landmark, I raised you better than that. Even if you are having a hard day," Grinny said.

She rubbed my back as if to soothe away the sting of her words.

"I know. It hasn't just been me though. She can't stand me." It sounded stupid as I said it. What are we, twelve?

"Marlow is nice to everyone," Sofie insisted. "But she's been through hell and I'm sure after driving from Texas to Landmark, she wasn't feeling her best. The reason I went to get her is because she caught her husband in bed, their bed, with another woman...they are both horrible human beings who deserve each other, but Marlow did not deserve to see that. And neither did Dakota." She made a face and I balked.

"Wait, Dakota saw that too?" I asked. I wanted to punch the guy without knowing any other details. "He was fucking someone else in their home?"

"Wyatt Henry!" Grinny tsked, but she patted my hand. "Isn't that the worst kind of scoundrel? That poor girl has been through a lot."

Guilt coursed through me. Shame over the way I've talked to her, taken out my own frustrations when she's going through hell herself...there's just no excuse for the way I've acted.

AND NOW MARLOW wants a job at my hospital. This place is my life. Okay, my family is my life, but this is the closest second. I have a simple existence beyond these walls and the only chaos I can handle is a busy ER. I want to help her—it's the least I can do after the way I've treated her—but I'm not sure this is the best way.

There's something about this woman that sends me sideways.

Unfortunately, we don't have any other interviews lined up. Poor Helen retired a long time ago and she deserves to spend her days the way she wants. Naomi was wonderful, but she wants to watch her granddaughter full-time and I can't fault her for that. Being on the board of directors hasn't been problematic until right now. I'd love nothing more than to walk out and let someone else deal with this.

I walk toward the table, the silence tense as I sit down across from Marlow. Emma pokes her head in the door and smiles when she sees us. I exhale my relief and motion for her to come on in. She wasn't planning on being part of the interview, but she falters when she sees my expression.

"Do you have time to sit in on this?" I ask, my eyes pleading.

Her head tilts as she studies me. "Well, I have a patient coming soon, so not really, but I *am* the one who suggested Marlow apply," she smiles at Marlow, "so she's got my vote."

Great.

"Thanks, Dr. Langley." Marlow smiles at her and when her eyes meet mine again, the smile drops.

She's like an iceberg. Good. Should keep me from my wayward thoughts where she's concerned.

Emma lifts her hand in a wave and walks away, leaving me alone with Marlow.

"Do you have any experience working in a hospital?" I ask.

"No, but I've worked in a temp agency for the past year and covered many different office environments. I'm adaptable and can handle anything fast-paced."

"Temp agency?"

Her face flushes. "I was looking for a change and the

temp agency worked great because I could try a lot of different places and provide help in a short amount of time."

"So your stay in Landmark is temporary?"

"No, I plan to stay here and build roots."

I look up from her resume and her gaze holds me captive. Her expression is bold, defiant almost. Her cheeks are flushed and her hair is a wild tangle of waves. She shouldn't look so stunning in her classic white blouse and black skirt, but she does.

"What made you choose Landmark Mountain?" I ask.

"Sofie."

I wait for her to say more and when she doesn't, I lean in slightly. "I want to pause this interview for a second, if you don't mind." I grip the papers in front of me. "I'm sorry for the way I've treated you, Marlow. There's no excuse. I had no idea what you'd been through and the first night we'd met, I'd just lost a little boy on the table..." I pinch the bridge of my nose and when our eyes meet again, hers are soft, warm. I take a deep breath, ready to keep apologizing, but she jumps in.

"I'm so sorry to hear about that little boy. I don't know how you do this job and don't lose it." She swallows and looks down for a second before her eyes meet mine. "I'm sorry for the way I've treated you too. I'm not normally so —" She leaves it hanging and smiles softly.

"Neither am I," I interrupt, smiling back. "Apology accepted. I hope you'll forgive me too."

"I do," she says.

We're quiet for a beat and the air feels thick. But it's still a thousand times better than any other time we've inter- acted. I glance at her resume.

"Do the hours seem like they'd work for you? Eight to five, Monday through Friday?" I finally ask.

"That would be perfect," she says.

I hold up her resume. "From the looks of this, I'd say you're overqualified, but I should make it clear too that working for a hospital in a small community—or at least at Pine Community—can sometimes mean taking on additional unexpected jobs..."

"I can assure you that I'm flexible, and as long as I have childcare set up for my daughter in the hours that I'd be needed, I'd have no problem taking on additional jobs around here."

I imagine her being flexible, stretched out in an exotic position, and I scrub my hand over my face. I need sleep, food, and to get laid, the latter preferably first if I'm going to survive seeing Marlow on the daily.

"Thank you for coming in today. I'll discuss it with the rest of the board and someone will let you know soon if we decide to move forward."

"Oh, okay. That was quick," she says. She picks up her purse and the folder lying in front of her and looks awkward for a second before she smiles and stands. "Thank you for your time."

She leans across the table and holds out her hand and I hesitate before taking it. She gasps slightly when our hands touch and it sets a fire blazing through me. Her eyes are wide as we shake and I can't read the expression in them, but all I know is that I have to get out of here. Now.

"Thank you," I manage to say before I bolt.

Working with Marlow is going to be torture.

CHAPTER SEVEN

NEUTRALS

MARLOW

"Ah, Sofie is engaged," I sing, as I click Sofie's glass with mine. "I'm so excited!"

Dakota lifts her Shirley Temple and clinks our glasses, and Scarlett and her friends, Holly and April, laugh as they join in. It might be a downer to some to have a little girl with them on a girls' night out, but Sofie asked specifically if Dakota could come tonight and everyone acts like they love having her with us as much as I do.

We're at The Gnarly Vine, which specializes in wine and fabulous charcuterie boards, so not necessarily the most kid-friendly place, but Dakota is in her element, hanging out with her favorite Auntie Sof and the girls.

"I'm so glad you're all here," Sofie says.

She is glowing and I have never been so happy for anyone in my entire life. My best friend has gone through so much and to see her this happy with Theo is all I could've wished for her.

"I've wanted the three of you to meet Marlow and Dakota for so long. Even before I knew I'd be back in Landmark, I imagined all of you getting to know each other. And I haven't gotten to be with you guys as much as I've wanted to since I moved back," she says to Holly and April, "but I hope that will change now." She looks at me. "I was closer to Scarlett and Holly and April than I was with people my own age because I was always at Theo's house, and Holly and April were always there too, hanging out with Scarlett. And when I went to Texas and met Marlow, she became my family..." She puts her hand on Dakota's back. "I was even there the day Dakota was born." She waves her hand in front of her face and laughs as her eyes fill with tears.

A huge charcuterie board is placed in front of us and we thank the waitress as Sofie continues.

"I'm still floating about marrying Theo, and now all my friends are here with me too." She shakes her head. "It's just too good to be true."

"It's meant to be and only going to get better," Scarlett says.

I like Scarlett. She seems to be a straight shooter and she's been kind to me. But I especially love how crazy she seems about Sofie. Holly and April too.

"I wanted to get together to see if I could talk you into

being my bridesmaids," Sofie says, leaning in, her eyes sparkling brighter than the twinkle lights surrounding us.

April puts her hand on her heart and Holly looks like she's about to cry.

"I'm so honored to be part of this," Holly says.

"You've always been so special to us," April adds. "And I can't wait for you and Theo to get married."

Scarlett reaches over and hugs Sofie. "You'll finally be my sister for real, and there's nothing I want more."

And then I hug Sofie. "No place I'd rather be." I sniffle and take a deep breath, trying to hold back the tears.

"I've cried more since coming to Landmark than I have in my life," Sofie says, laughing. "And it doesn't seem like it's stopping anytime soon." She turns and looks at Dakota, hugging her to her side. "And I want *you* to be my flower girl, peanut."

Dakota's eyebrows lift sky-high and she claps her hands, doing a little dance in her seat. "Yes! I want it!" she says. "What is a flower girl?"

We all laugh, and Sofie bends down and holds up a gift bag for Dakota. Dakota's eyes are wide as she carefully pulls out the tissue paper and then lifts a gorgeous little crown.

We all gasp, Dakota the loudest.

"It's the prettiest," she says in awe.

"You'll get to wear this crown and a pretty dress that we'll pick out together, and you'll sprinkle flower petals before I walk down the aisle," Sofie says.

"I love flower girls!" Dakota says.

Scarlett lifts her glass and Dakota grabs hers and we all clink again.

"This is going to be the most beautiful wedding Landmark Mountain has ever seen," Scarlett says.

"Well, as beautiful as we can pull off in a short amount

of time," Sofie says, making a funny face. "Think we can pull off an October wedding?"

Holly's mouth drops. "We're already into September."

"It's better than what Theo wanted," Scarlett says. "He wanted them to get married the night he asked her."

We all laugh and Sofie flushes.

"I don't need anything fancy. And we can do it on an odd day or a weird time if we need to, whatever we can all pull off. We'd like to do it down by the lake on Theo's property." Her cheeks lift with how big she's smiling. "Just something simple."

"*Your* property too now," Scarlett reminds her.

"That will be beautiful," I say. "And as long as you have the dress you want, it seems like the rest should fall into place easily since you're doing it at your place."

"I haven't even looked at dresses yet," Sofie admits. "But I love the one you made for Grinny's party. Something simple, but created by you," she says to Scarlett. "No pressure at *all* though. There might not be time for that."

"Oh my God, there is nothing I'd love more," Scarlett squeals. "I wouldn't want to do you wrong though. You know I'm not a wedding dress professional."

"Didn't that dress only take you a weekend?" Holly says, scrunching up her nose. "Insanely talented."

"I know. It's just not fair that you have that much talent," April says.

"Wow, I can't believe you made that," I add. "I thought your dress was so pretty that night, but I never dreamed you'd made it!"

Scarlett ducks her head modestly and thanks us before quickly changing the subject. "What colors are you thinking for us to wear?"

"I'm all over the place on this, so tell me what you

think," Sofie says. "You could all wear whatever pretty dresses you want, maybe in blues like my ring...or would it be weird to just say any kind of neutral? Cream or gold or silver?"

"I love those ideas," I say. "And we'll do whatever you want."

"Exactly," April says. "Whatever you want."

"October is such a beautiful time of year, by the water and with the fall colors, I love the idea of us wearing neutrals, and that should be easy to find," Scarlett says. "Should we do a Boulder shopping trip or do you want us to just work on finding our dresses on our own time?"

"I'd love to go to Boulder, but I'd rather not do an overnight," Sofie admits, pressing her lips together as she gives us a sheepish look. "Sorry. I promise I'm not going to be one of those people who can never do anything outside of her husband, but I was away from him for so long and I'm—"

I put my hand on hers. "You don't owe us any explanations, Sof. For once in your life, please be selfish. Say exactly what you want and let us do whatever we can to make that happen."

"Marlow, I *knew* I liked you," Scarlett says, her smile wide. She looks at Sofie. "Marlow's exactly right. The whole point of this is to give you and Theo the experience you want. We can make a day of it and get back by that night, or we can find things online...order them and try them on together at one of our houses. Whatever is fun and makes you happy."

"I'm so happy right now I don't even know what to do with myself," Sofie says, and we clink glasses again.

She turns to me when the others start talking about dresses.

"So, what's this I hear about you and Wyatt?" she whispers.

I put my hand on my throat as I stare at her, trying to figure out what she's heard. "Uh, what do you mean?"

"I didn't know you hit his car." Her eyes widen. "Why didn't you tell me?"

I make a face. "It was my first night here, you were as exhausted as I was...and I didn't even know it was him that night. We didn't exchange names. We've actually had some...heated conversations. He said rude things, I said rude things, yada, yada." I make another face and hold up my hand. "But...he apologized when I interviewed for the job at the hospital. I think maybe we've made our peace. Hopefully." I laugh awkwardly. "Since we have to be in your wedding together and all that."

She hasn't said a word and is just staring at me still.

"At least I'm assuming he's also in the wedding." I laugh and fan my face. "What?" I ask when she only smiles.

"Nothing," she says, her smile growing. "Yes, he's in the wedding too. I wish I'd known all this drama was going on all this time. I would've set him straight sooner."

"Oh, so you did that, huh?"

"Well, he did ask what your story was, and I forget sometimes that he's usually the last to know all the gossip around here because of his crazy schedule. I didn't think you'd mind me telling him. I hope that's okay."

I squeeze her hand. "Of course it is. He also overheard me talking to Cash before the interview, so I think he would've gotten the picture on his own eventually."

"But the two of you are good now, you're sure?"

I lift a shoulder. "We're for sure better than we've been. I guess I'll wait to see how he acts the next time I see him to make any judgment calls."

Our attention turns to the food then and I try to not laugh when I realize that while we've been talking about dresses, Dakota has been grouping like items together in little piles all over the board and has a stack of crackers Jenga-styled in the center.

"Kota," I say in a warning tone once I'm sure I won't laugh out loud. "We're sharing this board with our friends. Let's not touch any more of the food, okay?"

Dakota leans back. "Sorry, Mama," she says. "I ate a lot of chocolate and cheese." She makes a face.

I look at the board again and notice it's really only crackers and meat and a few pieces of dried fruit.

Scarlett winks at Dakota. "I didn't really need any chocolate or cheese anyway."

"Me either," whispers April.

The crackers crash onto the board and Dakota jumps, covering her mouth with her hand.

"I'll order another," I tell the table.

"No, it's okay! I wanted some soup anyway," Holly says, waving me off.

"Same," April says.

"Their Caesar is really good," Scarlett says. "I don't think we need another board unless you just want one."

"Ya'll might be the nicest people I've ever met," I say, feeling overwhelmed with a sudden rush of emotion.

I meet Sofie's eyes and she smiles, knowing that before her, I didn't have the easiest time with friends. And then being married to Cash, I lived on pins and needles.

"Welcome to Landmark," she says, leaning over to put her head on my shoulder.

"I think it might be even better than you told me," I tell her.

CHAPTER EIGHT

ALLURING CONDIMENTS

WYATT

I go into the office and pick up Marlow's file and walk into the courtyard when I see that no one else is out there.

Ever since Marlow came into town, I've had this nervous energy and it's so foreign to me, I don't know what to do with it. I didn't get nervous energy about my medical boards, for chrissake, I don't know why the hell this woman makes me look for the nearest paper bag to breathe into.

Emma's right, we desperately need the help. I came in

an hour early this morning to show Helen how to run the new copy machine. Although come to think of it...knowing that feisty old woman, she could very well be *pretending* to be slow just so I'll hire someone faster. The more I think about it, that really makes sense, dammit.

I walk around the courtyard staring at Marlow's number and dial it on my cell phone before I can talk myself out of it any longer. There's no answer, and before I know it, Marlow's raspy Southern voice is saying, "You've reached Marlow. Leave me a message and I'll get right back to you."

Her voice is like sexy butter.

Good God, there is nothing sexy about butter.

Did I hit my head somewhere along the way?

The beep jolts me out of my horndog thoughts and I start talking.

"Uh, Marlow. Dr. Wyatt here. I'm calling to offer you the job at Pine Community. We'd like you to start as soon as possible. Please stop by the Human Resources office this week and fill out the necessary paperwork." I sound like a fucking robot and close my eyes, swiping my hand over my face. "Thank you."

I hang up and then kick the rocks, sending them into the flowers where they don't belong. I try to kick a few of them back into place and hurry inside to get back to work. I'm ashamed of how this woman reduces me to someone utterly idiotic.

Before I go to my next appointment, I throw away my trash from lunch and get a text from Brooke, one of our pharmaceutical reps. She called a few days ago saying she'd be in town sometime this week to leave some samples and wanted to know if we could meet for a drink. The last time we met for a drink we ended up in bed in her hotel room, and that sounds like it could be exactly what I need right now.

> **BROOKE**
>
> I'm coming through Landmark around four or five and will be stopping by the hospital. Got time for a drink tonight?

> I get off at seven. Drinks and dinner at The Pink Ski?

> **BROOKE**
>
> Sounds perfect.

I put my phone in my lab coat and go down the hall to see my next patient, feeling much better about everything. It's been a busy time and an emotional time too, when I think of all that's happened this year. My heart isn't used to the workout it's been getting with all of the love and loss and emotions going around.

A little time with Brooke, someone I'm comfortable with and who wants the same things as I do—a little fun with no strings attached—and I'll be back to myself.

Just in time to see Marlow at work.

I PULL into the parking lot of The Pink Ski and when I walk inside, Brooke is already there. She walks toward me, her arms open wide. I don't really love the idea of hugging her so openly in public, since PDA is not my thing, but I don't want to embarrass her either, so I return her hug.

"The owner is working on a table for us. Hopefully Helen got the samples I left. You were busy when I got there and so were Dr. Langley and Dr. Brady," she says.

"Helen left before I was done for the day, so I didn't, but I'll ask her about it tomorrow."

Sally comes up and winks as she smiles at me. "Hey, handsome. Oh, are the two of you together? I've got your table ready," she says. "Follow me."

Sally usually doesn't miss a chance to flirt, but when she asked if Brooke and I were together, Brooke looped her arm through mine and nodded, so Sally doesn't even wink or try to feel my biceps when she hands me a menu. Which doesn't hurt my feelings. Sally is lovely and harmless and a little flirting never bothers me.

I just hope Brooke and I are still on the same page.

She grabs my hand as soon as we sit down and I flinch. Nope, we're definitely not on the same page. The last time we saw each other, she'd just gotten out of a relationship and said she didn't want to be in another for a long time. We didn't even touch until she pulled me into her hotel room.

"I've missed you," she whispers.

Yep, I think she's changed her mind.

I pull my shirt away from my neck to get a little breathing room and hear a throat clear next to me. I glance over and see light blonde pigtails first, her dark brown eyes staring at me and then down at my hand in Brooke's.

I untangle my hand and breathe a little better.

"Hi, Dr. Wyatt," Dakota says. "Is she your wife?"

"Hello. Uh, no, this is my friend, Brooke. Brooke, this is—"

Marlow rushes up behind her. "Sorry to interrupt," she says. "Dakota, let's get back to our table."

"It's okay," Brooke says. "Aren't you cute," she says to Dakota. She smiles up at Marlow. "She's adorable."

"Thank you," Marlow says, smiling back at her. Her expression sobers when she looks at me. "I got your message.

Thank you so much. I'm really excited about this opportunity."

I feel Brooke's eyes on me too, as I try to school my reaction to seeing Marlow. I couldn't even tell you what she's wearing, but everything about her just screams perfect to me.

"What opportunity?" Brooke asks.

Her sales skills are really coming into play now and she is pulling out those people skills. It's actually a good thing since I seem to be struck silent when Marlow's around.

"I got a job at the hospital," Marlow says.

"Oh, congratulations. That's great," Brooke says.

She looks at me and I nod.

"Congratulations," I tell Marlow, clearing my throat when it comes out gruff. "When can you start?"

"Well, the timing is perfect. I was able to get Dakota enrolled in preschool already, so I'm good to start whenever you need me."

"Excellent," I say, my lips turning in what feels like more of a grimace than a smile.

Brooke frowns slightly as she looks back at me and then at Marlow. "You don't sound like you're from around here..."

"Oh, yes," Marlow says, laughing. "I barely get two words out before people are asking where I'm from. My daughter and I just moved here from Texas."

I glance at her hand and where I know I saw a wedding ring that first day, there is now a bare finger. It looks damn good. I sit up straighter, my mouth going dry.

"Just the two of you?" Brooke asks, her tone a little sharper.

"Just the two of us," Marlow says, nodding. "We're

starting a new life together here and I could not be more excited about it."

"I *see*," Brooke says.

My shoulders straighten and something in me settles. I don't know why, but I feel better than I have in quite a while. More like myself.

"How about you come in tomorrow and spend a day or two with Helen? She can show you the ropes and then you'll be ready to go solo by Monday."

"Perfect," she says, smiling at me.

"Perfect," Dakota echoes, doing a cute little dance.

I smile at her and when I look back at Marlow, her eyes are light, happy.

Takes my damn breath away.

Brooke reaches over and takes my hand when Marlow and Dakota walk away. "I haven't been able to stop thinking about the last time. I can't wait to get back—"

"Brooke, we need to talk. Thanks for meeting me for dinner, but I need you to know...I'm only up for a friendship. You're great and I enjoyed our time together...but I won't be going back to the hotel with you."

CHAPTER NINE

BROUHAHA

MARLOW

I wish I could've gone shopping before starting my new job, but there's no time.

I wear an old green blouse and my trusty black Express pants and hope that it'll be fine. I'm excited and nervous, more so than I ever was for a temp job. Besides waitressing at The Dancing Emu, which might have to be my next option if this doesn't work out, I haven't seen any other openings. Sofie is working on starting a horse rescue and it's possible I could eventually help with that, but I need something that pays now.

I was surprised to see Dr. Wyatt out last night. I didn't realize he had a girlfriend. She was nice. Beautiful. Blonde and legs for days. The two of them looked like they belonged together. I bet she never does stupid things like run into his Lexus and chew him out for his attitude.

No, surely not.

But that's in the past. We've apologized, and working together is going to be just fine.

I hope.

I'm not even sure if he is *technically* my boss. It sounded like I have a bunch of people I still need to meet and that he's at least not the only one I'll answer to. Hopefully Dr. Langley will be more of my point person.

I walk into the hospital ten minutes before I'm supposed to start, and Dr. McGorg is the first person I see. I thought Dr. McDreamy was hot on *Grey's Anatomy*, but Dr. McGorg is...next level.

"Marlow," he says. "Good morning."

He's not wearing his scrubs today but a nice button-down shirt, dress pants, and a white lab coat. It's a toss-up which look is more striking on him, and I decide that's not something I should be considering anyway.

I start to say his name back and can only think of the funny ones I've thought about him...

This is why nicknames are very bad.

"Mornin'," I say.

He looks over my outfit and I wait to see if he has a comment. Cash always had something to say about what I wore. I was never dressed sexy enough for him or my outfit didn't scream money like he wanted it to. He thought since I had money from my grandparents' estate, I should use it to get a big house and wear designer clothes, and thank goodness I didn't listen to him because I wouldn't have been able to make this move and get away from him if I had.

"Helen isn't feeling well today," he says, "so she won't be here to train you after all. I was hoping Pam or Linda would be here by now to walk you through a few things, but everyone appears to be running late or maybe with a patient. I'm not working in the ER today, so on days like this, you can page me here." He points to his name on the list next to the phone.

I nod. "Great. I've worked in several offices, so it won't take me long to figure out this phone. As long as I have an idea of who everyone is and their schedules, it should be an easy transition."

He nods.

"Hey..." I flush and try not to show how embarrassed I am to be bringing this up after all this time, but I can't just let it go. "You never called about your car. I'd really like to take care of that soon."

"Oh, it's fixed already. I handled it."

"But why didn't you—"

He shrugs. "Don't worry about it. I had a friend fix it... Linda's husband, you'll meet her soon, if you haven't already."

"Well, just let me know how to reimburse you or..." I lift my hand, unsure of what to say.

He gives a slight shake, his lips lifting slightly. "It's all good, Marlow."

My cheeks flush slightly and I'm about to thank him or argue with him, I can't tell which. I didn't feel so bad when he just drove off that night, but now I feel bad that he covered the damage I did.

A good-looking guy in scrubs walks up to the counter

next to us before I can say anything, and the cute nurse who helped me when I first brought Dakota in isn't far behind him.

"It's a slow morning back there," the guy says to Wyatt.

Shoot, I need to think of him as Dr. Wyatt when I'm at work so I don't call him the wrong name.

The guy notices me standing there. "Well, hello. You're not Helen. I'm Dr. James Brady. Call me James," he adds. "Or *Doctor*. Or whatever you want."

Dr. James' tone is flirty and I'm not sure I'm reading the room right, but it's almost as if I can feel Dr. Wyatt Uptyatt —Dr. *Wyatt*—bristle all the way from over here.

I hold out my hand to Dr. James and he takes it, holding it for a few long seconds. Before I can turn it into a handshake, Dr. Wyatt taps the counter of the front desk and we turn to look at him.

"This is our new receptionist, Marlow," he practically barks.

Dr. James squeezes my hand tighter. I think he's distracted at this point, so I try to pull my hand back, but it doesn't work.

"Amelia, are you able to help Marlow get started?"

"Sure thing," Amelia says, smiling wide at me. "Good to see you again, Marlow."

"You too." I smile back, relaxing when she seems happy to see me.

"Excellent. We'll let you two get to work then," Dr. Wyatt says.

When Dr. James makes no move to let go of my hand, Dr. Wyatt puts his hand on his shoulder and gives him a little shake and says something under his breath.

It sounded a lot like *she's married,* but I can't be sure. What I do know is that Dr. James' hand drops out of mine as Dr. Wyatt pulls him away and steers him down the hall.

Dr. James turns to look back at me and lifts his hand up in a wave. "Nice to meet you, Marlow," he calls.

Amelia goes over the list of things I'll be doing as patients come in and out. We stop and direct them to the right place and I see a few people I met at Grinny's birthday party and from working on Sofie's stables. When Amelia has to attend to a patient, Linda steps in where she left off. I like both women. Amelia is friendly and easygoing, a little younger than me, I think, with light brown hair, full round cheeks, and a sweet smile. Linda is married and has two adult children, but she and her husband, Bill, moved here from Tennessee a few years ago, so we bond over being the Southern newbies around here. Linda loves a good gossip session, if the way she tells me tidbits about every person she knows who walks in is any indication.

When she starts asking me a bunch of questions about myself, I'm hesitant to spill right away since I can already see it might not stay in a vault, but she's so sweet and funny, she manages to pull it out of me anyway.

"So, you have a beautiful little girl," Linda points at the small frame of Dakota I set next to the computer. "What about a beautiful man to make the picture complete?"

I make a face as I laugh. "We're complete without a beautiful man, trust me."

Linda shakes her head and then nods, her brows furrowed as she emphatically pats my hand. "Girl, that is right. We don't need no stinkin' man to complete us, do we?" She pauses for a second and leans in. "But there *is* a man in your life, isn't there? I'm all for independence and all that, but come winter, when it's time to shovel, I want a little muscle in my life. And that's not the only muscle I want neither, if you know what I mean..." She throws her head back and laughs, and I can't help but join in.

Unfortunately, she's looking for my answer when we stop laughing.

"I'm in the process of getting a divorce, hopefully the quickest one possible."

Linda's forehead moves into a thousand creases as she makes the saddest face. "I am so sorry, I had no idea. I should have never said that. You must be devastated."

"Oh no, it's okay," I say, waving it off. "Honestly, I'm more frustrated at myself for not leaving him sooner than I did."

Throughout our conversation, I keep thinking about Dr. Wyatt covering the bill for his car. I can't believe he did that...especially when I've been so snarly with him. Well, it went both ways, but...that was really generous of him.

My cell rings and I hurry to turn the sound off.

"It's okay," Linda says. She looks around. "If you need to take that, go ahead. No one's here anyway and you're picking up everything so fast."

It's my mom and I don't want to talk to her, but I owe her a call. Maybe if I tell her I'm at work, it'll make the conversation go better.

"If you're sure it's okay. I won't be long at all."

"It's fine," Linda says. She rolls to the other side of the reception desk and puts the files away that she'd taken out to show me how to input certain things.

"Hello?" I say, annoyed with how tentative I sound.

"What is this I hear about a divorce?" my mom says.

"Mama, I'm at work, so I can't talk right now."

"You've avoided me long enough. Marlow Agatha Walker...Hennessy," she corrects herself to say my married name. "Divorce is a sin. What a terrible example you're showin' your daughter, boltin' at the first sign of trouble."

"It is not the first sign of trouble," I say, but she's still talking.

"God strike me dead if I'm about to have a daughter who not only had a daughter out of wedlock but is now divorcin' the man. Marlow Agatha, you should be ashamed of yourself—"

"Mama, I'm sorry you're ashamed of me, but I'd only be ashamed of myself if I kept putting up with him. I should've left the first time I thought he was cheating or when he didn't show up when I was having Dakota because he was out drinking and overdid it. It took seeing him in bed with someone else to knock some sense into me. So, I wouldn't threaten God with striking you dead because the second I can be free of Cash Hennessy will be the happiest day of my life."

I'm shaking and hold the phone out to see if there's still a connection or if my mom hung up on me. It's silent.

"Mama?"

"I just think y'all could do with some counselin'," she says in a much quieter tone.

"I tried that during our first year of marriage and we went to two sessions before Cash cussed out the therapist and told her we didn't need her psychobabble BS."

Cash didn't say BS, but the quickest way to shut Mama down is to say *bullshit* in the middle of the day. She wouldn't be able to hear another thing I said.

"Well, that was uncalled for," my mom huffs. "I bet he'd be open to it now though..."

"I've gotta go, Mama. Love you." I hang up before she can say anything else and roll back from the desk, fanning my face.

It's only then that I remember Linda is sitting right there, and she's looking at me with wide eyes.

Dammi-dalmatian.

Might not be long before the whole town knows my business.

CHAPTER TEN

GIVE ME MY MUFFIN

WYATT

Grinny calls as I'm parking and I answer as I linger outside the hospital.

"Are you able to make it to the family dinner tonight?" she asks.

"I'll be a little late, but I'll be there. Start without me and I can eat whatever is left."

"I'll make extra. We're having Marlow and that sweet little girl of hers, Dakota, over too. Have you straightened things out with her yet? I sure hope you're not still being a bear. That is not like you, and well, she is just a doll. And don't get me started on Dakota..."

I grit my teeth before answering. "Yes, we've worked things out. She's actually started working at the hospital recently."

"Oh, is she the one who took Helen's place?"

"She is."

"Helen is so happy to have her days back."

We're quiet for a moment.

"Are you there, honey?" Grinny asks.

"Sorry. Yes, I'm here. I'm just walking into work. Do you want me to bring dessert? I could stop by Happy Cow on a break and get something for all of us."

"No, don't go to that trouble. I thought I'd make a couple of apple pies. Does that sound good?"

"Your apple pie *always* sounds good."

"All right. That settles it then. I'll see you tonight. Don't work too hard."

I chuckle. "I'll try. I love you, Grinny," I tell her.

"I love you too, my boy."

I'm nearly to the hospital cafeteria as I hang up and I've been so distracted on the phone that I didn't realize Marlow is right behind me. When I pause and turn to look at her, she's smiling and her eyes are bright. It stuns me silent for a moment.

"The way all of you love your grandma is just so...I love it," she says, putting her hand on her chest.

"She's easy to love."

She smiles and we enter the cafeteria, both saying hello to all the regulars. I'm surprised that they seem to know Marlow already—she's only been working here for a few days. Even Charles, the grumpy cook that always looks ticked off to be working in the mornings, smiles when he pops his head out of the kitchen and says hi to her.

Once we get to the counter, our hands crash as we both reach for the last blueberry streusel muffin.

Since my parents and grandparents taught me right, I back off and let the lady have the muffin, but for whatever reason, I can't make it too easy on her.

"I've had this muffin every day that I've worked here. It's going to knock everything out of balance to have to eat—that." I point at the puny cranberry muffins left in the basket.

She smirks and moves toward the register. "Balance is overrated."

She buys the muffin and unwraps it right in front of me. I absentmindedly purchase the cranberry muffin and a coffee, unable to take my eyes off of Marlow. Just as she's about to take a big bite of the muffin, she leans over and holds it up to me.

"Sorry, I touched it. Take it. You should see your expression. I didn't know you were all about the blueberry muffins."

I chuckle. "I do love them. Take it, you'll see why."

"No, I insist."

"Like you said, you touched it."

She frowns like she's offended and then can't hold onto it without laughing. "I think I *have* heard something about you being a germaphobe. I guess it's true?"

I shrug. "I'm a doctor, what can I say?"

"Okay then. Your loss."

She closes her eyes for a second when she takes a bite and then moans. Damn...she's making that muffin look even better than it already did. Once she's finished chewing, she looks at me and nods.

"It's delicious. I can see why you're such a boring creature of habit over this muffin."

"You have me there. It is kind of boring to eat the same
thing every day, but it's a fucking good muffin."

Her face flushes when I curse and it's adorable. And she
smells so good, looks so good.

I run my hand through my hair and she watches, her
expression unreadable.

"How are you liking this place? Pine Community...
Landmark Mountain?" I ask.

"I love it. I haven't had one bad..." She laughs and looks
self-conscious.

"What?"

"I was gonna say I haven't had one bad experience since
I got here, but that's not exactly true." She makes a face.

I laugh. "First you take my muffin and then you throw it
in my face what a jerk I was—"

"I know, I know. Sorry." She shakes her head, still laughing. "I'm glad we've...worked through it."

"Me too." I smile at her and it's nice.

She's nice.

It's easy to see why everyone around here has fallen for
her—I seem to be the only one who has dragged my feet.

We both go our separate ways, although it's not the last
I see of her. Her melodic voice pages me throughout the day
and it's hard not to notice her long legs as she walks by me.
She gets off before I do, but the reprieve is short-lived
because she's already there when I get to Grinny's, smiling
and looking all cozied up to my family. And shit, she looks
amazing at work every damn day, but she's changed into a
dress and it's almost impossible to not stare.

I hug everyone but Marlow, and my nephew Owen and
Dakota are busy playing, so I just say hello and take the

plate Callum hands me, dishing up food. Dakota runs up to me and wraps her arms around my neck when I sit down.

"Dr. Wyatt! I'm so happy to see you."

"Well, hello there, Sweets. How are you doing?"

She holds up a LEGO and then holds up her other hand. "I'm *great*. Look, Dr. Wyatt, you were right. No more stink." She giggles.

This kid. How could anyone resist that face and that laugh?

"*And* Owen's letting me play with Hermioneep," she adds.

"It's Hermione," Owen says, trying not to laugh. "Hi, Uncle Wy."

"Hey, O." I ruffle his hair and he grins.

I take the LEGO from Dakota and hold it up to her. "Hermione is a solid character. You know what? You kind of look like her."

"I do?" Dakota gasps.

"You do. Did you like the *Harry Potter* movies?"

"I haven't seen them yet, but I really, really want to." She turns to look back and I see Marlow watching us.

"You should see them. Not as good as the books, but pretty great," I say.

"Mama, Dr. Wyatt says I should watch the *Harry Potter* movies!"

"Maybe sometime soon...when we're sure they won't give you nightmares," Marlow says, narrowing her eyes at me.

"Right," I say.

She smirks to let me know she's not too peeved, and damn, I sure am glad we've worked through things too because I like this playful side of her.

"Whatever your mom says," I tell Dakota, as if I'm only

speaking to her. "She knows better than I do when you'll be ready to watch certain movies." I lift my head and look at Marlow just in time to see her smile.

"What's it like working at Pine Community, Marlow?" Scarlett asks. "How are you getting along with this one?" She nudges me.

I roll my eyes and nudge her back.

Marlow pushes her hair back. "It's going well. I like everyone..." Her eyes lift to mine. "And Dr. Wyatt has turned out to be...very nice." Her teeth go over her lip as she tries not to laugh. "Just don't get in the way of his blueberry muffins."

"Are you still eating those every day?" Theo says. "No wonder Lar and Mar are hassling me about not seeing you often enough. Get your ass over to Happy Cow."

"I'm over there plenty," I say. "They're doing just fine." But I'm laughing too. "It's a great muffin," I insist.

"What do you get when a snoop and a donkey enter a room?" Owen says.

"What?" Dakota giggles.

"Bray Watch," he says. He eyes the book he got the joke from and frowns. "I don't get it."

The room is quiet for a second and then everyone but Owen and Dakota cracks up.

"Or a Peeping Tom and a Jackass," I add.

Marlow's eyes widen and then she laughs along with everyone.

Dakota has her hand clamped over her mouth and when she drops it, she stares at me and then Grinny. "Does he have to put a quarter in the jar?"

Grinny laughs. "Yes, he does. Pay up, Wyatt."

Dakota takes my quarter and leans across the table to hand it to Grinny. "Thank you, Dr. Wyatt."

"You can just call me Wyatt if you want." I smile at Dakota. Her cheeks lift and a dimple appears. She has the Hermione LEGO walk down my arm.

"And you call me Sweets," she says, beaming.

I grin and shrug. "Seems to fit you pretty well, I think."

"That's nice," she says shyly.

"Dakota, let Dr. Wyatt eat," Marlow says.

"I'm eating just fine with Hermione." I grin at Dakota. "Does she like blueberry muffins?"

Dakota giggles. "I don't think she eats. She's made out of plastic."

That cracks me up and Dakota's eyes light up when I laugh.

"Hey, any more trouble with your ears at all?" I ask her.

Dakota nods happily. "You made me all better."

"Excellent." I make Hermione do a little dance, which Dakota loves.

Her laugh is infectious. When I look up, Marlow is watching us with a strange, almost pained expression.

"Hey, Wyatt, you missed our discussion earlier about going to The Gnarly Vine tomorrow night," Sofie says.

"We already know your schedule is clear, so don't even try to get out of it," Scarlett says when I start to shake my head. "Theo was smart to ask for everyone's schedule, so the two of you can't weasel out of things." She points to me and Callum.

I scoff and look at Callum for support. He shrugs.

"You're putting up with The Gnarly Vine?" I stare at him in disbelief.

"At least it's not The Dancing Emu," he grumbles. "We committed to the wedding." He points at Sofie. "And to do whatever that one right there wants for the rest of her life."

Sofie puts her hand on her heart and then goes over to

hug Callum. He pats her awkwardly on the back and she turns to me next, giving me that sweet smile. Of course, I melt. The girl is like family, always has been, and dammit, she deserves the world.

"I'll be there," I say.

Sofie beams and hugs me. Over her shoulder, I see Marlow watching us, her eyes brimming with emotion.

I'm so screwed.

CHAPTER ELEVEN

HANG ON

MARLOW

As I get ready for my night at The Gnarly Vine, thoughts about Wyatt sneak in.

I don't know why he's invaded my brain—I guess our tumultuous start probably has something to do with it. And possibly because when I got to work this morning, there was one of those fabulous blueberry streusel muffins waiting for me on my desk.

Being around him feels like going on the Tilt-A-Whirl at the State Fair. I like the ride, but it makes me dizzy.

And that's confusing.

Why does he affect me at all?

At first I disliked him so much, but since I've gotten to know him a little better, I'm starting to see why everyone thinks he's so great.

I just don't trust my feelings much anymore. And it's not just the number Cash did on me. I have sky-high mother issues on top of that, and for a long time, Sofie was really the only one I trusted.

But it's been easier than I expected to let my guard down here. I've always been friendly, working at temp jobs all the time, it's part of it, but I've had a hard time letting people in. Being around the Landmark family and working at the hospital, I often find myself watching the way everyone interacts so comfortably with one another, and I think maybe...I'm ready to want that too.

At work, Dr. Wyatt is the favorite...of *everyone*. People like Dr. Emma and Dr. James too, but when they see Dr. Wyatt, they light up, stand a little taller, and try to gain his attention. And it's impressive how he treats everyone with such kindness and is generous with his time.

The few times I've seen him with Dakota, something shifts inside of me. He's gentle and attentive with her, and she eats it up. She loves being around the Landmark family, and since Sofie and Theo's wedding is coming up, we're going to be around them a lot more.

I put on a dress that I got at the lodge boutique. Holly works there and Sofie and I have gone in to see her a few times. She's funny and easy to be around, and so is April. I thought I might feel like the odd one out for a while, but they've welcomed me right in.

I should probably save this dress for another occasion since I don't have many clothes, but I feel like wearing something pretty. It's a short, flirty, colorful dress and when I turn to see the back, Dakota walks into the room.

"Ooo, pretty Mama," she says.

"Thank you, Kota. Are you ready to go to Grinny's house?"

"Yes!" she says. "I'm ready!"

She's been talking of nothing else since Grinny offered to watch her and Owen tonight while I meet Sofie and everyone else for this planning get-together.

"All right. Make sure you have a toy or two and let's go."

"I hope Owen brings that Hermioneep."

I smile. "If he doesn't, he'll probably have something else fun."

"Yeah," she says, sighing wistfully. "Prolly so."

We get to Grinny's and Owen is running around in the front. He waves when he sees Dakota, and she runs to catch up with him. Grinny's sitting in a chair on the grass, and she smiles when she sees me sigh.

"She won't forget you," she says. "These two have just hit it off fast as can be."

"I'm so happy that she already has a friend. She looks forward to seeing him more than going to preschool, I think. Owen is sweet to be so patient with her."

"I like the way she makes him slow down a bit," Grinny says, laughing. "It's nice for him to have a friend in the family to play with. It's been him and the grown-ups since he was born." She shakes her head and we watch the two of them sneaking up on a bird.

I'm so touched that she's scooped me into the family already, I stand there for a moment, soaking it in.

"Well, I better run so I get there on time. Bye, Dakota. I

love you."

"Love you, Mama," she yells, running over to give me a quick hug.

Grinny smiles as she watches us. "My, you sure look pretty," she says. "Enjoy your night and don't let anyone give you any sass." She winks and I flush, wondering if she means Wyatt.

I pull into the lot at The Gnarly Vine and wave when I see Sutton walking in.

"Marlow, I actually hoped we could have a minute. How are you doing?" he says, pausing at the door of the bar.

"I'm doing well. What's up?"

"I was just going to ask if you have someone pulling some strings for you in Texas. I've never seen a divorce case move faster than this seems to be going. Of course it's not final yet, but I wouldn't be surprised if it is by next month."

"Really? That's great. I'd hoped since neither of us was contesting anything, it would go fast, but next month would be shocking. Thanks for whatever you're doing to move it along."

"I've done my best, but I don't think it's me. Maybe they're having a slow season, maybe someone there is pushing for it to go faster too, or I could be wrong about all of this and it will go longer...I should've just said things are looking good so far, so I wouldn't get your hopes up."

I smile at him. "I'll try to remain cautiously optimistic."

"Good plan." He smiles and opens the door for me and we walk inside.

Sofie stands and holds her arms out when I get close, hugging me. Over her shoulder, I see Wyatt talking animatedly with Theo, but as soon as he sees me, he stops in mid-sentence and stares at me.

I take a deep breath and when Sofie and I separate, I

hug Scarlett and then Holly and April. Theo and Jamison say hello and Callum nods at me. I wait to see what Wyatt will do and Theo says something before he has to.

"I'm so glad you're all here. Thanks for making this work with such short notice. We wanted to start the ball rolling with the wedding. We have a few dates to throw out there and thought it would be easiest if we just got together and went for it."

Theo and Sofie are glowing. It's hard not to smile whenever I see the two of them together. Jamison and Scarlett too...I've had to fan myself several times with the way he looks at her.

The waitress comes up and takes our drinks and apps order and when she walks away, Theo clears his throat.

"Attention, everyone," he says, chuckling. "Let's set a wedding date."

He sets a sheet of paper on the table with a few dates written on it, all of them right around the corner, and we quickly agree on the third Saturday next month. There are weddings and Halloween festivities surrounding the date on either side, but that Saturday works for everyone.

"Well, that was easy," Scarlett says. "And now, we have a proposal for the two of you." She slides her hands together in excitement. "I'm sorry I didn't get a chance to talk about it with you yet," she says to me and Holly and April, "but my brothers and I were talking about it..." She holds up her hands in front of her and her eyes go wide. "Picture this: all of us, in Vegas, for your bachelor and bachelorette parties. Since the two of you don't want to spend the night away from each other...and I don't really want to spend the night away from Jamison either..." She gives him an adoring look and his look back at her is scorching hot.

I fan my face with the drink menu while she continues.

"We could take the lodge's charter helicopter, maybe even both, depending on the schedule. If not, it'd take two trips back and forth, but that's doable. I've already okayed the possibility with our pilot George. We could go for two nights..." She pulls out her massive planner and opens it up, pointing at the weekend before the wedding. "And still have time to rest for the wedding. Or we could even do the Monday and Tuesday of the wedding week."

There's a pause as we wait to see if she's throwing any other dates out. When she doesn't, answers start coming.

"I love this idea," Theo says.

"Me too," Sofie says, dancing in her seat. "I'll need to make sure Aunt Hilary and Abby can take care of the horses, but they enjoy doing it, so it should be okay."

"That weekend would probably be better for me than that particular Monday and Tuesday," Sutton says. "As long as Grinny is okay to watch Owen."

"Either should work for me," Wyatt says. "Emma wanted to work that weekend and the next, so I'd cover a few weekends for her this month, so I'm set."

All I can think about is what the cost of the hotel might be, but it shouldn't be bad with all of us girls staying together...well, I guess it would only be three of us...and then I don't know why I'm even considering it.

I can't leave Dakota.

"And we'll cover everything," Scarlett adds, pointing between herself and her brothers. "It's part of our gift to you guys."

"Wow, that's...thank you," Theo says, reaching over to squeeze her hand. "But let us help. There are a lot of us."

"Absolutely not," she says. "Back me up," she says to the rest of her brothers.

"Yeah, we've got this," Wyatt says. "You've gone easy on

us as far as wedding expenses go. It's at your place, we don't have to wear a tux...I think we can splurge on a trip to Vegas for you."

"I've never spent the night away from Dakota," I admit.

The table goes quiet and I wish I'd waited to bring it up with Sofie one-on-one.

"Well, now I feel so selfish, not wanting to be away from Jamison when you've never even been away from Dakota," Scarlett says.

"I don't have to go," I say, shaking my head.

"Well, then we won't go," Sofie and Scarlett say at the same time. They look at each other and laugh.

"No, you have to. This sounds so fun. I just...I don't know what options I'd really have," I say.

"We could do two things. One, I'm sure Grinny would be thrilled to have her stay with her, if Dakota would be okay with that, but the other option...what if Grinny went and you could see Dakota whenever you wanted and even if Dakota spent the night with Grinny, you'd still see her before she went to sleep and all that." Scarlett lifts her eyebrows. "What do you think?"

"That sounds like a lot of work for Grinny," I say, making a face.

"I'd love to have Dakota and Grinny around for what-ever festivities they could be part of," Sofie says. "And I bet Grinny is up for anything. She always is."

"We'll figure something out," Scarlett says. "But set aside those dates, everyone, because *wherever* we end up, we'll be there together."

My eyes meet Wyatt's and his dark hair falls over his forehead, his green eyes unreadable and yet mesmerizing. I can't help but feel like I need to buckle up because this ride is just going to get bumpier.

CHAPTER TWELVE

CURRENCY

WYATT

I walk outside on my break and stop when I hear Marlow.

She sounds upset and I look around to see her pacing between the trees in the courtyard, talking on the phone.

"You have a lot of nerve calling me," she says.

I've been on the receiving end of Marlow's anger a few times now to know that was nothing compared to this. It feels wrong that I'm hearing this conversation, but she sounds so agitated that I don't want to leave her alone either.

"No, trust me, the fact that you're in Cash's bed these days only means that you should lose my number and never call me again."

Shit. The girl who slept with her husband called? That's beyond ballsy.

"Oh, he's all yours, honey. You can have him," she says and pauses, stopping just past the tree.

I can tell the moment she sees me because her shoulders go even more rigid. Dammit. There's still time to leave, but I don't move.

Her head tilts and she stares at me, her eyes narrowing.

"By all means, if your daddy can get things moving faster, so be it," she says. "I hope you and Cash have a nice life."

She hangs up, and her chest rises and falls faster and faster. I walk toward her when I see her hand shaking.

"Are you okay?" I ask.

I hold my hand out to touch her and leave it suspended in the air, hovering over her shoulder.

"I can't believe she called me," she says, choking out that painful laugh again. "What an awful human."

She puts her fingers on her forehead and takes a deep breath. When her eyes finally meet mine, she lets out an exhausted exhale that nearly brings me to my knees. She looks so weary, so beaten.

"I'm sorry you had to hear any of that," she says.

I shake my head slightly. "You don't need to apologize—"

"Yes, I do. You keep seeing me at my worst."

I want to argue with her. If this is her at her worst, my heart stands no chance of surviving her best.

"Do you want to talk about it?" I ask instead.

"I honestly don't even know where to start. I feel so stupid."

"Marlow, the last thing I'd think about you is that you're stupid. No one is faster with comebacks than you."

Her lips press together when I say that, like she's about to laugh, which feels like a win.

"You're taking care of your little girl, who is one of the smartest little humans I've ever met, and I've met a lot."

Her eyes get shiny.

"The little I've heard about Cash—he sounds like the stupid one. And the girlfriend doesn't sound much better."

She lets out a shaky breath. "I just—I shouldn't have ever married him...I knew it then."

"You're making it right now. That's all you can do. Take the next step toward your better life, and from where I'm standing, that's exactly what you're doing."

She presses her hand to her mouth, her eyes shinier than before, and nods. "Thank you, Wyatt. Really. Thank you."

"What can I do to help? Name it," I say.

My early infuriation with her turned on its head when I heard what she'd been through, when we had our moment of apologies. Seeing the way she is with Dakota, the way she is around here—I don't know exactly why I feel such a need to help her, protect her, but something about her just tugs at me.

"I could use a friend," she says, lifting her shoulder, as her eyes meet mine. "And to know that there really are decent guys out there."

I nod slightly, my hand itching to touch her, just on her shoulder to console, but I keep my distance. "Done. At least I hope you'll consider me a friend. You've seen that

I'm not perfect, but I think I can handle decent pretty well."

She smiles and reaches out, her hand squeezing my arm for only a second, but I feel it long after she lets go. She takes a step back, another deep breath, and her shoulders straighten as she turns and walks away from me. I watch her until she's out of sight, her sweet scent lingering in the air.

When I snap out of my Marlow-stupor, I go inside and stop by the break room to see if any sales reps have dropped off treats. I avoid them like the plague most of the time, but I wouldn't say no to a bear claw from Happy Cow right about now. Sadly, no bear claws, but Linda is digging into a bowl of candy like she's on a mission.

"What are you looking for?" I ask.

"Bit-O-Honey. Thought I saw one, but nope." She digs around a little more and holds one up, waving it in front of me.

I smile and start to back out of the room then stop. "Hey, thanks again for getting Marlow set up. Thanks to you, she's already a pro."

She laughs and waves me off, but her cheeks are lifting with pride. "It's all her. She picked everything up so fast and it's already like she's been here forever—she fits right in!"

I nod. "Yes, she does. I'm glad we hired her."

I grab a Reese's peanut butter cup out of the candy dish and get back to work.

Brooke messages me and I'm polite back but don't engage. I thought I made it clear that I'm not interested in our sporadic arrangement any longer, but it seems like I might have to reiterate it.

Earlier, Theo texted asking if I'll be bringing a date to the wedding and I said no. He insisted that I should, but I insisted I didn't want to be distracted with a date at his wedding.

And yet, the truth is, I'll already be distracted by Marlow...affected...whatever this is.

It'd be better for everyone involved if this fascination with Marlow fazes out and I can get back to normal. She's not single yet, and she needs a friend. That's what I'll be.

The ER fills up when I'm done with my break and I'm grateful for the reprieve. It's twisted to like a full ER, but that's where I am these days...and I'm not very proud of it.

CHAPTER THIRTEEN

DEFROSTING

MARLOW

On Saturday morning, I have energy to burn and Dakota is hyper too.

The fall colors have already started to show up and I love how vibrant everything looks. The cooler temps compared to what I'm used to in Texas around this time of year are also nice. I won't know what I'll do with all the snow this winter, but I'll worry about that when the time comes.

"How about we go for a walk before we go out with the girls?" I check the clock and there's plenty of time since we're up early.

"Yes!" Dakota yells, running to put on her shoes.

"Oh, you're ready right now." I laugh. "Okay, one sec."

I go into the bedroom and put a bra on under the T-shirt I was already wearing and change from my shorts to my yoga pants.

Dakota is singing by the door and bounces from foot to foot as she waits for me to get my tennies on.

"Where are we going?" she asks when we step outside.

"How about we walk to Heritage Lane and get something at Happy Cow?"

"I love Happy Cow!" she says.

We start walking, Dakota happily singing next to me. I take a deep breath and it feels so cleansing, I wish I'd done this days ago. I've had all this pent-up energy since Maggie called a few days ago.

The one good thing that came out of the call is that she let me know that her dad is friends with the lawyers and the judges in the county where I filed for divorce, so in her words, he's "pulling strings" to make it go as fast as possible. I guess Sutton was onto something.

Maggie is so eager to be with Cash and I can't be divorced soon enough.

Dakota takes my hand when we get to Heritage Lane and then skips as we walk toward Happy Cow.

"What are you gonna get, Mama?"

"Hmm. I think I need a bear claw. I sure hope they have them! What are you getting?"

"Welllll...I would like a jelly donut and...that one thing that has the chocolate inside."

"A chocolate croissant?"

"Yes, a chocolate crossy..."

I smile and absolutely do not correct her because she so rarely says her cute versions of words anymore. "Anything else?"

"Yes. And a donut with sprinkles and a donut with the white stuff."

"Powdered sugar?"

"Yes, that."

I grin at her. "Sounds like we need to fill a box."

"Yes! Fill a box!" she says, jumping up and down.

She fills my heart with such happiness, so much love that I don't even know what to do with it all. I can't imagine anyone not wanting to know her, much less her own father.

She's been mentioning him more lately. I guess we all start out believing the best in our parents. At first, I thought she might not even miss him, that maybe she hadn't had him around long enough *to* miss him.

He'd leave before she got up, come home after she went to bed, and on the occasions he was around when she was awake, he wasn't present. He was on his phone, watching TV...doing just about anything to avoid interacting with his daughter. I gave him a pass initially because, growing up, he didn't have a great example of loving parents. They lived in Arkansas and in the four years we were married, they came for two visits, and we visited them once. There was a general feeling of indifference from them, so it shouldn't have been a surprise to me that their son was the same.

My parents were another breed altogether.

Not indifferent but *very* invested...in what I've always felt were the wrong things.

Sofie is one of the few people that knows I was put in beauty pageants at three months and it continued until I was seventeen.

My mom believes in three things: God, beauty, and reputation.

And not in that order.

Beauty came above all else, with reputation almost tied for first. For her, the more awards I won, the better her reputation.

My brother is a year and a half older than me, and it's shocking that he loves me at all since, growing up, everything revolved around me. I won titles and prizes and awards at every pageant, even while begging my mom to let me stop competing, and it wasn't until I was seventeen that I finally got the nerve to sabotage myself in a pageant.

It was the only way out.

I flopped on purpose...however, it was at one of the most crucial times of my life and a pageant where the stakes were high. I didn't get the scholarship I needed to go to college, and my mom had gone through all the money I'd earned in previous pageants. But standing up to her in that way gave me the momentum I needed to leave home.

I think my mom has hated me ever since.

"Whatcha thinkin', Mama?" Dakota stops right in front of me and shades her eyes with her hand as she looks up at me.

"Ugh. Sorry. Mama got distracted with—" I shake my head and make a face. I bend down and put my hands on her cheeks. "Do you feel my love, baby girl?" I ask. "All the time?"

"I do," she says, grinning wide.

I kiss the tip of her nose and stand back up. "I'm so glad. I want that more than anything. For you to feel my love and for you to be happy inside out."

"I feel your love all the time, Mama," she says. She taps her heart. "Right here." She looks down at her stomach and rubs it, frowning slightly when she looks back up at me. "Maybe when I eat all those donuts, I'll be happy inside out too."

I laugh and put my hand on her shoulder. "Good thing we're here."

I point to Happy Cow, and she does a little skyrocket jump that's so impressive but quick, I would've missed it if I hadn't already been looking at her.

We walk inside and Dakota does another leap, thankfully, this one a little more contained, and I think she's just excited to be here, but then she says, "Wyatt!"

I've been replaying the words he said to me in the courtyard over and over. I didn't know how badly I needed to hear that I'm doing a good job with Dakota. It's one thing to hear it from Sofie and the friends I'm making here, but another from my boss...the guy I've considered problematic since I got here.

His kindness to me that day has helped balance some of the tension I felt from talking to Maggie.

He turns and breaks out into a smile when he sees Dakota. "Hi, Sweets!"

His eyes meet mine briefly and he says hello, still grinning, before turning back to Dakota to ask what her favorite pastry is. She runs down the long list, and he laughs. Ugh. Why does he have to be so charming with her? It's a heady combo—warms me up inside and rips my heart out at the same time.

I want her to have a relationship like that with her dad, and it just doesn't seem like it'll ever be.

Lar and Mar smile at Dakota and me, Mar dusting the powdered sugar off her apron.

"Did you hear all that, Mar?" he says.

Mar nods. "I sure did."

"It'll be my treat," Wyatt says.

"Oh no," I jump in. "That's not necessary. I'll—"

His expression is cautious when he looks back at me. "My bad. I should have checked to make sure you're okay with her having all that sugar."

"Well, we're here, so I was planning on getting a box—"

"Okay then. My treat. Put that bear claw in their box, Mar."

"You sure? It's the last one," Mar says, grinning at me. "You must be on his good side for him to give away his beloved bear claw."

"First the last muffin and now the last bear claw? You're going to dread seeing me coming, Dr. Wyatt," I say.

He mutters something under his breath and his ears turn pink.

"What?" I ask.

"Consider it a welcome to Landmark," he says.

"We've been thoroughly welcomed for a while now," I counter.

He pauses before saying, "How about we just say it's my pay-it-forward to a sweet little girl and her mom who brought some sunshine into Happy Cow this morning?"

I stare at him and swallow hard. For some reason, I feel like crying *and* hugging him.

I blink up at him, momentarily blinded by his green eyes and the long black lashes, the way his jaw is peppered with scruff, unlike the times I see him at work. Every nerve ending in my body is fired up just being near him.

Terrifying and wrong, but true.

"Thank you," I say, turning away from him so I can get a grip.

Mar and her husband, Lar, are staring at the two of us

like we're the most interesting specimens they've seen in a while. And then Mar gets busy finishing up our box.

Wyatt points at something. "Throw one of those in there too, please. And that fruit tart." He smiles at me and then Dakota, who claps her hands in approval, and as hard as I'm trying to hold onto the walls I've erected, the armor I've always needed, my heart thaws and the barriers begin to crumble.

CHAPTER FOURTEEN

EVERY SINGLE AFFLICTION

WYATT

I feel good about the exchange with Marlow at Happy Cow over the weekend...until I see her on Monday morning.

The way she steals my airways, causing my heart to stutter every single time I see her...it's just not right.

It should send me running in the opposite direction, but it's such a bizarre phenomenon for me that I only want more.

This is not how a friend acts.

All week I find reasons to walk by the front desk when I have to go anywhere in the hospital, even if it takes me the farthest route. I can use the steps, right?

My strategic and somewhat frequent lurking is how I notice that I'm not the only one intrigued by Mrs. No-No.

This is how she must remain to me until she is no longer married.

There are a couple of patients who are becoming regulars. We've always had patients who enjoy their hospital time.

Agnes Freeman comes in every time she gets a mosquito bite.

Jim Landon is prone to thinking he has an incurable disease and so far, he's only had a sinus infection and Athlete's foot.

But this is different.

There are two men who have been visiting Landmark Mountain for a few weeks and once they came in that first time, Pine Community has become their revolving door.

Bobby Hymer, age 30, 190 pounds, stats all within a healthy range. I first saw him about a twisted ankle, and the next time was for an upset stomach. When I saw him come in a third time and linger by Marlow's desk a good twenty minutes before his appointment, and his reason for coming in was a sore on his big toe, something clicked.

David Lowell, age 42, 220 pounds, high cholesterol. He came in for heartburn and keeps coming back like it's a surprise that it hasn't gone away overnight while he's still doing the same things he was that first visit. He hangs out at Marlow's desk long after his appointments are over.

When I walk past the reception desk on my way to the cafeteria for lunch and both Bobby and David are standing at Marlow's desk, competing for her attention as she gives them a pained smile, I'm compelled to step in.

"Gentleman," I say briskly. "If only the hospital were like an airline and had a frequent flier club, am I right? You'd both have lots of miles accumulated after all these visits."

Both men look startled and then laugh, David more boisterously than Bobby, who eyes me suspiciously. *Yeah, buddy, I see you.* Marlow stares at me as if she can't believe I'm stepping in here. I can't blame her for that.

"I need to ask both of you to make your stops at the reception desk brief—"

"No one is here," Bobby interrupts, turning around to show me the obvious...there's no line behind him.

Fortunately, someone walks in just then and Bobby rolls his eyes. But that person ends up sitting down by the front window like they're waiting on someone else.

"I still have work to do when no one is in line," Marlow says quietly. Her tone is somewhat apologetic but firm, and she glances at me gratefully after she's said it.

It's ridiculous how my chest wells up. I probably need to make an appointment myself...see if something is wrong with *me.*

"Well, in that case, can I have your number?" Bobby says, grinning wide.

What a piece of work.

David glares at Bobby and then smiles at Marlow, turning the charm on. "I'd love to take you out to dinner sometime."

This is not going how I intended at all and I'm about to shut them down when Marlow stands up and picks up a folder.

"I don't date patients, hospital policy," she says sweetly.

She then walks past the three of us and leaves us staring at her stunning legs and the mesmerizing sway of her hips and perfect ass. Her long hair bounces slightly with each step.

Damn.

Bobby and Dave grumble under their breath and before Bobby walks away, he looks at me and says, "Sucks to be you. Since she can't date patients, I'm sure she can't date doctors either." He shrugs and walks away.

Bastard.

But I'm not even slightly mad.

I turn and go in Marlow's direction. When she hears me behind her, she turns and pauses. I grin at her and she eyes me suspiciously. Again, I can't blame her for that.

Her eyes narrow. "Are you being...*smug*?"

"Uh, no?" Yes. I chuckle and she smirks. "What?"

"Are you sure you're not having indigestion or something? Do I need to find Dr. Emma and ask her to fit you in?"

"No, you're mistaking me with your friends back there. They're the ones with the indigestion and various other issues. Good thing we cleared that up."

"I handled it." She shrugs, but she's grinning wider now.

"So, this hospital policy...what page is that on again? I've never seen that about patient fraternization...I just want to make sure I'm following the rules."

Now she's trying not to laugh. "It's on page five, section 3.a., second paragraph."

The way she can bullshit on the spot is sexy as hell.

"Ahhh. Got it. Very helpful, thank you."

"You really should refresh on the rules, Dr. Wyatt."

The sass on this woman.

There's a quiet beat of silence and yet, it's the most

comfortable it's been between us. Of course, I nearly ruin it by staring at her mouth too long, but I think I curb it in time.

"All joking aside, I'm glad you stepped in today and forced the issue," she says.

"Anytime."

She leans in slightly and I catch her citrusy gardenia scent. I inhale greedily.

"I'm really glad we're not biting each other's heads off anymore," she says under her breath.

"Me too," I breathe out.

Those familiar *she's married* bells do eventually go off, albeit more delayed than usual, but I'm just happy that we're having a conversation where I can walk away without guilt over how I've spoken to her or confusion over the way she's spoken to me.

Maybe we're on our way to finding a professional friendship balance.

Her words come back to bite me in the ass: Balance is overrated.

Because when we get right down to it, there's never been anything *balanced* about the way I look at her...or the way I *think* about her.

But if I can just ignore the way I'm starting to want to kiss those lips senseless, maybe, just maybe, we can survive being in the same space all the time.

CHAPTER FIFTEEN

PAGEANTS AND PROGRESS

MARLOW

Just as I think we're making progress and maybe actually becoming friends, Wyatt backtracks.

Our exchange over the hospital *rules* was lighthearted and playful.

But he's avoided me ever since.

And now it's the weekend and I don't know why I'm thinking about him at all. He shouldn't occupy my mind as much as he does.

I drive down Theo and Sofie's driveway and Dakota gets out of her booster before I've fully parked.

"Hey, slow your roll. Someone's sure in a hurry," I tease.

"I'm excited to see all my aunties," she says.

Sofie's Aunt Hilary and her wife, Abby, will be here today while the bridesmaids try on dresses. When Dakota asked them if she could also call them Auntie, you'd have thought a party was going on, the way they laughed and carried on.

Holly opens the door when I knock and Dakota runs in, beelining to her Auntie Sof first and then making her rounds hugging Hilary and Abby. Scarlett, Grinny, and April come in a few minutes after me, and they fawn all over Dakota too, like she's the princess of all. It brings tears to my eyes the way everyone dotes on her. She hasn't had that in her life before coming here, and I'm just so grateful that she does now.

"There are brunch-y things to eat...these little egg bites and mini pancakes and salad...apple juice, orange juice, and mimosas," Sofie says, holding her hands out toward the spread on the island. "I've been so excited for everyone to get here today, I just kept making more things." She laughs.

"We should have been doing all of this for you!" I say. "Oh my goodness, these are so cute!" I hold up the little cookies that have our names on them.

"My aunts have helped and we've had so much fun," she says. "Things are slower for me right now, and all of you have full-time jobs. I've put everything on hold with Morgan's Sanctuary until after the wedding. This has been a lot of fun." She grins.

"How is everything going with that?" April asks.

Sofie is starting a nonprofit horse rescue that she's

named after her mother, and I'm in awe of how much she's already accomplished getting this new venture underway.

"It's going great," Sofie says. "We have a ways to go before we're fully running, but it's coming along slowly but surely."

"Don't let her fool you," Hilary says. "Between wedding stuff, she's exercising the horses, designing the new space over at the other property, and doing the finishing touches on the stables here. I don't know how she's pulling it all off."

"How do you get all that done with my brother hanging on you every minute?" Scarlett asks, tapping her chin like she's so curious.

We all laugh and Sofie throws a smiley face pillow at her. Scarlett pretends it guts her but then tosses it back.

"Morgan's Sanctuary is going to take a while, and I'm not taking in any new horses until Theo and I are back from our honeymoon, so it's been good timing...almost like a stress reliever to work on wedding stuff," Sofie says.

"I have never heard anyone talk about wedding planning as a stress reliever," Holly says, laughing.

I put my arm around Sofie's waist and she leans her head against mine.

"I love seeing you so happy," I tell her.

She turns and faces me. "I want you to be happy too."

"I am..."

She makes a face.

"I am," I insist. "At least way more than I was in Texas, and more than when I first got here."

"Are you liking your job? I haven't been able to tell for sure."

"I actually love it."

"Really?" Her voice lifts with excitement.

"Stop worrying about me."

She pulls me in closer. "You know we'll never stop worrying about each other when things aren't quite right. That's what we do."

"I know. And I'm grateful that I've got someone like you who loves me like that." I swallow the lump in my throat as she puts her hand on my shoulder and squeezes.

"Always," she says.

We both laugh when we fan our faces to keep from crying.

"See? There's something in the Landmark water," Sofie says.

"I've noticed that." I dab my eyes and take a deep breath.

The space clears in front of the food, so I call Dakota over to pick out what she wants.

"There's room at the table," Grinny says.

"I think we can all fit if I just bring these chairs over," Sofie says.

Once we're all settled and eating, the wedding talk picks up again. We've each ordered at least two dresses—April has the most with four. Holly and Scarlett both have two, and we'll return whatever we don't wear...although it sounds like April and I will be the only ones returning anything.

"We found Dakota's dress first. It was easy. I think it'll be perfect," I say. "Right?" I look over at Dakota and she nods, mouth full.

"Perfect," she manages to get out. "I want to wear it every day."

We laugh and I nod. "We need an alternative dress for her to wear in the meantime because, yeah...I have to remind her several times a day that the dress has to stay special for Auntie Sof's wedding. But you do finally get to try it on today."

"Girl, I don't blame you," Scarlett tells Dakota. "That's how I feel about the one I think I'm keeping."

"I have three dresses and I think I know which will be my favorite, but it'll depend on if it goes with what everyone else picks out," I say.

"Yeah, I definitely have different levels of sexy," April says.

"Same," I say, laughing.

"I love this," Sofie says, her smile so wide. "I cannot wait to see them all."

"You're the easiest bride ever, Sof," Scarlett says. "Has anyone broken the agreement and tried on a dress?" She looks around the table.

"No! We agreed to wait until we were all together to try them on," April says.

"You look guilty." Holly points at Scarlett.

Scarlett's eyes go wide. "No, I have *not* tried on either dress and it's been torture!"

We all laugh and look slightly guilty ourselves. I've almost tried my dresses on at least twice since they started arriving.

"I can't wait to see your dress, Sofie," I say. "The pictures Scarlett's been sending in the group chat look incredible."

"It's not quite finished yet, but it's close enough for her to try on today." Scarlett makes an excited face as she tilts her head from side to side.

THE HIGHLIGHT of the day is when Sofie tries on the dress. It's exquisite. Champagne lace with bell sleeves and a low neckline that fits Sofie so perfectly, it's a dream. She looks like a bohemian fairy.

I decide to return only one of my dresses and keep the other two—the prettiest one for the wedding and the sexier one for Vegas. Something I probably never would've considered if I hadn't tried everything on with the girls.

By the end of our trying-on session, Grinny and the girls have talked me into going to Vegas.

"I'd be absolutely thrilled to watch Dakota. We can do a trial night before you go, if that will make you feel better," Grinny says. "And if anything at all came up, we have pilots that work at the lodge that could come pick you up, right, Scarlett?"

"Absolutely. George is a gem," Scarlett says.

I already knew Sofie was special, but I thought for sure that a little weirdness would come up between the group at some point. Weddings can bring out the worst in people, and any time females are thrown together, I've found it to be volatile.

Or maybe that's just my experience from being in pageants.

And dance.

And high school.

"Do y'all really treat each other like this all the time?" I ask as we're changing into the clothes we arrived in.

"What do you mean?" April asks.

"I haven't picked up on any jealous vibes or any of that competitive crap I'm used to...I mean, Sofie's not that way, but she's...Sofie. She's the best person I know."

Sofie smiles at me. "*You're* the best. And yep, we do treat each other like this all the time. Well...I've been away for a long time, so if they've had any cattiness while I was gone, I don't know about it."

Scarlett laughs. "Having four older brothers, I was so happy to be around other girls, I never thought to be jealous or competitive. And growing up, Grinny and the Golden Girls were always the best examples of women loving and supporting other women."

"It must have been wonderful to grow up here together," I say wistfully.

"It took you a while to believe I genuinely liked you," Sofie says, using my shoulder to balance as she puts her shoes on.

"You were such a surprise," I admit. "And now all of you are. I realized a little bit ago that I keep holding my breath, waiting for a backhanded compliment or a snarky comment to sneak through here and there, but y'all just keep being great." I laugh and they do too, but I feel the need to explain myself. They've opened up to me so easily, and I want to let them know why it could seem like it's taking me longer to be as open. "My mom put me in pageants my whole life, and there were times it was brutal. *Everything* and *everyone* was a competition. And if I met someone that it seemed I could be friends with, my mom forced it into a competition. I've told you about some of it," I say to Sofie, "but I've tried to forget most of it." I make a face and my nose starts to burn when tears well up. "I'm just really glad to be here."

The next thing I know, I'm surrounded in a group hug, Grinny and the aunties included.

"We're so glad you're here," Scarlett says. "It's felt like you're one of us from the day I met you."

"I know, it really has," Holly says. "And now you're not getting rid of us."

April does her best scary laugh, which sounds more like a goat than a wicked witch.

Dakota squeezes in an opening and gets in on the hug.

"I like this," she says.

"Me too, Kota." I pull her in closer and squeeze everyone tighter. "I think we've found our home."

CHAPTER SIXTEEN

WINNER, WINNER, CHICKEN DINNER

WYATT

I stop by Theo's on my way home from work, tired but needing a break from the hospital.

It was a hard shift.

Jeffrey Franks, thirty-nine and with no health issues to speak of, was visiting Landmark for the first time with his wife and fell a good thirty-five feet while hiking. He's in critical condition and his wife is, understandably, a wreck. I stayed past my shift and I'm not on call tonight, but I'll be going back later to check on him, or calling in for frequent updates if he starts improving.

I start to back out of the driveway when I see Marlow's SUV there, not wanting to intrude on the girls' time, but then she steps outside, and I'm caught. I pause and pull back in, parking next to her. She puts something in her car and pauses when I get out.

"Wyatt," she says cautiously.

"Hey. I thought everyone might be gone by now. Is everyone still trying on dresses?"

"Dakota and I are the only ones still here," she says. "We'll get out of your way soon though..."

I exhale, the weight of the day catching up with me.

Her features tighten and she shakes her head, saying something under her breath that I don't catch.

"What was that?" I ask.

She rolls her eyes and mine go wide.

"Uh...did I do something to—" I start.

"I just never know what to expect with you," she says, her hands landing on her hips. "But I've had the best day I can ever remember having, so I'm not going to let you ruin it."

I stare at her, my brain failing to catch up. "Oh. What's going on?"

"Why don't you tell me? I thought we were past the weirdness, but you've been avoiding me for days," she says.

I swallow. She's right. I have. I've been all up in my head about her and as a result, I thought it'd be best if I just steered clear of her for a few days until I could be around her without wanting to reach out and touch her.

"I really like Dr. Emma and Dr. James, but you've gotta admit, it's strange when you have them pass along messages for you. And when you see me coming and turn to go in the other direction." Her voice rises and she takes a few steps forward, until she's within a foot of me.

Her cheeks are flushed and she's close enough that I could reach out and pull her against me with little effort.

"Dakota and I love it here," she says, her voice cracking, and the next thing I know, her fingers are jabbing into my chest. "And we're not going anywhere, do you hear me?"

Her face crumbles and before I know what I'm doing, my arms are around her and I'm holding her against me in a hug. I can feel her heart or mine, maybe both of ours, pounding out of control, and then I feel the calm that takes over when she relaxes into me.

"The last thing I want is for you to go anywhere," I finally say, my voice gruff.

Her body feels like heaven, curves in all the right places, and the perfect fit against mine.

"Well, you could've fooled me," she says into my chest. "I mean, I also wasn't expecting *this*...uh...whatever this is that we're doing right now—"

"I think this is a hug," I say.

"Right. A hug. You are all over the place. Constant whiplash...the rudeness, the pastries, the sweetness, the bolting, and now this...hug. Why are you so exhausting?"

I chuckle and reluctantly step back, letting my hands drop from her.

It really, *really* sucks to let her go.

"I apologize for all the whiplash," I start carefully. "I promise it's not that I don't want you around. It's...the opposite of that."

Her nose crinkles up and she looks so adorable and sexy and tempting, I take another step back.

"What do you mean?" she asks.

I take a second, and then it comes to me. "Did you ever see *Love Actually?*"

She frowns again and nods. "Yes?"

"You know that guy who holds up the signs? He's been awful to his best friend's girlfriend their whole relationship and when she finally calls him out on it, he has to admit that he's had feelings for her all along..."

"Yes? What does that—"

"I always hated that part," I admit. "Like, why didn't he admit it sooner, when he might've had a chance? Or why didn't he get the hell away from her, so his feelings didn't grow? But I think I'm starting to get it now."

"Well, I don't—I'm more confused than ever," she says.

"You know what I thought when I first saw you in the hospital with Dakota?" I ask, running my hands through my hair.

Her nose flares as she takes a deep breath, her eyes widening again as she stares up at me. "What?" she says quietly.

"I thought you were the most beautiful woman I'd ever seen. I could barely get a coherent word out of my mouth because I was so consumed by your beauty. The night I met you, I was too upset, but when I truly saw you..."

She starts to laugh, but it dies when she sees that I'm serious.

"That's never happened with me before...ever," I say. "And it doesn't excuse the way I've treated you, but—"

"I'm having a hard time believing this," she interrupts. "If you think I'm *so beautiful*, it seems like you'd be a lot nicer. Most guys with crushes flirt or at the least...don't behave like cavemen."

I bite the inside of my cheek to keep from laughing.

"That's fair. And I admit, I don't know what to do with myself...how to act around you. Caveman sounds about right."

Her cheeks burn brighter and she licks her lips, looking at me and then away like she can't stand to settle on me for very long. But when she does, her eyes are curious and her chest is rising and falling more rapidly the longer our conversation goes.

"So you've been acting this way because you think I'm attractive," she says, her eyes narrowing.

"I think you're more than attractive. I think you're fucking amazing. The way you've come in and captured the hearts of everyone here is remarkable. The way you are with Dakota, and the way you'd do anything for Sofie. I've noticed everything about you. *Too much* about you."

"I don't know what to say," she whispers.

She puts her fingers to her puffy lips and I stare transfixed. I clear my throat and tug on my hair to get ahold of myself.

"You don't need to say anything, Marlow. I'm sorry for even putting this on you now. You're married," I say softly, "and there's no way I'd ever normally say this to a married woman. I've never had these thoughts about a married woman...or anyone," I groan. "Sorry. I can't seem to stop." I hold up my hand. "Trust me. I won't keep talking like this. I just wanted you to know I can't bear the thought of you leaving. I only want to know you better."

Her mouth parts and she starts to say something and then pauses, shaking her head.

"I'm in the process of a divorce, as I believe you know," she finally says, looking past me before frowning up at me again.

"And you have a girlfriend," she adds.

"Me? No, I don't."

"Brooke?" She emphasizes it as if that will help me remember.

"Brooke's not my girlfriend."

"Well, she wants to be."

"Yeah, I think she does, but I made it clear after that night you met her that I don't feel the same."

She studies me and the moment changes the longer she looks at me, the energy around us crackling.

"Dr. Wyatt?"

"Please don't call me Dr. Wyatt when we're not at the hospital. For all I care, you don't have to call me that there either."

"I've called you plenty of other things in my head, believe me," she says, her cheeks lifting with her grin.

I can't help it, I smile back. "I bet you have."

"I'm attracted to you too," she says, her voice barely above a whisper. "Even though you've been such a jerk." She puts her hand over her mouth and laughs. "Wow, it feels really good to say that. The jerk part. I'll probably regret saying the other part."

I stare at her, my body pulsing with the desire to touch her, to claim that mouth, to—

Her shoulders lift as she drops her hand from her mouth and I force myself to look in her eyes.

"But I've been married to a cheater," she says, "and there's no way I'd ever do that to anyone."

I swallow hard, anger and indignation flooding through me. "How anyone could ever cheat on you is beyond me."

Her eyes heat and I drag in a deep breath.

"But we're on the same page regarding cheating," I say, my voice husky.

I cannot believe this conversation is happening.

She swallows and I watch the pulse in her neck flutter. "Sutton's helping me with the divorce," she says. "He thinks it'll go through soon."

"That's great...right? If Sutton said that much, it's true. The guy is annoyingly right about most things."

We stare at each other for a moment, the sunset leaving streaks of color in the sky and on her face with the last light.

"I feel like I've already let you down. I said I'd be a friend and I haven't done a good job of that yet," I tell her.

She's quiet and then lifts her shoulder in a subtle shrug. "It helps that you've explained yourself. I'm still having a hard time wrapping my mind around it, but...it helps."

"I'll try to do a better job of...everything," I say.

She takes a step forward and my chest feels like it's going to cave in.

"That hug was maybe the best thing I've ever experienced, just so you know." Her smile is shy as she looks at me.

I hold my arms out, already anticipating the second she'll walk into them for another hug.

She shakes her head. "No, not yet. It was a little too nice."

I nod. "Okay. Got it. No hugs yet. But Marlow?"

She tilts her head. "Yeah?"

"The moment you're divorced—" I leave the words hanging and the way the heat builds between us, and she swallows hard, tiny goose bumps skittering across her skin, I know she hears everything I'm not saying.

It's a promise.

"You going inside?"

"Sure, buddy," I tell her, smiling.

She smiles back but shakes her head.

"Too far?"

"Yeah. We're friends, but don't be friend-zoning me," she says, smirking.

And I feel like I've just won the fucking lottery.

CHAPTER SEVENTEEN

NO BENEFITS

MARLOW

Wyatt and I walk inside Sofie and Theo's house, my head reeling from everything that just happened.

Wyatt is *into* me?

How did I not see even a single sign of this?

I look at him shyly out of the corner of my eye and smile nervously when he glances back at me. My heart is still palpitating over that hug. I didn't see that coming either and it was...epic.

"Wyatt!" Dakota yells as she comes flying at him, her arms wrapping around his waist like a little koala. "Hiiiii," she sings.

"Hi, Sweets," he says, laughing as he looks down at her.

And then I hear both of them yelp and Dakota backs up with her mouth gaping and we all look at Wyatt's pants that now have something brown dripping all over them.

Dakota gasps and covers her mouth, mumbling under her hand, "I forgot about my chocolate milk."

She turns to me, her eyes welling with tears and I put my hand on her shoulder before rushing to get something to wipe it up.

"I'm sorry," Dakota whispers.

"No worries," Wyatt says.

"Easy fix," Sofie says, tossing me a towel and then one to Wyatt.

Wyatt helps me sop up the chocolate milk from the table and the floor and then he dabs his pants.

When I get it cleaned up, I look at Dakota and she still looks crushed. I'm about to say something to her when Wyatt leans down and puts his hand on her shoulder.

"Hey, it's just a little chocolate milk. At least it's not horse...poo. Although you could've chosen a different color to spill on me...brown does make me think of you-know-what."

She giggles when he plugs his nose and shudders.

"And you know what? That was the best hug-and-hi combo I have *ever* been given."

Her full cheeks lift as she smiles up at him.

Good lord, I think my ovaries just twitched.

She turns carefully and grabs her crown sitting on the dining room table.

"You're not supposed to see this yet, but I think it's okay

since you're my Wyatt." She plops her crown on her head and he puts his hand up to his chin, nodding as he assesses her.

"It's official," he says. "You are a princess. Theo," he calls, "did you know you have a princess in your house?"

Dakota laughs and Theo comes over to study her too.

"Yes," Theo says, his voice serious. "I had a feeling when she stayed here the first night. I put a tiny rock under her mattress to test it and sure enough, she moved out a few days later to finer dwellings, just like *The Princess and the Pea.*"

Theo knows we have an adorable version of that book, but I'm still impressed that he pulled that out so fast. Dakota's eyes are wide as she takes her crown off and carefully sets it back on the table.

"No, I only left because Mama said so." She looks at me for backup, and I lift my hands in a shrug but wink at her.

She grins, comfortable now that she knows they're joking. "Mama knows I don't need any rocks!" She shakes her head emphatically. "Right, Mama?"

"That's right. No rocks for my princess." I hold up my hand and she gives me a high five.

I glance at Wyatt, who is watching us with a sweet grin on his face. Before, I would've thought it was only because of Dakota, but after our conversation, either something has changed between us or I'm seeing who he really is now.

Or maybe both.

"What do princesses eat for dinner?" Sofie asks. "Pizza, maybe?"

"Pizza!" Dakota cheers.

"Perfect. I thought maybe we'd order a pizza from Pierre."

"Who's Pierre?" I ask.

"Oh, he owns The Dancing Emu," Sofie says. "But he's been gone for a while, just got back into town, I guess. I ran into him at Happy Cow. He said he had to work out some family drama."

"I didn't realize he was back. I wonder if Jack knows," Wyatt says.

"Who's Jack?" I ask.

Sofie makes a face. "Sorry, we need to do a better job of catching you up on who everyone is."

"I'm learning a little bit from working at the hospital, but honestly, besides work and hanging out with you guys, the occasional Happy Cow trip, and the one night at The Pink Ski, Dakota and I don't get out much."

Wyatt leans in closer and says, "Jack owns The Gnarly Vine, but he's a bit of a recluse. Stays in the kitchen most of the time. He and Pierre stay out of each other's way."

"Did something bad happen between them?" I ask.

"No one really knows," Wyatt says. "But Jack was a lot happier with Pierre out of town."

"When do you see Jack?" Theo asks.

"We have a little barter situation going on. He gives me free wine, I take care of his doctor visits. I get the better end of the deal." He laughs.

"Did everyone figure out the dresses?" Theo asks Sofie.

While they're talking about that, Wyatt looks at me. "Have you met Jo yet?"

"No, I haven't."

"She owns Sunny Side with her husband, Mark. And we really need to get you to Tiptop. You'd love it. One of my best friends, besides my brothers, owns that restaurant... Blake and his wife, Camilla. They have a view like you won't believe."

"For being such a small town, Landmark has so much to do. I've really only barely scratched the surface."

"Are you doing anything next Saturday?" he asks.

"Uh, no, I don't think so. Unless I'm forgetting wedding stuff. Why?"

"There's something I think you and Dakota would love. If you're free, dress in layers and I'll pick you up at ten."

My mouth parts as I try to come up with a reason why we probably shouldn't spend time together outside of the hospital and wedding activities, but it seems harmless. Dakota will be with us and this is what friends do, right? Hang out with each other?

Except my cheeks feel flushed and I'm sweaty and I know that's not friend behavior.

"Okay," I say reluctantly. "Maybe."

Dakota's hand pops between us as she sits on the stairs, her hand fitting easily through the railing. She waves. "I can't wait. What are we gonna do, Wyatt?"

He grins at me before placing his hand on the railing. His arms are so ripped, not bulky but toned to perfection. I swallow hard and look away.

"How about a surprise? Do you like surprises?" he asks Dakota.

"I love surprises! But where are we going?" she asks.

He laughs. "That would ruin the surprise."

I bite the inside of my cheek and then laugh. "Good luck with that. She can grill like nobody's business."

Sofie sets something down and I look at her. She and Theo are watching the three of us like we're their only entertainment.

"What?" I ask.

Sofie's eyes go wide and she looks at Theo, shaking her head.

"Nothing," Sofie says. "Right?"

He clears his throat and grins, nodding. "Right."

I narrow my eyes. "You guys are being weird."

"Get used to it. I swear, Theo and Sofie have their own language. Just be glad that you missed being here after they first got together," Wyatt says. "I'm just now getting used to seeing them again. They didn't show their faces for weeks."

"Not true," Theo says.

"Well, maybe for a minute or two because Grinny forced you to family dinners," Wyatt says.

Sofie flushes and can't stop smiling.

"I guess I got here at just the right time," I say.

"Yes, you did," Wyatt says under his breath.

My stomach drops a little in an excited lurch.

Friends, friends, friends, friends, I remind myself.

CHAPTER EIGHTEEN

ROYAL TREATMENT

WYATT

I stop by Happy Cow on my way to Marlow's the next Saturday morning.

They're out of some of the things Marlow and Dakota ordered when we were here before, so I fill a box with chocolate croissants and bear claws and the one donut with sprinkles left in the case.

I've been up for hours. Cleaned my condo from top to

bottom, worked out, showered, and still made the trip to Happy Cow and to Marlow's with ten minutes to spare. I watch the clock impatiently, ready to just go bang on the door already.

I look at myself in the rearview mirror.

Who are you and what did you do with the chill version of yourself, man?

I run the little duster Grinny gave me for my car over the dashboard and the controls and a minute doesn't even pass.

"Wyatt!"

I turn and Dakota is standing in the door, waving. Busted.

I get out of the car and walk toward her, smiling when I see her space buns.

"Nice hair," I tell her.

"Mama did it. She said since we don't know where we're going, I should be prepared for anything."

"She's right."

"Did you bring us treats?" she asks, her eyes on the box.

"Oops, I didn't hide that surprise very well, did I?"

Her mouth drops and she claps her hands together.

"Is that the surprise?" she says excitedly. "I can't wait."

She is too cute for words.

"That's just one of the surprises."

"There's *more*?"

This girl is going to make my heart double in size, I swear. She takes my hand and leads me inside.

"Yes, there's more."

"This is the best day ever," she cries.

Marlow is standing in the living room when we walk in, looking unbelievable in jeans and a long-sleeved T-shirt that both fit her just right. This might've been a bad idea. My thoughts are anything but honorable right now.

She looks at me shyly and I grin, trying to cover my nervousness. She's looked at me this way since I laid it out in front of Theo's, how into her I am. I wasn't planning on doing that, but I didn't know what else to do. It wasn't working to avoid her or to keep it bottled up—all that was accomplishing was making me seem like the biggest prick in Landmark Mountain.

"Wyatt brought treats!" Dakota says.

"Treats for Sweets...and her mom," I say.

Dakota claps and Marlow's cheeks flush. "That was nice of you. Thank you," Marlow says. "We're getting the royal treatment, Kota."

She points to the coffee pot and I nod, moving to take a mug from her. Our fingers brush against each other and my whole body is aware of it. We take our coffee to the table and sit on either side of Dakota, forming a triangle around the donut box.

"And this is not the only surprise," Dakota says, carefully opening the box and then squealing when she sees the donut with sprinkles.

"Is that for me?" she whispers.

"I thought you might like that one." I nod.

She does a little dance and picks it up, taking a big bite and sending sprinkles flying on the table.

"Oops," she says with her mouth full. "Don't worry, Mama, I'll take care of it."

She sets her donut on the table and then tries to meticulously pick up each sprinkle. Some are harder to capture than others, but the payoff is great when she pops one in her mouth—she does a little dance, her head tilting side to side.

"Is she always this entertaining?" I ask Marlow.

"Always." Marlow laughs. "I don't think I've ever been that excited in my life. She makes me want to be though."

We smile at each other and then reach for the same bear claw. I lift an eyebrow when she grins and I motion for her to take it.

"I guess pastries will continue to be an ongoing fight between us," she says, her tone playful.

"Keep smiling at me like that and I'll gladly hand over anything you want," is out of my mouth before I can stop myself.

I run my hand through my hair and exhale, silently admonishing myself to pull it back a notch.

Her smile widens and she points at the other bear claw in the box as she takes a bite out of hers. "Oh wow. So good. Better grab it before I decide to get greedy."

Her head tilts back and forth, matching Dakota's and I just watch them both for a minute before ever taking a bite of mine. A memory of my dad comes back to me, a moment in the kitchen when he was watching my mom and he leaned over and nudged my shoulder with his.

"When you get married one day, make sure you find someone like your mom," he said. *"Kind and beautiful and generous."*

I blink and Marlow's watching me.

"Are you okay?"

I swallow hard and nod.

"I'm so happy about this new relationship with pastries," Marlow says.

"What do you mean?"

She makes a face. "We didn't have sugar in our house growing up and my mom would have a fit if she saw me eating this now."

"Sugar's not the best thing for us, but I can't imagine

never having it. I do indulge more than I should," I admit. "Is your mom super healthy?"

She snorts. "God, no. She is thin at all costs and expects me to be the same. Her diet consists of Diet Coke, cold cuts, and cheese...well, the cheese comes and goes if she's trying to cut back on dairy."

I frown. "That's not...great."

"No. I'm still trying to learn to balance myself and I've been out of her house for over a decade. It's hard sometimes to dismantle the way we're raised." She looks over at Dakota, her smile not as free after talking about her mom.

I wait for her to keep talking. I don't know if it's because I lost my parents so young or what, but I have an unusual curiosity about relationships with parents. When my brothers and I used to go to Blake Gamble's house, I'd hang out a little longer at the dinner table or help in the kitchen to see the interaction with Blake's parents and the rest of his siblings.

When she doesn't say anything else, I speak up. "I don't think I'd ever thought about what a gift Grinny had given me until med school. She always taught us to eat in moderation and to listen to what our bodies are telling us. I couldn't listen to everything my body told me, which was *sleep, idiot*, but my peers who lived on junk food and partied instead of not sleeping every chance they got during that time...they had it a lot harder than I did. Didn't mean I always got it right, still don't. But moderation has served me well."

"I like that," she says. "I want that for Dakota. Moderation and a healthy balance. And fun!"

"Speaking of fun...are we ready to go see what's next?" I ask.

Dakota nods, eyes wide. "I'm ready!"

I hold my hand up and she slams my palm with hers. I look at Marlow, eyebrows lifted.

"Ready," she says, laughing when I hold my hand up for her to slap.

When she does, I stand up and they do too. We make quick work of clearing off the table, and I set the pastry box on the kitchen counter. They're staying in one of the furnished condos at the resort, but it has their personal touches with pictures and Dakota's toys. I pause to look at the pictures of Marlow and Dakota. One of them in a sunflower meadow laughing makes my gut hurt it's so beautiful. There's another one of them with Sofie and one of Dakota with a guy I'm assuming is Cash. I don't see a resemblance, but he's a good-looking guy. And then there's one more picture of a much younger Marlow with a guy who favors her. His arm is wrapped around her shoulder and their smiles are wide.

"Is this your brother?" I ask her.

She grins. "Yep, that's Logan. He's trouble, but I love him."

"Where is he?"

"It's hard to keep track of where he is. He travels nonstop." She shakes her head. "I'm trying to get him to come visit. I don't know if he'll ever settle in one place..." She looks at me wistfully. "You're lucky that you live close to all your siblings. Logan and I are close, but we both got out of the house as soon as we could, and Logan hasn't stopped moving since."

"Sounds like there's a story there."

"Yeah, if I can ever get him to slow down long enough to tell it."

We make our way to my car, after grabbing Dakota's car seat, and she bounces all the way. I'm excited to show her the surprise, but I'd be just as happy hanging out with them here.

Every little bit of revelation into who Marlow is intrigues me.

I just want more.

CHAPTER NINETEEN

COMPETITION

MARLOW

I think Dakota and I both gasp at the same time when we see the long slides that disappear up into the mountain.

I've never seen anything like it. There are two carts going side by side, one a few feet ahead of the other.

"What is this?" Dakota asks, a bit awestruck.

"This is the resort's alpine slide. It's only open in the summertime, along with the coaster...which you can go on when you're a little older. What do you think? Do you want to try the slide?" Wyatt asks.

"I can try it?" Dakota asks. "I'm not too little?"

"I thought maybe I'd go in one cart and you and your mom could go down the other and we'd race down the hill."

I turn to look at him, mouth gaping. "And that's safe?"

"Yes. I haven't ever treated anyone from accidents on this...everything else in town, yes, but not the alpine slides."

Dakota looks more excited than nervous and I reluctantly nod.

"Okay, if you're sure." I'm smiling when I tear my eyes away from the view in front of us. "It looks really fun."

We make our way to get in line for the chairlift ride.

"The lift up is almost as great as the slide," he says.

He looks animated, much looser than at work, his eyes lit with excitement. It's hard to notice anything else when he looks like this. He puts his hand on the small of my back as we get closer and I feel warmth radiating into me. It's more than his touch, which I can't think about for too long because it feels so good...

It's the way he wants to do something special for Dakota and me.

The time he's already invested in us this morning, and every time he sees Dakota.

It's the way he listens to her like she's the most interesting creature he's ever heard.

The way he looks at me.

We get on the lift and the ride for the next few minutes is breathtaking.

Dakota points out things and can hardly contain her excitement now that we're going up.

"I can't believe there are places in the world like this

that I almost missed out on seeing," I say. "Why was I content to stay in my little box all that time?"

"Sometimes it's easier staying in what we know, even if it's not comfortable," Wyatt says. He turns to look at me and smiles. "But I'm glad you're here now."

"Me too."

"I thought I was scared to go down that slide, but I'm not. Maybe a little scared," Dakota says.

"I'm a little scared too, but we'll be okay," I tell her.

"There's a way down other than the slides, if you change your mind," he says. "But I think you'll really like it."

Dakota nods and gulps. "I don't want to change my mind."

"It's totally okay if you do, but don't miss out on this view," he says. "Look, there's a golden eagle. Do you see its nest?"

"We're flying even higher than her," Dakota says. "Do you think she wants to catch up to us?"

"I bet she does," Wyatt says. "Anyone who sees you wants to say hello."

Dakota smiles and waves happily to the bird as he takes off in the other direction.

"Hello, eagle. Goodbye, eagle," she sings.

Wyatt waves at the eagle and I watch the two of them with a lump in my throat. I think Wyatt has already spoken to her more than her dad has, and he's certainly shown her more affection.

When we reach the top, we're shown how to handle the cart and then we're buckled in. The next thing I know, we're cascading down the hill, the breeze in our faces, and Dakota is squealing with joy.

"Faster, Mama, faster. I think we're gonna win."

I glance over at Wyatt and she's right. We're ahead by a yard at least. I don't tell her I'm almost positive he's braking so we will win, and when we reach the bottom first, the way her head falls back and she claps and then throws her hands up in the air make it all worth it.

We get out of the cart and she's jumping up and down.

"We won! Can we go again?" she says.

He gives her a high five. "How about we check out the games inside?" He points at the arcade beyond the ticket counter. He lifts a shoulder. "You can try to beat me at Ms. Pacman."

"Oh, Mama will beat you at that," she says. "She's better than *everyone* at that game."

I laugh and nudge her. "Let's make sure we're good sports."

"What does that mean again?" she asks.

"It means we can be excited when we win, but it's not nice to brag about it."

Wyatt pretends to pout. "Can I brag a little bit if I beat you at Ms. Pacman?"

I try to hold back my smile. "I'm sorry to say you won't get the chance to find out...because I'll win."

I'm laughing before the words are all the way out...that I said it and his reaction to it. He leans over me, his face getting close to mine as he laughs and says, "Game. On."

Dakota plays Skeeball next to us and gets a long line of tickets to choose a prize.

It ends up closer than I'd like with our game—he's really good—but I beat him soundly.

I don't think he can quite believe it.

"Best out of three?" he asks. "Loser buys dinner at Sunny Side?"

"Sure," I agree.

And I beat him every game.

"You weren't lying about your mama being really great at this game," he says, laughing. "I think I need to go drown my sorrows at Sunny Side."

Dakota puts her hand on his arm. "Are you so sad?" She looks up at him and then back at me with concern.

"I'm just teasing," he tells her. "I need to practice before I play your mom again. And I'm hungry. How about you?"

"So hungry! Can I pick out a prize first?" she asks.

"Of course." He looks at me and shakes his head. "She really is the sweetest kid I've ever met."

"Thank you. I sure like her a lot."

"I like you both a lot," he says softly.

My words get stuck in my throat. I smile at him, feeling all stuttery inside, and we watch as Dakota picks out a pen with a sloth on top and a small bouncing ball.

"That was so fun. I loved that," she says as we walk to the car.

"Thank you, Wyatt, for all this fun," I say and tilt my head to her to remind her to thank him.

"Thank you, thank you," she sings.

"You're welcome. I'm the one who should be thanking the two of you. If I wasn't with you today, I'd still be cleaning my condo and maybe washing the car or browsing medical journals."

"Yucky," Dakota says.

"Exactly."

I sneak a look at him and he's looking at me, his mossy green eyes darkening slightly.

"Maybe I can convince you guys to spend the day with me again sometime," he says so only I can hear.

I lift a shoulder. "Maybe." All nonchalance.

But inside, my insides are zipping around like they're on speed.

When we get to Sunny Side, a cute diner that I've only had takeout from, we order burgers, fries, and shakes and Wyatt lifts his shake glass to ours.

When we lifts ours, he clinks them and says, "To making new friends..."

I repeat the words after him and Dakota repeats after me, but I already know my heart is long gone.

CHAPTER TWENTY

TV AND TACOS AND TREATS

WYATT

After spending Saturday together, I find myself eating lunch with Marlow almost every day the next week.

Okay, true confession: Once I figured out her schedule, I was able to move a few things to make my lunch coincide with hers.

Creepy? Hell yeah.

Which is why I'll never tell a soul.

But getting to sit across from her every day this week

has been fucking great. This quest for friendship is paying off. She's not looking at me with such suspicion anymore, and I don't assume everything she says is a rip on my personality like before.

I've also been filing things away about her.

"Oh my God, I love taco day," she says, taking a huge bite out of her taco.

It's weird how much I love watching her eat.

I pull out a big bag of Reese's Pieces and she lights up.

"How did you know those are my favorite?" she asks, opening the bag while still chewing her taco.

"I saw you ciphering through the candy bowl in the break room." I laugh. "Easy deduction."

She also passionately loves hospital ice.

Coke. (Never diet.)

Thunderstorms.

And today, during breaks and now continuing during lunch, we're discussing rom-coms.

"I'm one of the few people I know who's okay with the way *My Best Friend's Wedding* ended," she says, pausing for my reaction. "You saw it, right?"

"Yeah, Scarlett made me watch it. I think she was crushing on Blake at the time and she bawled at the end."

"Sofie hated the ending too...it made her think of Theo even though they were never just best friends. But Cameron Diaz won me over in the karaoke scene," she says, shrugging. "I liked how vulnerable she was...and if Julia and Dermot were supposed to be together, something surely would've happened long before he was getting married."

I nod. "Maybe they were both afraid of ruining a good thing."

She raises her eyebrows. "But if it was meant to be, it

would've only made them better…" She leans in. "I did also cry at the end because I felt really bad for Julia."

I smile and feel that pang in my chest every time I look at her. I didn't know being her friend would be a physical pain, but it is. She literally makes my heart hurt, and I keep coming back for more.

"How did you feel about Ross and Rachel?" She takes another bite of taco and watches me carefully for my response.

"Uh. I liked them? I never watched the whole show."

"You never watched *Friends*? It's like a rite of passage."

"I've seen reruns, but I've never watched it from beginning to end," I admit.

"Well, I'm also one of the few who actually rooted for Rachel and Joey because Ross turned into such a whiny baby. The whole *we were on a break* thing made me so angry I never fully got over it, and I liked how loving Joey became when he and Rachel got close." She lifts a shoulder. "His soft side was really nice. But I was also happy for Rachel and Ross because…it's Rachel and Ross."

"Hmm. I guess I'll have to watch the show now."

She nods. "Let me guess, you were more of a *Grey's Anatomy* first season kind of guy…"

I shook my head. "Too unrealistic. I did like *House* though."

"Only saw part of one episode, but I did see that guy in a British show and was shocked by his accent because he was hysterical in *Sense and Sensibility*."

"Never saw it."

"Oh my God, iconic. Willoughby," she cries. "Willoughby." She stares into the distance and when she looks at me again, her eyes are misty. She shakes her head. "Iconic," she repeats.

"Wow. I guess I'll have to watch."

"Do you have a favorite show or movie?" she asks.

I look down at my plate and nod. And then I take a bite of taco so I won't have to answer for a while.

But she's patient and when I'm done chewing for what feels like forever, she's still waiting for my answer.

"Well?" she says, motioning for me to come out with it.

I look across the cafeteria and sigh, saying under my breath. "*Ted Lasso.*"

"What?"

I clear my throat and say it a little louder. "*Ted Lasso.*"

She leans in and makes a face. "Why are you whispering it? There's no shame in liking that show. It's amazing."

"I'm not ashamed. I just...I watch it every day."

She presses her lips together, but her smile is still growing by the second.

"Every day, huh?"

"I've watched the whole series four times already."

"No way. I haven't finished season three yet, so don't tell me any spoilers."

I shake my head. "I would never. That show must be experienced firsthand."

"I have to say you keep surprising me, Dr. Wyatt," she says, full-wattage smile going now. "Who knew you were such a softie?"

"Let's not mention this to my brothers..."

We finish and pick our trays up, chatting all the way to where we drop them off. Her talking about Keely's style and me throwing in that Ted even makes a mustache look cool.

"No, I wouldn't go that far," she says. "But he is really endearing."

We walk toward her desk and I feel that familiar pang

that our time together is about to come to an end. I've never felt that way about any friend in my life. I'm so screwed it's not even funny.

"How do you feel about *Bob's Burgers*?" she asks as she steps behind the huge desk.

I lean on the counter and frown. "I've never had them. Are they good?"

She laughs. "It's a show. And I think you'll love it. Report back to me after you've watched at least three episodes. I think that's a good amount to get acclimated to the show."

I grin and nod. "All right. I'll see you later."

"Later, Dr. Wyatt."

I walk away and turn to look back before I turn the corner. She's looking at me and her cheeks get rosy. I lift my hand in a wave, and she lifts hers, smiling before looking down at her desk.

IT'S like a gift from the gods when I get groceries that night and open the trunk, only to find Dakota's sweatshirt that she didn't end up needing the other day. I could totally wait and take it to work tomorrow—that would be the right thing to do. But what if Dakota needs this sweatshirt? What if she's been missing it all this time and forgot where she last had it?

Instead of calling...which would also be the right thing to do...I stop by their condo and knock on the door, my fist death-gripped around the sweatshirt.

It's barely a second and Dakota opens the door, her face breaking into a smile when she sees me. She tugs my hand, dragging me inside, and says, "Hi, Daddy!"

I stare at her in shock and then notice she has the phone up to her ear. It was hiding under all her hair.

"Hello?"

Even hearing the man's voice on speaker gives me a visceral feeling of rage.

"It's me...Dakota," she says. "I, um...I was wondering if you could come to Donuts for Dads? It's at school and—"

"Uh, no, I'm not...I can't do that," he says.

I squeeze her little hand that's still tucked in mine when her face drops.

"But it'll be lots of fun. You get free donuts! I bet you could even have five or six...and I'll be there and you can meet my friends. Owen isn't there though because he's too big for my class, but—"

"Dakota," Cash says harshly. "Put your mom on the phone."

Dakota looks up at me, worry on her face. Marlow calls from the other room.

"Dakota, who are you talking to? Come get in the tub, your water's ready."

"Bye, Daddy," Dakota says. She hangs up and tosses the phone on the couch. Her eyes are big when she looks at me. "I'm not 'sposed to use Mama's phone like that," she whispers. "Or open the door either, but I saw it was you..."

I don't know what to say, whether I should correct her for making that call or tell her it's okay for her to call her dad.

"It's important for you to listen to your mom," I say. "Do what she tells you to do, okay?"

She nods solemnly. "Okay. Would you go to Donuts for Dads, Wyatt?" she asks.

"When is it?"

"It's tomorrow." She runs and picks up a paper with the

details. "Here." She wraps her arms around my legs and her head rests against my side. "I don't want to be by myself."

I swallow hard and look up to see Marlow standing there watching us.

"What's going on?" she asks. "I didn't know you were here."

"I let him in," Dakota says.

Marlow gives her a look and I mouth *sorry*.

"I should've called and let you know I was here." I lift the sweatshirt. "Brought this over."

"I called Daddy and he's not coming to get donuts tomorrow, so I asked Wyatt to come instead," Dakota says.

"Oh, Kota, that's—" Marlow pauses when her phone rings.

Dakota moves toward her toys and sings to herself as she plays.

Marlow makes a face and holds up her phone to show me it's Cash. "I'm sorry, I should take this. Don't go yet..."

I nod and she answers the phone, walking toward the front window.

"Hey. No, I didn't have her call you."

I try to act like I'm not listening while also straining to hear her quiet words to that jackass of a man.

"You're her dad," she whispers. She turns back to look at Dakota, who's still singing happily in her own little world. "It's normal for her to want you there. No, I'm not guilting you, I'm just telling you how it is." She puts her hand on her head and takes a deep breath. "I've gotta go."

When she hangs up, she looks back at me and shakes her head, her cheeks splotchy with anger.

"I'd be happy to go, if it's okay with you," I say to Marlow.

She swallows and nods, looking at Dakota, who starts dancing her way over to me.

"I'll be there tomorrow," I tell Dakota.

"Yes," she sings.

She does a little leap and twirl and I grin and attempt the same moves, and her head falls back as she laughs.

"I'll never turn down treats...with Sweets..." I sing...or attempt to.

Marlow's still wearing a concerned expression, but she's smiling too by the time I turn to leave.

When I open the door, she reaches out and touches my arm. "Listen, Wyatt," she says under her breath. "You don't have to do this. I'll talk to her."

"I'm not letting that little girl down," I whisper. "Let's not make it more complicated than that. Okay?"

She's somber as she lifts those hazel eyes to mine, nodding. "I didn't know they made guys like you, Wyatt Landmark."

CHAPTER TWENTY-ONE

ANXIETY PRECIPICE

MARLOW

I pull into the preschool parking lot and see Wyatt's car already here.

I'm hanging somewhere between mortified and so moved that he would come to this. I don't want anyone to get the wrong idea...I know how it looks. Here I come, crashing into town, quite literally, with a little girl and in the middle of a divorce, and from the outside, it could seem like I've not wasted any time, going after the town's most eligible bachelor, snagging a job at his hospital and then luring him in through my daughter.

I jog inside the door, grossed out by myself, even though I know that's not what I'm doing. Wyatt is rounding the corner ahead of me and I turn just in time to see him walk in Dakota's class. She bolts to him, hugging him hard, and the teachers, kids, and parents all swarm around Dr. Wyatt like the star he is.

Not wanting to ruin the moment or make anyone think about how weird it is that I showed up...I turn and hurry back to my car.

Since when do I care what everyone thinks about me?

I'm amped up like I've had three cups of coffee and I haven't even finished one yet. In my hurry to go by Dakota's school and get to work on time, I put my coffee in a to-go cup and haven't gotten back to it. I call Sofie as I pull into the hospital parking lot, still a few minutes before I'm supposed to clock in, but it goes to voice mail.

Scarlett, April, Holly, and I are supposed to go over there tonight to work on these little gift baskets all the guests can take home at the wedding. I love how much fun Sofie's having with all the details. Cash and I eloped—it was a Tuesday at the end of our lunch break. A justice of the peace did our vows and we were married and back to work by one thirty in the afternoon. That night after work, we went out to dinner with Sofie and Cash's friend, TJ, and I was so exhausted and nauseated from my first trimester, I think I was asleep by nine o'clock that night.

I was already an embarrassment to my mom for ditching the pageants and a baby out of wedlock really didn't help. So I went with quiet and didn't even bother with the simple touches I could've done to make a wedding more beautiful and enjoyable.

Seeing Sofie's joy in making their day special, not only for her and Theo but for everyone who loves them, has been an eye-opening experience of how it should be. Her bridal shower is this weekend at the lodge, in the sunny atrium with the gorgeous mountains as the backdrop, and I love that she's surrounded with such beauty during all the wedding festivities, but I honestly think the two of them could get married in their barn with no decorations whatsoever, and it would still be the most spectacular wedding ever. Their love is that pure, that true.

I've talked myself somewhat down from the ledge by the time I've worked an hour. And then Wyatt walks up to my desk, catching me by surprise after I've leaned down to pick up something off the floor.

"I was properly donuted," he says, knocking on the counter.

"Excellent," I say awkwardly. "I really hope that wasn't too uncomfortable for you—I know you're not—"

"Are you kidding? It was great. Free donuts. Your ray of sunshine daughter...what better way to start my day?" His eyes crinkle at the edges and I blink in slow motion, momentarily stunned by everything that is Wyatt Landmark.

"Did anyone ask why you were there?"

"I jumped in before anyone could ask and said her dad can't be here as much as he wants, so she invited me since I'm a friend of the family."

"It was really...so nice of you to do that—"

"I'm honored she asked me, but I'm sure any of my brothers would've done the same for her too. The two of you are part of us now. You're not alone, Marlow. Remember that."

My air catches in my chest and I pick up a folder to fan myself, hoping I don't start crying right here at work.

He smiles and knocks on the counter again before walking away, and I'm left here speechless and all up in my feels.

I'M the first to get to Sofie's that night and Theo takes Dakota out to see the horses, so it's just the two of us.

"I'm sorry I didn't call you back this morning. I tried you later, but it sounds like your day got busy," Sofie says as we're grabbing a drink.

We take our drinks to the table and get comfy before we get started on our mini assembly line of wedding basket goodness.

"Oh, it's okay. I was just having a little meltdown. I'm better now."

She looks at me with concern. "Are you sure? You still seem a little—"

"No, I'm fine. It's just..." I flip my hand nonchalantly and laugh, but it sounds off. I lean in and whisper, even though it's just us. "Dakota asked Wyatt to go to Donuts for Dads at her school since Cash said he wouldn't come...and he went."

She waits and then says, "Oh," when I don't say anything else. "And you're upset because?"

"Because so many things!" I stand up and start pacing around her dining table. "But mainly...I'm afraid Kota's going to get too attached to Wyatt."

She nods. "Are you worried about that for her and Theo? Because I promise, he's consistent and when he loves someone, he loves them forever." She puts her hand on her heart, and I know she's right. Theo has loved her from the time they were little.

"No, I've never even considered it about Theo. I know you're right. But Wyatt..." I trail off.

"Wyatt is consistent too," she says. "All of the Landmarks are. When they open up their hearts to someone, you're in for keeps." She grins. "I'm really glad you and Wyatt have worked out your differences. It seems like it's going so much better. You guys seem...almost...close." Her head tilts as she eyes me carefully. "Is...do you—"

I shake my head, not wanting to know what she's about to say. "Theo is sort of stuck with us...with you being my best friend and all." I laugh. "The rest of the Landmark family have been great and it's like a bonus to have them love us too, but...Wyatt and I work together and...Dakota has really developed a fondness for him—she loves Theo too," I rush to add, "but she and Wyatt have this, I don't know, something I can't fully explain yet. It's really sweet." I take a deep breath and plop down in my seat, feeling exhausted.

I hadn't realized how much this was all weighing on me until I started trying to say it out loud.

"No one feels *stuck* with you, trust me," Sofie says, reaching over to squeeze my hand.

I start sticking all the cute things in the basket, happy for the distraction.

"And Wyatt will do right by her," she adds. "If he went to that this morning, it's because he knows it means something to her and he'll be careful of her feelings."

When I don't say anything, she puts her hand on mine again, and I stop and look at her.

"Is there more to this than what you're saying? What has you so worried?"

So many things, I want to say.

I don't want my daughter to make Wyatt a father figure when the guy is just being nice.

I don't want to scare Wyatt away before we even get a solid friendship off the ground.

I don't want us to get our hearts broken.

But instead, I say, "I'm sure I'm making a bigger deal out of it than it needs to be. It was nice of him to go, and it made Dakota really happy. Cash has disappointed her so many times, I should just be glad for her to have all the positive experiences she can with the new male figures in her life. She deserves it."

Sofie nods, her eyes wistful as she smiles. "She does... and so do you."

CHAPTER TWENTY-TWO

RETIRED TEATS

WYATT

It's Saturday morning and I'm antsy.

This time last week I was about to go pick up Marlow and Dakota to spend the day with them, and this week I'm off since I worked an extra-long shift yesterday and have no plans.

I love days with no plans.

But even after a hike I'm restless, and it annoys me because I've never been bothered by how quiet my condo is or that I'm waking up alone, eating alone...existing *alone*.

Most of the time, my family makes up for any lack I could possibly feel, and I don't know why hanging out with Marlow and Dakota only makes me ache for more.

They're busy today anyway, I remind myself. Sofie's shower is this afternoon and I'll see Marlow at work this week...and the Vegas trip is next weekend.

I think the last time I moped around was in seventh grade when I was stuck inside with the flu on a day I was supposed to go skiing. The fuck is wrong with me?

I wish I could blame this melancholy on a fever.

After staring inside my refrigerator for far too long, I pick up the phone and call my brother.

Callum picks up on the third ring.

"Wyatt." He never says hello.

"What are you doing?"

"Delphine got into the house again. And I just barely managed to keep Irene from following her."

"Good God. When are you gonna get rid of that goat?"

"The hell?" he snaps.

"It's a reasonable question. Next thing you know, she's gonna be holding seances in your living room with her cow buddy and you'll be out in the barn."

"Don't be stupid. I've been skimping on the peanut butter with her this week and she was just having a little protest."

"Just having a little protest," I repeat. "You do realize I'm not the one talking stupid, right?"

"Shut up," he grumbles.

I gasp in mock outrage. "It's a good thing Grinny's not hearing this conversation."

Growing up, there were a few things Grinny was firm

on. She didn't love cursing, but she absolutely would not tolerate *shut up, idiot,* or *stupid.* We're at two out of three right now.

"I stand by it," he says. And then under his breath, he adds, "Idiot."

"You did not." I laugh.

I think I might hear him laugh a little too, but it was probably my imagination.

"What do you want, Wy? Some of us have things to do."

"Oh, am I keeping you from Delphine? It's no wonder you're single, brother."

He snorts. "Say that to me when you've got a woman."

"I thought maybe you'd be up for a beer or something...I can come over and...help with Delphine."

"You all right?" he asks.

I don't know.

"Yeah...I'm fine."

"I'll see you soon." He hangs up.

Jerk never says bye either.

I head over to his house with his favorite beer—Laughing Lab—and get a call from Sutton as I'm pulling into Callum's driveway.

"Hey, Wy. Got a sec?" he asks.

"Sure. What's up?"

"I was just talking to Jamison about the flights for Vegas. I've had a change in my schedule. I'll be able to pull off the weekend, but I need to be on the first flight back, and since we have to take two flights both ways to accommodate everyone, I'm calling everyone in the wedding party to see who's able to stay a little longer and who's able to come back slightly earlier than planned."

"What are the options?" I ask.

"We're taking two helicopters at eleven on Saturday, so

all of us will get there that afternoon, and then some of us will come back Sunday night, the rest on Monday morning."

"I'm off Monday, so I can come back then, but if most want to stay, I can come back Sunday night too."

"Oh good." He sounds relieved. "I saw Scarlett with April and Holly at Sunny Side this morning, and April and Holly said it'd be better for them to get back Sunday night too. I'll let you know what I find out from everyone else."

"I think Marlow took Monday off too, but you should still double-check with her."

I wish I could ask him about the status of her divorce. It's not my business...but damn, it's at the forefront of my mind.

"I'll call her next," he says. "I need to talk to her anyway."

I flick the beer bottles I'm holding and am otherwise silent, my ears perked for any Marlow news. What the hell is wrong with me?

"It'll be nice to get away," he adds. "I wish I could stay both nights. I need some time to chill...and time in a different state than Tracy. She's beyond difficult right now."

"You sound exhausted, man. What's going on with Tracy?"

Sutton's ex-wife is not a favorite of anyone in the family. She was difficult before he married her, but he didn't see her true colors until it was too late. We should've tried harder to tell him how we felt about her, but we went the supportive route because it's one of those things—telling someone in love that they're marrying a b with an itch is a surefire way to cause conflict...

"I don't know what her deal is. Maybe just the typical Tracy shit and I'm just not up for it right now. She's always tried to make things as hard as possible for me, but it's amped up over the summer. It's all I can fucking do to have a conversation with her right now without her losing her shit, and for Owen's sake, I just want to keep the peace. Work is chaotic. I need a fucking vacation. God, listen to me. I'm sorry. This is the last thing you need right now. You need a vacation as bad as I do."

"No, you actually sound like you need it a lot worse. I actually just got to Callum's—why don't you come over and have a beer or two?"

"I wish I could. To make next weekend work, I need to work through this one. Thanks for listening to me vent. I promise I will be in full party mode by then. Count on it."

"You be however you need to be. Everyone will understand."

He chuckles. "You might regret saying that."

"Nah. I'm here for you. And listen, it won't hurt to get out this weekend too. Get some work done, but relax a little too."

"When did you get so smart, little brother?" he asks. "Oh wait—you've always been the smart one."

"Uh, no, I think you're confusing me with Callum."

"Wait a minute. You were supposed to say I was confusing you with myself..." He laughs.

"See? You should call me more. I already made you feel better."

"Message received. Love you, Wy."

"Love you, man. Talk to you later."

He does say bye because he spends his days speaking with lawyers and judges and not goats and cows like someone else I know. I trudge up to Callum's door, feeling eyes on me. I turn and jump when a cow is next to me, giving me a pointed look.

Callum opens the door and points to the cow. "Go, Irene. I have had enough of your shit today."

She looks at him as if to say *I'm leaving only because I want to* and trots off, stepping over a place in the fence that's in need of repair. Callum grumbles and it's then I notice the tools in his hand.

"I've gotta fix this fence or this morning's episode will be nothing. Delphine is in the barn right now, so it's a good time. The rest of the cows are grazing. It's this one that just can't cooperate." He hustles to the fence and gets to work while I set down the beer and try to assess how I can help.

"You ever think of selling her? Seems like you'd have a lot more peace around here."

Every other week, Callum's telling the family about some mischief or another that either Delphine or Irene have gotten into.

He shoots a glare my way and then tilts his head up for me to steady the woven-wire steel mesh fencing for him to secure it.

"She was one of my best producers," he says.

"Was? Doesn't that mean you sell her and get a new one who can keep the milk production up?"

"Wouldn't feel right to do that just because her teats have retired."

I snort and shake my head. "For the foulest of us, you sure are the softest hearted."

"Shut up."

We work our way down the fencing until it's completely sturdy again and he lifts his beanie long enough to push back the hair that's going in every direction.

"Thanks," he says.

"Anytime."

He points at the beer. "You leavin' that out here to tempt the animals or what?"

I chuckle and follow him inside. I don't care much for this beer, but after two, it's going down a lot easier.

After a few hours, I walk the miles between his house and my condo instead of driving. And even with the distraction, the exercise, the fresh air, the beer...at the end of the day, my mind is still on Marlow Hennessy.

CHAPTER TWENTY-THREE

THE VIEW FROM HERE

MARLOW

"But Owen won't be there the whole time?" Dakota asks on the way to Grinny's house.

We've talked about it every day this week. We even came over to Grinny's a couple nights to hang out so Dakota would be completely used to it—more for my sake, I think, than for Dakota's. She loves every chance she gets to be at Grinny's and seems excited to be a big girl staying overnight somewhere.

"Remember Sutton said Owen would be at Grinny's, but his mom is picking him up after lunch on Sunday?" I look at her in the rearview mirror.

She nods. She remembers, she just wants to discuss it.

"And remember, if you need me, you can call anytime, or I can fly home."

Since I'd taken off Monday when I agreed to go on the trip, I told Sutton I could come back then if that helped, but he said the pilot had told him this weekend was reserved for us, so any variation of travel we needed to do would be fine.

It puts my mind at ease to know I can get home quickly should the need arise.

I've been all over the place about this trip. Leading up to it, I've been mostly anxious, but each time we're with Grinny has helped. And then yesterday, I finally got excited.

I smile giddily as I pull into Grinny's driveway. If I didn't still have some nerves going about leaving Dakota for the weekend, I'd feel light as a feather. Lighter than I've been in years.

Because not only am I going away for the weekend to celebrate my best friend marrying the love of her life, but I am celebrating my freedom from Cash Hennesy.

My newly single status.

It feels wrong to be yelling it from the rooftops when the whole point of the weekend is to celebrate Theo and Sofie, but in my heart I am on a *high*.

Starting my new life in Landmark, and every day since walking out of Cash's life...all of it has culminated in a joy I never saw coming. I wake up happy, excited to face the unexpected, and more content than I've ever been in my life.

I love living here, and I love the fact that I never have to see or speak to Cash again...unless he changes his mind about seeing Dakota and then I'll deal with that when the time comes. But for now, I am free of that man and nothing could be better.

"We're here," Dakota cheers, interrupting my thoughts.

"Yes, we are." I park and turn around to look at her. "Are you sure about this?" I don't know if I'm asking her or myself.

"I'll miss you," she says softly, and my heart melts. "Owen says he'll make sure I don't get sad."

"Aw, that's sweet of him. I know Grinny is really excited about you staying with her too." Just then I look up and Grinny and Owen are waving from the front door.

We get out of the car, Dakota wheeling the little suitcase that Sofie bought her for this weekend. She's just as excited about the suitcase as she is about the crown.

"I love you, Mama!" she says, turning to hug me tight before we get to the door.

I'm still saying, *"I love you, Kota,"* as she turns and runs inside. Grinny picks up her suitcase and sets it inside before stretching her arms out to hug me.

Her eyes are compassionate when she sees that I'm a little wounded by how easy Dakota let me go.

"It's the newness of it all." Grinny holds the tops of my arms as she leans back to look at me. "She will be even more excited to see you on Monday, I have no doubt about that."

"I'm happy she's excited." I roll my eyes as I blink up at the sky and fan my face. "I'm ridiculous."

"You are no such thing. You're a good mama through and through, and the confidence you've instilled in that little girl is priceless. Go and enjoy yourself. Call whenever you want to, and try not to worry. Owen and I will try to keep her too busy to get homesick."

I hug her again. "Thank you so much. I can't even tell you how grateful I am that you're doing this."

Grinny smiles and gives my arm another squeeze.

"Love you, Kota," I yell into the house. "I'm leaving. Y'all have fun."

She comes running back with Owen on her heels and he smiles and waves as Dakota hugs me tight.

By the time I get to the resort, my tears are already drying. The guys are getting on a helicopter and Scarlett and Sofie motion for me to get on the one they're standing by. Wyatt is standing next to Theo outside their helicopter and he lifts his hand when he sees me. His lips curve into a smile when their engine starts and my sundress flies up with the sudden gust. I yelp and try my best to hold it down.

"I thought for sure I heard you say it was going to be a *plane*, but this is safe too, right?" My voice is shaky when I reach the girls, and I clutch Scarlett's arm with a sudden rush of nerves.

"Oh, I might've accidentally said that, but this is what we've got, and trust me, they're safe," she says. "Do you get motion sickness?"

I shake my head and I must look terrified because Sofie puts her arm around me.

"We can be terrified together," she whispers, making a face.

Theo jogs over and kisses Sofie. "I want to be in your helicopter," he says.

Scarlett pretends to gag. "Get out of here with your sexual innuendos." She shoos him away and the rest of us laugh, including Theo. "You're already getting your way by having her in your hotel room. We get to have her some of the time." She gives him a little shove and motions for Sofie and me to get in our helicopter. "We'll see you soon enough," she yells over the sound of the engine turning on.

Once we're inside, we get headsets and Holly hands us champagne. I take it reluctantly but lift it in a *cheers* as we clink the glasses. One sip and I set it down so I don't prove myself wrong about the motion sickness. For the next two hours, we chatter happily about the weekend and the wedding, and I see the most incredible view.

From up here, every problem seems tiny, every hope infinitely possible, and I can't wipe the smile from my face.

Life is good.

CHAPTER TWENTY-FOUR

UNDERCURRENT

WYATT

After being slammed all week at work and barely seeing Marlow except in passing, the anticipation has been building about this weekend.

There was one lunch when we had the same schedule, but I was called to see a patient five minutes after we sat down. Still, when she steps off the helicopter and I see her head fall back as she laughs and tries to keep her dress from flying up, I'm not expecting the intensity of my feelings.

That steady undercurrent that keeps the reins on me is there, *she's not yours yet* on repeat, but when she sees me, she smiles at me with a shyness I haven't seen from her in a while. I feel it too.

Maybe it's just us being far from home.

Maybe it's Vegas.

I wish all rules could fly out the window, that whole *what happens in Vegas, stays in Vegas* crap that you hear everyone say, but as tempting as it might get while we're here, I refuse to cross that line.

But damn, that smile. It's like she's lit up from the inside out.

We pile into a cushy SUV limo and Sutton appoints himself as bartender. I end up directly across from Marlow and her cheeks flush as her eyes meet mine. Her tongue peeks out to lick her full lips, leaving them glossy.

Fuck me.

I start to sweat.

This is going to be harder than I thought.

When we all have the bubbly in hand, Sutton says, "To Theo and Sofie!"

The ride is over in no time, and Scarlett, Jamison, and Sutton go inside to check us in and are back a few minutes later to hand out the keys.

"Suites for all," Scarlett says, shimmying her shoulders.

She gives Theo and Sofie their room keys, hands Jamison theirs, and gives Sutton, Callum, and me our own keys, rolling her eyes.

"I don't even want to know why the three of you can't stay in a suite together—you could've gotten one as big as the girls' if you needed some space, but whatever. Just make sure you're at all the planned activities. Without extras," she adds.

"Yes, ma'am," Sutton says. "And relax. We'll keep our prowling on the down-low, right?" He smirks at Callum and me.

"Speak for yourself," I say.

Sutton shakes my shoulder and laughs, and I realize he took that the opposite way I meant it.

I look at Marlow and her mouth parts. A flicker of something crosses her face, and I wish I could read her mind. If she could read mine, she'd know there's only one woman I want to be around this weekend, and she's standing right in front of me.

"A few of our activities are at different times than I'd hoped ...due to when they could fit us in, so I hope that's all right." Scarlett gives Sofie an apologetic look. "For example, fancy drinks probably would've been better second in our lineup, but we're starting off there. Can everyone meet there in an hour and a half?"

"This is amazing, Scarlett," Sofie says. "We're up for anything, right?" She looks around at the rest of us and we agree.

"Remember you said that." Scarlett grins. "Put on your pretty dresses and ties." She points at Callum. "That goes for you too."

He just stares at her but then grins at the last second.

"You're such a closet softie," I say under my breath.

He lifts a brow at me, grin gone.

I hold up my hands like I'm backing down but smirk nonetheless. He knows I'm right.

We pile into the elevator together, and I groan inside when Marlow stands in front of me, squeezed in so tight that her back is against my chest. Just as I glance down, she looks at me over her shoulder, laughing nervously, her hazel eyes darkening when she sees how close I am. She bites back her smile and turns around quickly. My dick jerks to life and I try my best to not jab her in the hip with it.

This longing for her just seems to be multiplying by the day…the hour. I have no idea what she feels for me at this point. Our friendship has grown, but we've both been so careful to keep things in that lane, that I wonder if we're going to be stuck there.

Everyone calls out their floor number and April pushes the buttons. Sutton and Callum get off first, my room is on the next floor, the girls' suite is two floors up, and the couples' suites are on the highest level.

Right before I get off, Scarlett is saying, "It would've been fun to rent a house for all of us to stay in, but—"

"It's probably best that we're not all sharing walls," Holly says, laughing.

"Right." Scarlett laughs.

The elevator dings and I shift past Marlow. Her breath hitches as I brush against her and I'm glad that I can escape to my room before my hands get a mind of their own.

AN HOUR AND A HALF LATER, I walk into the over-the-top bar and laugh when I see my brothers and Jamison already there with their drink of choice—well, all but Theo. They're surrounded by massive floral arrangements, the chandeliers and brocaded wallpaper not quite the vibe we're used to in Landmark Mountain.

"No sign of the happy couple?" I ask.

"Nope." Sutton grins. "And since they can't seem to keep their hands off of each other for more than five minutes, I suspect they'll be the last to show."

"Scarlett went to get ready with the girls—only reason *I* got here on time." Jamison smirks.

Callum shakes his head at him, his voice a low rumble. "No."

"No?" Jamison repeats.

"What Callum is trying to say so eloquently is that we don't want to hear about our sister's sexual exploits." I make a face with those last three words, suddenly feeling slightly ill.

Sutton and Callum both groan in unison.

"Sorry." I shudder.

Jamison laughs. "Fair enough. I wasn't raised with a sister, so I can only compare it to hearing my niece Ivy being talked about like that one day." His face pales. "Shit," he mutters, gulping down his drink.

"Party's here," Scarlett calls.

We all turn toward the door and the girls walk in, dressed to kill. My eyes zero in on Marlow and holy fuck, I can't even breathe right. I loosen my tie, determined to ditch it the minute Scarlett's back is turned.

Marlow's in a skin tone dress that shimmers in the light and accentuates every curve. Her long, wavy hair bounces down her back, and her legs look a mile long in her short dress and heels. Her nipples peak just enough to be completely tantalizing, and so help me, I don't know what I'll do if she turns around and reveals her perfect ass in that dress.

Being around her is becoming brutally painful. I run my hands through my hair, giving it a hard tug. Sutton frowns at me and turns to see what I'm reacting to, and it's a good thing Theo and Sofie walk in when they do. We all cheer and pink drinks are brought out for the girls, while the bartender tops off the rest of ours.

We clink glasses and Sofie and Theo kiss. Everyone cheers and sips their drinks, and I'm so focused on Marlow that I see the moment Sofie squeezes Marlow's shoulder, a shocked expression on Sofie's face.

"I just realized this is the day, right?" Sofie lifts her glass in the air and does a loud yelp.

Marlow's eyes dance, her smile huge and happy. "Well, it's not something I was going to advertise when we're celebrating your upcoming wedding, but yes."

She presses her lips together and her eyes flit to mine for a second, barely landing on me before looking away again. She swallows and I watch the way her neck moves, the slight flush rising on her skin.

"My divorce is final," she says.

I gulp. My stomach dips down to the floor and up again within a matter of seconds.

"Her divorce is final," Sofie yells. "Woohooooo!"

Theo starts cheering and then Sutton, and everyone else joins in...except me. I stand there taking in this beautiful woman. I'd like to say I'm a gentleman and I'll give her a chance to revel in being single, but fuck that. She can shoot me down if she needs time, but I'm not wasting another second hiding how I feel.

CHAPTER TWENTY-FIVE

BE STILL MY RACING HEART

MARLOW

A huge part of me is protesting as we leave the guys and go to the next surprise Scarlett has for all of us.

The other, very small part of me is relieved.

Because the look Wyatt Landmark sent my way when it was announced that my divorce is final...

I swear it incinerated the pretty lacy bra and panties I'm wearing right off of me.

I remember the words he said to me that day outside Sofie's house.

"I think you're more than attractive. I think you're fucking amazing. The way you've come in and captured the hearts of everyone here is remarkable. The way you are with Dakota, and the way you'd do anything for Sofie. I've noticed everything about you. Too much about you."

And then the conviction in his eyes when he said, *"The moment you're divorced..."*

He left those words hanging there and hasn't said anything like it since, but that, combined with the fire in his eyes tonight, made it feel like a vow if ever I've heard one.

I shiver and Sofie puts her arm around me.

"Are you nervous to try this?" she asks.

I look around, my mind too occupied with Wyatt to realize we've walked into a room full of poles and mirrors.

"Oh. Wow," I whisper.

Sofie giggles. "This should be interesting."

We change, and the next hour is an intense class with an instructor who must have magical powers. By the time she dims the lights and turns on a new set that spotlights each one of us, calling out, "From the top," I feel like I am one with this pole. It's fun and I'm sure I don't look anything close to knowing what I'm doing, but I feel beautiful and liberated when I drop back down on my feet.

Wyatt is the first one I see, his eyes swallowing me whole. He stands there, still in his dress shirt but tie gone, his hair looking like he's run his hands through it. I gulp as he stalks toward me, forgetting everyone else in the room.

"That was...*fucking incredible*," he rasps, his husky voice tugging my insides.

My mouth opens to...I don't even know what—thank

him? Whimper? Beg him to have mercy on me and stop looking like Dr. McSex?

But the commotion of Theo trying to escape with Sofie saves me.

"You are not stealing our bride during her bachelorette party and you're not escaping your bachelor party to go off and..." Scarlett leans in to whisper loud enough for all of us to hear, "*Have sex.*"

"Then why did you invite me here to see her do *that*?" Theo asks Scarlett, as she motions for the guys to drag him out of there.

Wyatt sends me a heated glance over his shoulder before disappearing with the guys. I wipe my face with the towel and try to calm my racing heart.

We're all laughing as we go to the spa and shower, Scarlett apologizing again that she's making us get ready twice. But when we come back out, there are makeup artists and hair stylists waiting to help us.

"My God, woman, what else do you have up your sleeve?" Holly asks Scarlett. "Were you afraid we'd back out of the pole dancing if you told us about it ahead of time?"

Scarlett laughs as powder is dusted on her nose. "Maybe."

"I can't believe how much I loved that," Sofie says.

"Same!" I say. "I've never thought I could be coordinated enough to get on a pole."

"I freaking loved it," Holly says. "I think we need to figure out how to get a pole class going in Landmark Mountain.

April giggles. "You know who would be all about it? Peg!"

We all crack up. I don't know Grinny's best friends, Helen and Peg, as well as everyone else, but I've seen them enough around town to know they're friendship goals. And she's right, I can picture that little firecracker Peg whipping around a pole easier than I could've imagined myself on one.

"God, I hope I have as much energy as the Golden Girls when I'm that age," Scarlett says.

"Me too," we all chime in.

"Your hair looks stunning, Sofie," I tell her.

All of us have our hair down and in loose waves, but Sofie's is up, and with her red hair, the thick braid on the side and twisted perfectly in the back, it's enchanting.

Scarlett puts her hand over her mouth and her eyes fill. "You should do it like that for the wedding."

"Can you fly to Colorado in two weeks?" Sofie asks the stylist, laughing.

Carla laughs. "I wouldn't be opposed. You guys are fun."

Scarlett points at her. "We'll talk." And then looks at Sofie, nodding with wide eyes as she mouths, "Let's do it."

It still catches me by surprise that Sofie has money now. We were both trying to make ends meet when we were in Texas. When her estranged father died, she suddenly had money. She's still the same practical Sofie I know, but it's so fun to see her building her dreams with the new business and marrying into a family that has charter helicopters at their disposal.

While the guys are at a swanky steakhouse, we opted to eat salads and fruit since we had appetizers with our drinks earlier, and there's a huge charcuterie board full of delicious meats and cheeses, chocolates, and fruit. The champagne flows as we finish getting ready.

I FaceTime Dakota and she's having so much fun, she can hardly sit still. The conversation is sweet and brief.

When I step back into my dress, I look at myself in the three-way mirror. I thought I looked my best earlier tonight, but with this hair and makeup, I feel *beautiful*. Despite all the pageants I've won, between my mom's comments and my *ex*-husband's—God, it's good to say ex—I've always been more aware of my flaws than my beauty. It's nice to look in the mirror now and like what I see. I think being content has a lot to do with that.

Sofie grabs my hand and Scarlett's and motions for Holly and April to come close too and we huddle around her.

"I'm so happy," she says. Her eyes fill and she shakes her head, laughing. "Gah, I am not going to make us all cry, I promise. But I love you all so much, and I'm pinching myself every day that I have this life. Thank you for being part of it with me!"

We're all a teary mess despite her promise, but no one's makeup gets botched over a few tears.

"Are you ready to hit the club?" Scarlett asks, lifting her hands in the air and shaking her hips.

"Saying I'm ready for bed is not the right answer, is it?" I tease.

Seriously though, at home, it would be bath and story-time and I would not be about to go dance the night away.

"Vodka Red Bull coming right up," Holly says.

She's not kidding. She manages to find one for me within minutes. Only in Vegas. I drink it and get a burst of energy.

Sofie pulls me close as we're walking out.

"Hey," she whispers. "Anything you want to tell me about you and Wyatt?"

I shake my head but can't stop the obnoxious smile that gives me away.

She nudges me. "There *is* something going on! What are you not saying?"

I look at her with wide eyes and still can't get the words out.

"You *like* him," she says. She puts her hand over her mouth and squeals. "I can't believe it. I mean, I can...I totally can." She takes my hands and shakes me in a little dance.

"Hold on." I stop and hold my hand up. "Nothing has happened—"

"Yet," she cuts in. "Maybe nothing *much* has happened *yet*. But I saw the way he looked at you when he heard you're divorced."

It's a good thing you were distracted with Theo after the poles because that *look was on a whole other level than the one you saw.*

I wisely keep that to myself.

"He's attracted to me." I lift my shoulder nonchalantly. "But he's made sure not to cross any lines..."

"And now there are no lines to worry about," Sofie says excitedly.

The girls turn back to see if we're coming and we walk a little faster.

"We work together...and you and Theo are the closest people in our lives, so if it went south, it'd be awful—"

"Or it might be the best thing either one of you have ever experienced in your life," she finishes.

I fan my heated face. "I just got out of a marriage. Do you think it's too soon to go out with Wyatt?"

"Cash was never right for you, and it was over long before now. You deserve someone who worships the ground you walk on, Marlow, and the look Wyatt gave you earlier... what if he's that guy?"

I look at her skeptically and her smile just grows wider.

"Don't be scared to give him a chance." She leans in closer and puts her hands on my face. "If you have feelings for him, put me and Theo and any other concerns you may have aside, and go for it. Okay?"

I nod slightly, and she does another excited little leap before we rush to catch up with the others.

CHAPTER TWENTY-SIX

PALM KISSES AND LACY MYSTERIES

WYATT

I've had a semi throughout the best meal I've had in a long time and it has nothing to do with the food.

What fresh new torture is this to experience Marlow having her way with that pole? Her lean body with curves in all the right places, that ass in the leotard so mouthwatering I want to bite it, and those nipples pointed right at me as she landed on her feet.

I've never felt this way in my life.

Horny? Yes.

Up for a mindless fuck? Sure.

Obliterated? Never.

It's not just her body I want. I want her smiles. I want her focus. I want to give her everything I have and—

"Where are you, brother?" Sutton's hand lands on my shoulder.

We've moved on from the restaurant and the blackjack table, and now we're standing in the club sipping Manhattans, Jamison's drink of choice. I'm nursing it slowly because I want to be fully present for everything about this night.

In the next second, I suck in a breath when Marlow walks in. She always looks good, but the way her shoulders are back, her expression almost defiant as she makes her entrance, she looks like a fucking goddess.

"I *see*," Sutton muses under his breath, chuckling. He leans in closer. "It's about time someone turned your world upside down. Enjoy the ride." To Callum, he says, "Looks like it's you and me..."

Callum mumbles something, but I'm already moving toward Marlow.

When I'm standing in front of her, she surprises me by holding out her hand. I take it and her mouth parts in a grin. I wonder if she feels the same rush of heat as I do.

"Marlow Walker," she says, her voice husky.

My eyebrows lift slightly as I smile down at her, my own voice raspy when I say, "Marlow Walker, I like it. A beautiful name for a beautiful woman."

She takes a step closer, all sultry sass. "And you are?"

"I'm Wyatt Henry Landmark, and I'm whipped over you, Marlow Walker."

Her eyes are shining as she leans in and says, "Agatha. Marlow Agatha Walker."

I nod, lips puckering as I pretend to contemplate this. I lift her hand to mine and kiss her palm, and her gasp is like damn music to my ears.

"I'm whipped over you, Marlow *Agatha* Walker," I say, pressing another kiss to her palm.

"So you *are* still attracted to me?" she whispers, looking around to see if anyone hears us.

I glance around too. It's too loud for anyone to hear us, the music pulsing so hard I feel it in my gut, and our group has moved near the bar where the girls are getting their drinks. Scarlett and Jamison are already wrapped around each other, and I don't even see Theo and Sofie.

"Oh, it's way more than that," I say over the music.

She stares up at me, her brow creased slightly in contemplation before it clears and she laughs. "But we haven't even danced yet." She lifts one shoulder up, her expression coy.

I set my drink down on the closest high-top and put my hands on her hips, tugging her toward me. Her hands land on my chest and she lets out a shaky laugh.

"I think we've been doing our own little dance with each other from the moment we met," I whisper in her ear.

She shivers and I grin, pulling back to meet her eyes again.

"I just got out of—" She starts then shakes her head. "We should be careful, Wyatt. This...itch between us...if we...scratch it and it doesn't work out—" She looks back toward our group.

"This is more than an itch and you know it." My palms tighten around her waist and I pull her flush against me.

Her eyes widen when she feels what I'm no longer trying to hide. "But we can call it whatever makes you happy."

Her eyes flutter when I lift my hand and skate it up her neck until I'm cupping her jaw. I lean down until my lips almost touch hers but don't go there, not yet.

"Dance with me."

And then I don't wait for her answer.

I take a step back and thread my hand with hers, and we walk through the crowd of people dancing to find a place in the middle of it all. She's shy at first, her movements gradually getting looser as we begin to move together. At first we're close but not touching, our eyes swallowing each other whole as we sway to the rhythm, but then I can't take it anymore.

I have to touch her.

My hands go low on her waist, her arms wrapping around my neck, and I want to yell a fucking victory cry with how good she feels against me.

For the longest time, her eyes never leave mine as we dance from one song to the next, the desire so thick between us I can almost taste it. With my leg between hers, I feel her heat as she swivels those hips against me, driving me out of my mind. Her hair sticks to her neck and I hold it back, leaning closer to blow on her glistening skin.

"You're so good at this," she says, breathless.

Her eyes glaze over, and I'd love nothing more than to make her come right here grinding against my leg, but she takes a self-conscious step back.

"*We're* good at this," I say, twirling her around and around before pulling her back against my chest. When she rolls that ass against me, I groan, my hands roaming from under her tits and down her body.

Her head tilts up as she looks at me over her shoulder, and I'm right there, breathing her in. Her breath hitches when she moves and my dick lines up between her cheeks. I hold her there, my hand on her hip keeping her movements slow and steady as my other hand slides up her body, up her neck, up to her face where my thumb glides over her bottom lip.

"Wyatt," she whimpers.

"What do you need, Marlow? Say the word. I'll give you whatever you want."

"What are we doing, Wyatt?" She puts her hand over mine and pulls it to her mouth, placing a soft kiss on my palm like I did hers.

I let out a ragged breath and she smiles shyly.

I turn her around in my arms and push back her hair, my hand lingering on her face. I love her fucking mouth, her soft as fuck skin.

"I want to worship every inch of your body and make you lose all inhibitions, see how many ways I can get you to come...but I'm also happy to dance all fucking night right here with you."

Her mouth drops with my first words and something flashes over her face before she presses her hand to her mouth and stares at me in shock.

"Did I say too much?" I ask.

A laugh bursts out of her. "Um...*no*. I...liked it."

"Do you wanna get out of here?" I ask.

She nods but then looks around. "Is it wrong to bail on the party?"

"I think we lost the couples a while ago, and the others will look out for each other. But we can text them, make sure of that before we go."

"Sofie and Theo left?" She laughs again, pulling her

hair off of her neck. "I guess we have been dancing for a long time."

Her hair spills over her shoulders when she drops her hands, her expression suddenly intense as she lifts her short dress on one side. I watch intrigued, no idea what she's doing, but here for every second. High up on her thigh is lacy material that matches her dress, and she pulls her phone out of it.

"That's fucking genius. How did I never feel that?"

She shoots me a look that goes straight to my dick. Who am I kidding? Everything about her goes straight to my dick.

"You were distracted," she teases.

"Damn right. I still am." I run my hands through my hair and try desperately to think of anything but her.

Now that she's not grinding up against me, the tent in my pants is unavoidable. The lights are dim and everyone around us is preoccupied, so fortunately I'm not too obvious.

Before she glances down at her phone, her eyes fall to my dick and she swallows hard. Her eyes fly to mine and I lift my collar away from my skin to try and cool myself off.

"Trying to think of everything but your heat against me, but it's not working yet," I say under my breath.

"Oh God," she whimpers.

Her hands are shaky as she looks at her phone and fans herself with her hand. "There are a few texts in the group chat. Sof and Theo called it a night and the rest are at the blackjack tables." She bites the inside of her cheek as she looks me over again. "What should I tell them?"

"Tell them we'll see them at the eleven o'clock brunch."

"We're not going to at least *try* to hide what we're about to do?" Her head tilts and I laugh, moving in to touch her again.

"If they saw us out here, I'm pretty sure they have a good idea. But you can tell them we're taking a walk if you'd rather."

She nods and taps out a response.

I lean down and kiss her shoulder. "Now, can we please, *please* get out of here?"

CHAPTER TWENTY-SEVEN

MORE

MARLOW

I cannot believe what Wyatt said about worshipping every inch of my body.

It took everything in me to keep it together, the way my panties practically caught on fire.

I stick my phone back in the lacy garter, happy it worked so well. I bought one for all of us girls for this trip. When I look at Wyatt again, I try to act unaffected as I push my hair off my shoulders and smirk.

"We'll discuss the ground rules on the way to your room," I say.

He smirks back and holds out his hand for me to start walking. "I can't wait."

When I move through the crowd, winding through the club and then the casino, Wyatt's hand oh, so low on my back, I try to get my thoughts together before we reach the elevator. I thought getting out of the club and away from the seductive beat drumming through my skin would help tone down the desire that's taken over every rational thought.

But no.

It's even more pronounced when we step into the elevator and I pointedly step away from his hand and go to the opposite side. His eyes never leave mine, his expression amused, cocky, and filled with such promise. I shiver, running my hands up my arms to still the goose bumps. He steps closer, his hands lifting to replace mine and I hold up my hand, pausing him.

"One night, and we don't let this affect our relationship at work or around our friends...your family...and you're still the same with Dakota, no matter what."

Hurt skitters across his face and then he nods and looks at me more intently.

"I'd never treat Dakota differently. I swear to you that will never happen. I love the relationship I'm building with your little girl and as long as you'll allow me to be, I'm in her life to stay."

Tears fill my eyes and I blink rapidly, trying to will them away.

He takes another step closer but doesn't try to touch me this time.

"As far as one night goes, I want so much more than that. But I know you've been through a lot and I'll be respectful of what *you* want. I've proven I can stick to boundaries, and that will remain true. But make no mistake, Marlow...I want you and I don't care who knows it."

A whimper escapes my lips just as the elevator dings and he props his hand up high on one side of the door to keep it open as he looks at me.

"Do we understand one another?" he asks.

"I think so," I answer, my voice barely above a whisper.

He smiles and my chest squeezes with a surge of wonder and fear and lust. Gathering my courage, I take a deep breath and step underneath his arm and off the elevator. He's by my side in seconds, his hand on the small of my back as he leads me to his room. He opens the door and I walk inside, taking in the suite, the lights of the Strip brightening the living room.

"Beautiful," I say, shy again. "Ours is too, but this is—"

He takes my elbow and turns me so my back is against the window, his face lowering until his lips touch mine. Our kiss starts out soft, slow, and so so sweet, our mouths moving in sync just like our bodies on the dance floor. And then it's a rush of tongues and heat as our heads angle to take it deeper.

Kissing Wyatt feels familiar, like coming home, and yet, it's wild and without abandon, something I've never once experienced before this moment.

We kiss and kiss and kiss, his hands on my face and mine in his hair for the longest time before our hands eventually start exploring. My body feels languid and drugged, heavy with want.

My lips are swollen when he drags his away from me, kissing down my neck.

"One night with you will never be enough for me," he whispers across my skin.

I arch into him, and his palm cups my breast, his thumb brushing over my pebbled nipple before he pinches it between two fingers. I arch into him more, his lips coming up to catch my gasp.

I'm afraid one night with him will never be enough for me either, in fact I already know it won't be, but I'm too scared to think about what that means right now. I don't want to think about the future or about anything but what we're doing right here, right now.

I reach behind me and start pulling down the zipper on my dress. He takes over, unzipping the rest, and when it's all the way down, I tug the strap of my dress and let it fall to the ground.

He curses under his breath, his eyes sweeping down my body and leaving fiery sparks behind.

"You're so beautiful, it physically hurts." His voice is a low rasp as he rubs the middle of his chest like he's trying to dissolve the pain.

He bends and picks me up, his mouth locking with mine as he carries me to the bedroom. He sets me on the edge of the bed, still leaning over to kiss me senseless. I scoot back to catch my breath and to get his clothes off of him.

As I'm unbuttoning his shirt, I lean in and kiss his bare chest. I glance up at him and he sighs, his hand coming up to sink into my hair.

"Did you bring condoms on this trip?" I ask.

He blinks and grins. "Once you left to get ready, I told the guys I had to run to my room but went to the gift shop instead and bought so many...it was wishful thinking on my part," he clarifies. "But I wanted to be ready for *whenever* you might be too."

I grin and tug his shirt out of his dress pants, unbuttoning the rest of the way before working on his pants. He hisses a breath as I unzip his pants, his steely hardness jumping at my touch. I wondered on the dance floor if he could possibly be as big as he felt, and so help me, yes. He's wearing grey boxer briefs that are all kinds of obscene, the tip of him peeking out the top more evidence that he's got a *lot* to work with. Makes me breathless too, and I don't know what I want to do with him first, the possibilities endless.

I reach out to touch him and he pauses my hand.

"Lie back," he says. "There's something I need to do first."

I do as he says, heart jumping in anticipation. He leans over me, and I can't keep my hands off of his chest. He reaches under me and unhooks my bra, hissing out a curse as he tosses it behind him.

His mouth is around my nipple in the next breath, his tongue flicking and sucking as his hand teases my other side. I try to tug his body flush with mine, but he's unmovable, his body hovering over mine as he takes his time with me. I never knew my breasts were so sensitive, but the things he does—I get so close to coming before he backs off, once, twice...

And then he's moving down my body, the intent in his eyes clear as he looks up at me. He drags the lace down my legs and then just places his face on me, *there,* and inhales.

I'm about to say something, anything...everything. *Is it okay? We don't have to do this. I don't really ever get comfortable with this, so...*

But when he looks up at me again, his face is lust-drunk, and he grins the sexiest grin I've ever seen in my life.

"I cannot wait to get my tongue on you, *in* you. Your scent just became my addiction, and I haven't even tasted you yet."

"*Fuck,*" I whimper, and his grin gets darker, predatory.

"In a little while, my queen," he murmurs, running his nose along my slit and planting a kiss at the top. "But I have to spend some time on my knees before you first."

The things he says—I'm already soaking before he ever touches me.

But then he proceeds to get to work.

He spreads me wide, his fingers parting me, and his tongue explores and flicks and plunges inside while he groans his approval with every sound I make. Once he's thoroughly licked me from top to bottom, while I squirm and moan and wreak havoc on his hair, my breath coming out in tiny moans as I writhe beneath him, he gets serious, sucking my clit like he's starving...and I fall over the edge.

It shocks me, the force of the orgasm, and it goes on forever.

"Wyatt," I whisper, pounding my hand on the bed.

He dips his finger inside and I arch into him, as his tongue flicks persistently in the best spot. Another finger inside and the sounds of us are loud, but I don't care. Every ounce of inhibition disappeared under his devotion, and I can't believe it, but it's not long before I'm trembling again with wave after wave of bliss.

I grip his hair with both fists and he doesn't let up until I let go of him, my hands collapsing by my side.

"What did you do to me?" I say, laughing.

He hasn't even taken off his briefs yet, and I reach for him, my eyes hungrily skating over every inch of him.

"Are you up for more?" he asks, leaning in to kiss me one more time *down there*.

I put my hand over my eyes. My God. This man.

I lean up on my elbows and his eyes land on my breasts, his pupils dilating with lust.

"Get up here *now*," I tell him.

CHAPTER TWENTY-EIGHT

FUN, FUN, FUN

WYATT

"Yes, ma'am." I laugh and stand up, moving to get a condom.

When I toss a strand from my bag in the nightstand drawer, her eyes get huge.

I smirk. "You said one night...I've gotta make it a night you won't forget."

"You already have," she says.

"Oh, Marlow. We're just getting started." I take my briefs off and my dick can hardly stand it when she licks her lips. I slide the condom on and she watches like she's spellbound.

"You okay?" I ask.

"More than okay," she says.

She leans up and pulls me down, and this time, I let myself lie flush against her, skin to skin. We both moan at the same time.

"I'm not even inside you yet, but you feel perfect." I brush her hair away from her eyes and they flutter closed when I lean in to kiss her neck and then her lips.

Her legs part, and I press my way in, just enough to make her eyes fly open. She bites her bottom lip and I lean in and bite it myself.

"More," she whispers.

I press in another inch and it's so tight, her breath hitches. She wraps her arms around my neck, her legs wrapping around my waist, and I go in a little deeper. She clenches around me and I curse, burying my head in her hair as I push in deeper and deeper.

"Wyatt," she says, her hands coming up to my face. "You feel so good."

"I hope it's as good as the way you feel to me," I say, groaning as I go the rest of the way. "I already can't wait to do this again."

She grins, but then her eyes squeeze shut when I pulse inside of her, her walls tightening in response.

"Mmm, I won't last long if you keep doing that," I warn her.

She gives me a sexy smirk and tries it again, but I drag all the way out, and she whimpers, her hands clutching my ass to pull me back in. I slide into her this time with less resistance, her tits bouncing as I thrust in a few times before pulling back out, and the next time she's ready for more. I go even deeper, giving her all of me.

"So. Fucking. Perfect," I pant.

We're still for a minute, both chests heaving with restraint. But then I can't be still another second.

I lean over her, my hands on the bed near her shoulders as I pick up the pace. The sounds of us are so fucking obscene, I love it.

"Listen to us," I say.

Her mouth parts as she looks up at me, eyes trusting and so full of desire it takes my breath away.

I want to do too many things at once. I can't take my eyes off of her. I want her chest against mine, but I want to watch her. I love how she's taking every bit of me and meeting me with her own thrusts, the way it feels like there are no barriers between us at all. Like every reservation she's had about me is gone and she feels this, knows whatever this is between us is real.

I lift her leg over my shoulder and her head falls back when I keep up a punishing pace, so deep now that I'm lightheaded.

When her walls begin to clamp around me, I'm so not ready for it to end, but I reach between us and rub that sweet clit, and she cries out. Her orgasm is so intense and so tight around me, I'm a goner. I'm hoarse as I unload into her, spots dot my eyelids, and I fucking see the stars.

When the twitches slow down, her pussy still clenching around me, I lean my forehead against hers. I thread our fingers together and with the other hand, I run the back of my fingers over her cheek and kiss her.

"Are you okay?" I ask against her lips.

She gives me a shaky smile. "I have never...ever been better."

I laugh with relief and she pouts when I pull out of her slowly. I kiss her again before getting up to take care of the condom.

When I come back, she gets up to go to the bathroom and comes back a few minutes later with the hotel robe around her.

"Nope," I tell her, pointing at the robe. "There are no clothes at this party."

"We're having a party?" she teases, fingering the belt.

I tug it until she falls on top of me and tickle the robe off of her. She wiggles and her eyes go wide when she feels my cock straining for her.

"You're not worn out yet, huh?" she asks.

"Marlow, I could be going without sleep for a month straight, and my dick would be happy to see you." I reach up to palm both breasts and my dick jerks against her heat to prove my point.

She lifts an eyebrow and reaches over to grab a condom, sliding it on me. I hiss out a staggered breath when she grips her little fist around me.

"I won't make you prove that point," she says. "You need your rest after all, Dr. McGorg."

I hold onto her hips as she lifts up and sinks onto me. "Dr. McGorg?" I wheeze out. "Because I'm always engorged around you?"

She sputters out a laugh and then bites her lip when I press my fingers against her sweet spot. When she catches her breath, she shakes her head. "No, because you're so gorgeous."

I pick up the pace with my fingers and she moans, swiveling her hips on me.

"*Are* you always engorged around me?" she finally bites out.

"Yes."

She starts to laugh again, but it hitches in her throat. "Mmm, Wyatt..."

"Yes?"

"How do you know how to make me feel so good?" she asks.

I sit up, her tits brushing against my chest, and my fingers don't stop against her. I live for every gasp and moan that comes out of her mouth. I lean into her ear. "Your pussy is telling me everything I need to know...that and your sweet sounds."

She clutches my neck. "The things you say. You're making me so—"

"So what?" I ask, my fingers never slowing.

"So greedy for everything with you," she says, her voice catching at the end.

My fingers falter then, but she's already falling apart, her hips bucking, her insides spasming around me in the sweetest death grip. I kiss her hard, trying to swallow every gasp, every cry, as I crash over the edge with her.

When we finally slow, our bodies slick and hearts pounding hard, I push her hair back and look her in the eyes.

"You already have everything with me if you want it, Marlow. I'm handing you my heart freely. It's yours for the taking."

She stares at me without saying anything for a long time, so long that I start to get nervous. Her lips are puffy, her hair wild and messy, and she's never looked more beautiful.

Finally, she smiles shyly and leans up to kiss me softly before lifting off of me. We both flinch at the loss, but she goes to the bathroom and I throw the condom away in the bedroom's garbage. I'm walking toward the bed when she steps out of the bathroom and moves past me, picking up her panties and bra.

When she moves toward the door to the living room, I follow her.

"Hey, what's happening?" I ask, watching her put on her bra and then panties, my foggy sex brain slow to catch up when she looks so fuckable.

"I should get back to the room," she says. "This is supposed to be a bachelorette party, not me disappearing for hours to hook up with a groomsman."

Ouch. But no, I'm not going to take offense at that. She's clearly having a momentary freak-out. It'll pass. It has to.

"Hey, if I said too much, I'm sorry. I just—I want you to know where you stand with me. I can pull back on that though if you're not ready. Come to bed. I'll let you sleep, I promise."

"I should get back," she says, picking up her dress and stepping into it.

Her slipping away right in front of me is such a helpless feeling.

"They know we're together," I tell her, "and I'm sure they're either sleeping by now or still at the tables."

She takes a deep breath and slides into her heels.

"I'll never forget the way you made me feel, Wyatt. No one has *ever*—" She pauses and reaches out to touch my face, her eyes shiny in the moonlight. "But I *just* got divorced. We're in Vegas. It was fun. *So* fun," she adds.

I put my hand on her hip and lean my forehead against hers. She stands there for a second before pulling away again.

"I can't just jump right into something else the second I'm free. I have to be smarter than that for Dakota's sake."

I grab her hand and put it to my lips, kissing her palm. She closes her eyes for a second and sighs.

"Tell me you know there's more to us than one *fun* night."

She smiles and squeezes my hand. "I do. And it terrifies me." Her voice is shaky. "We're friends. And I feel like I've won the jackpot with you, Wyatt Landmark. I'm *desperate* not to ruin this friendship."

"You can't ruin it," I say hoarsely. Even though inside I know she *can* ruin *me* if she closes the door to more.

Her eyes are sad as she smiles again. "Thank you for the most magical night I've ever had."

She walks out the door, and I call out, "Wait for me and I'll walk you to your room."

But when I reach the door, she's gone.

I stand there for the longest time, wondering how I managed to screw this up when it felt like I was finally getting everything I've ever hoped for.

CHAPTER TWENTY-NINE

HOT AND TIDY

MARLOW

I did the right thing, didn't I?

I'm wiping the tears away as fast as they fall the whole walk back to my suite. My body aches in the best ways where Wyatt has been. I've been thoroughly loved up and when we were in the thick of it, I thought nothing could bring me down from that high.

My fingers brush against my lips, puffy from his kisses. My skin tingles all over with reminders of him.

I slump against the wall outside my suite and wipe the rest of the tears off of my face.

I just had the most incredible night of my life.

The tears start falling again and my exhale is long and aggravated.

"Get it together, Marlow," I whisper.

My best days with Cash or anyone else don't even come close to being as intimate or earth-shattering as this night with Wyatt. I know it's wrong to compare, but it's hard not to when I'm leveled with the truth.

I press my fingers under my eyes and lift my head to the ceiling, hoping no one witnesses my breakdown. Everything in me wants to rewind my steps, fall in his bed, and never look back.

It'd be crazy.

Even though I brought up being greedy for everything with him, the risks we're taking by falling into this so fast didn't sink in until what he said after.

His response was perfect, but there's just no way it's true.

We didn't even kiss until tonight, and yes, we had the most amazing sex I've ever had, *twice*, but...that doesn't mean I'm ready for...whatever he means by everything.

He can't possibly even *know* if he wants everything with me.

And yet, somehow I know that he's set the bar now for the kind of man I want and no one else will compare to him.

I take one more deep breath, brace myself, and go into the suite. There's a light on in the living room, but the girls' doors are closed, lights out. Wyatt was right—they're asleep. My text to them said we were taking a walk, so maybe no one else has to know what happened tonight.

It's almost four in the morning, but I get in the shower and lose it once again.

My head aches, and as hard as I try to shut it down, my mind won't stop.

What I've been through the past four years in a terrible marriage.

The relief of that finally being over.

The most incredible orgasms breaking something inside of me.

The realization that I just walked away from one of the best things that has ever happened to me...

It all floods down the drain, along with the broken pieces of my heart.

I GROAN when the alarm goes off but text Grinny and Dakota to see how the night went before dragging myself out of bed.

Grinny sends a picture of Dakota and Owen at the table, eating waffles piled high with berries and whipped cream.

I send back a ton of heart emojis and tell them I'll Face-Time later when I have more time.

The girls are laughing in the living room, and I hurry to the bathroom to get ready for brunch. My voice echoes in the bathroom when I see myself and say, "*Noooo.*"

Hickey on my chest...not sure if my outfit will cover it or not.

Hair = rat's nest.

Tiny slits for eyes.

My hands go to my head, and I squeeze my eyes shut as I count to ten.

Same disaster going on in the mirror when I open my eyes, but I get to work. I find the eye masks I brought in case of a hangover and put them on my eyelids *and* under my eyes. I can barely see through the masks as I step in the shower just long enough to wake me up.

I try to tame my hair as best I can with product and brush my teeth, trying to put off doing my makeup until my eyes have had time to de-puff.

Makeup tones down the hickey but doesn't make it disappear entirely, and when I put on my yellow sundress, it's all I see. Hopefully, everyone else will be too tired or preoccupied to notice.

When I take off the eye masks, it's better, but I still look like I've cried all night. I try my best with the makeup, refusing to let my mind go to the dark place it was before I finally fell asleep. It'll have to do.

I put my sandals on, grab my purse, and pause when I pick up my phone. A message came from Wyatt half an hour ago.

WYATT

Good morning. I hope you got some sleep. I slept like shit, wishing you were in my bed. But that's not why I'm texting. I want you to know two things before we see each other today. One: I'm going to be the same as I always am around you. And two: I'm not giving up on us.

MY HEART GALLOPS and I put my hand on my chest, willing it to slow down.

I jump when Holly raps on my door and calls out, "Marlow, how are you doing in there?"

"Good," I say. "Coming right out."

I walk into the living room, a practiced smile in place. Holly's standing near my door, and April turns to look at me as she grabs her purse from the table.

"Mornin'," I say in my best chipper voice. "How's everyone feeling this morning?"

Holly smiles, her eyes full of mischief. "We're good. How are *you* feeling?"

A heated flush spreads over my cheeks and down my neck and I nod briskly, walking past her and toward the door. "I'm good too. Didn't get enough sleep last night, but...who does in Vegas?"

They fall into step behind me.

"You and Wyatt were *so hot* on the dance floor last night," April says. "Soooo hot."

"Tell me you made that man boldly go where no man has gone before," Holly says.

I trip over my feet. "What?"

April laughs. "Ignore her. She thinks her *Star Trek* brain makes sense to everyone. Interpretation: we hoped you were getting some wild and crazy sex last night on that walk." She does air quotes around *walk,* and I laugh nervously.

"Oh." I fidget with the strap on my purse and laugh again. If my fake laugh doesn't give it away, my red face will surely broadcast the truth. "He did surprise me with the way he can dance."

I feel their eyes on me, but mine stay trained on the elevator ahead.

"Hmm. Well, there's always tonight." April giggles. "You're staying back with Sofie and Scarlett, aren't you?"

Oh shit. I'd planned on it, but now the last thing I need is to be a third wheel with them and their men...or alone with Wyatt.

"Those Landmark men." Holly sighs. "They sure grew up hot. Too bad I think of them as brothers."

"I know," April says. "It'd be so convenient to fall for one of them since there are so few year-round single men in Landmark." She presses the button once we're inside the elevator. "Not that you need to go looking, Holly. If you'd just get over your fear of talking to Magnus, we'd be planning another wedding."

Holly groans and I turn to her.

"Yeah, I keep hearing about the great staredowns you guys do," I say. "What's the deal with him?"

"There is no deal," she says. "Back to Wyatt."

"That reminds me! Holly had a crush on Wyatt for a while," April says.

Holly makes a face at me and laughs. "I did...when I was like, nine, and he was fifteen." She puts her hand on my arm. "Don't worry. I haven't had a crush on him in years. It was fleeting. He was just so hot and *so* tidy. I love a tidy man."

We all laugh.

"Is that your hang-up with Magnus?" April teases. "All that long Viking hair isn't tidy enough for you?"

Holly fans her face, flushing. "I am trying to talk about Wyatt and Marlow here!"

"Well, he's all yours. Wyatt is still hot, and I've never been to his place, but I bet he's still tidy too." I almost sound convincing.

They look at me, both smiling, and like they know I'm full of shit.

When the elevator dings and we're stepping off, Holly leans in. "I saw the way he looked at you last night, and the only one who has his attention is *you*."

The lobby is loud and the perfect escape. We step off

and Sofie and Scarlett are standing nearby, looking beautiful and happy. We all hug and Scarlett motions toward the door.

"The guys are waiting for us over there. The place is close enough to walk," she says.

I look in that direction but don't see Wyatt. The nervous anticipation is killing me.

Sofie loops her arm through mine. "You look so pretty. I love your dress."

"Thank you. You look gorgeous and surprisingly well-rested."

She laughs. "I felt bad that we left as early as we did, but Theo managed to talk me into it." Her grin drops when she gets a closer look at me. "Are you okay? Did you not sleep well?" She makes a face. "Are you not having fun?" she whispers.

"I've had a great time," I tell her. "Didn't sleep much, but that's to be expected here, right?"

She's still looking at me with concern as we round the corner. She knows me too well.

I try not to react when I see Wyatt. He's highlighted by the sun from the window, looking like perfection in jeans and a button-down shirt, hair much *tidier* than the way it looked when I left him.

His body leans over me, muscles straining. Hair falling over his forehead and eyes piercing through mine, he thrusts into me so deep that I feel complete.

I swallow and blink, trying to clear the mental picture, but even fully dressed and walking toward me, I see what he looks like naked, how he felt inside me, the ecstasy of his—

"Hey." He grins at me and it catches me off guard.

He said he'd be the same, but...how can he be after the night we had? And what I did after...

Theo takes Sofie's hand and they walk toward everyone else gathered by the door. Wyatt falls into step next to me.

"Pretty girl, pretty dress," he says, voice low.

I look up at him and his smile leaves me weak in the knees.

"Pretty mark I left on your chest," he finishes.

I gasp, and he leans in and whispers in my ear, "Don't worry. It's barely noticeable. I just know the places I've been."

I lean back, my eyes narrowing on him and he laughs, coming toward my ear again.

"I should be sorry, but I have to say, my mark looks *really* good on you."

A choked laugh comes out of me, and I shove him back, pointing at him. "This is not being the same as you always are."

He lifts a shoulder and smirks. "Maybe I was just trying to put you at ease. Or...this is me being the same I always am now that you're single and I can say what I want."

"Well, knock it off," I say between my teeth.

I smile at the rest of the guys when we walk to where they're waiting.

"Hey, everybody. Good morning," I say, trying to move away from Wyatt, but he maneuvers next to me as we step outside.

"Okay, so...do I have this right? Your interpretation of the *same* is me pretending last night never happened." His tone is conversational, like we're talking about the weather.

"Something a little more like that, yes." I nod.

"Can't do that. Did you read the rest of my text?"

I sputter, holding my hand up to argue with him, when Sofie turns to look at me. I smile and wave, my pageant skills coming out like second nature. Her brow creases as she studies Wyatt and me before turning around.

"I did read the rest of your text," I whisper-shout. "And I was relieved that you were being an adult about it. I can see my *interpretation* was all wrong."

He chuckles and I want to shake him.

"I'm being an adult about it, Marlow," he says calmly. "I'm not in denial about what I feel for you. I loved every second of being buried deep inside of you. The taste of you is something I woke up thinking about. My only regret is not chasing you down the hall when you left. If I'd thrown you over my shoulder and licked the panic away, we could've woken up this morning and fucked without abandon the way we were meant to."

CHAPTER THIRTY

PICKING A PERSONA

WYATT

A whimper escapes her lips and she places her hand over my mouth, her expression a mixture of anger and desire.

I kiss her hand and when she doesn't move it, I flick my tongue across it and she drops it.

"Oh, you're being an adult all right," she huffs. "What was that you said about being able to pull back if I wasn't ready?"

I grin and bend down until I'm in her face. I can almost

taste her peppermint breath. "Every single thing we did last night felt like you were ready."

"*Ugh.*" She rolls her eyes and tries to stalk away from me but halts when she nearly runs into Jamison.

"We're here," Scarlett sings.

We walk inside the restaurant and Marlow rushes over to Holly and April, sending a scathing look my way.

I chuckle. I have to. Every time I went to the dark side during the night, I remembered the way she gave herself to me. The times she lowered her guard and let me in, not just physically, but in every way. We touched the sky last night and I'm not about to go down without a fight.

Sutton sends me a look of his own.

"You sure this is the way you want to handle this?" he says under his breath.

"You heard us?"

"I heard enough. And I know I can't really give advice since I'm divorced and haven't gone on a real date in so long I can't remember, but something tells me the cocky bastard routine isn't going to work in your favor."

I run my hands through my hair. I wanted to cry when she left last night. *Cry.* There's no fucking way I can go there. So, sometime during the night, I settled on this.

"Cocky bastard, huh? I was going for more of a confident swagger."

He snorts. "I don't think her looking like she wants to punch you in the nuts is what you're going for, regardless of how we want to title it."

"Fuck," I mutter.

"You poison Marlow during that *walk* of yours last night?" Callum sidles up to the other side of me.

"Now is *not* the time for you to get talkative," I snap.

Sutton squeezes my shoulder while Callum chuckles.

"Settle down, little brother." Sutton leads me to a chair directly across from Marlow. I start to sit down and he blocks me, pointing to the end of the table. "Nuh-uh. This is my seat. You're down there. Have some coffee, maybe a Bloody Mary or whatever will do the trick, and you can try out some new moves later."

I grumble all the way to my seat and when I sit down, I glance at Marlow. She looks beautiful but exhausted and... fragile. It makes me physically ache with the need to fix it, but I'm not sure how.

The truth is, I expected her to put on the brakes sometime *before* we had sex. When that never happened and not only that, when what we shared felt life-changing, I thought we were in the clear.

Wishful thinking, I know.

Our drink order is taken and the chatter around the table is happy. I try to pull myself out of my brain and focus on the conversation.

"Did you hear about Callum winning big last night?" Holly asks.

"Really? How much?" Theo clinks his water glass to Callum's.

"Forty-k," he mumbles.

"Holy shit," Theo says. "You playing today?"

"Nope."

"Come on. Let me live vicariously through you since I can't do it," Sutton says.

"It'd be okay in Vegas, wouldn't it?" Jamison asks.

"Wait—can judges not gamble?" Marlow asks.

"He could, he just avoids everything that could paint him in a bad light, publicly or privately," Scarlett says.

"Not everything," Sutton says, rubbing a hand over his jaw.

"Oh, every single person at this table would've divorced Tracy's ass long before you did." Holly laughs, and the ones of us who aren't verbally agreeing are nodding.

"She didn't make it easy, but I tried." He shrugs. He lifts the mimosa the waitress just set in front of him. "Fortunately, the two of you will never be miserable with each other," he says to Theo and Sofie. "To a happy marriage and a peaceful home."

We all lift our glasses and clink them together.

"Shouldn't that kind of toast be saved for our actual wedding day?" Theo asks, after he drains his glass.

"We'll up the ante for the wedding, don't you worry," Scarlett says, sending Theo a mocking wink.

He rolls his eyes, laughing. My chest wells with emotion and I clear my throat.

"I'm glad I have my little brother back," I say. "Theo was still trying to make the best of his life, Sof, but he was sad without you...hollow." I look at Theo and he swallows hard, his eyes glistening and dammit, I feel that urge to cry again myself. Instead, I barrel through. "Seeing the weight off your shoulders, how happy you are...I wasn't sure I'd ever see you this way again, and I'm grateful to you, Sofie, for bringing him back."

"Oh my God, I love this family," April cries, wiping her face.

I glance around the table and the girls are sniffling, Callum is staring at his plate like he's willing it to levitate, anything to get out of this emotional moment, and my eyes pause on Marlow. She blinks and a tear rolls down her cheek, but somehow I manage to stay in my seat instead of rushing to her side to kiss it away the way I want to.

"To happy beginnings," I say, still looking at her as I lift my glass.

"To happy beginnings," the rest of the table echoes.

Everyone but Marlow.

Her gaze flutters away from mine and I feel the loss, but at the same time, I'm hopeful.

The fact that I haven't known her for long doesn't deter me in the slightest. I'm almost thirty fucking years old, a man knows when he's in love...at least this one does.

I just hope to God I don't have to wait eight years to have my happy beginning like Theo and Sofie did.

But if it comes to that, I will.

Marlow is worth waiting for.

CHAPTER THIRTY-ONE

CODE

MARLOW

Damn him.

Why does he affect me so much?

It's like I can never settle on one emotion when it comes to Wyatt. From the day I crashed into him, it's been a never-ending series of twists and turns when it comes to my heart.

He got me all riled up before brunch and then swept me away all over again with the things he said to Sofie and Theo.

On our way back to the hotel, I feel Wyatt's eyes on me, but he doesn't try to talk to me, and I can't help but be a little disappointed.

It's official: I'm a mess.

The guys leave for their afternoon of golf, while we go shopping and have cocktails by the pool. It's relaxing and yet, as hard as I try, I can't seem to shake the thoughts of my night with Wyatt out of my mind.

I'm certain I cover it well, though. I'm determined to make this weekend special for Sofie.

I FaceTime with Dakota while I'm getting ready for dinner, and she tells me all the games they've been playing. I promise her I'll be home soon, and she leans in to kiss the phone before hanging up.

When I come out in the dress I bought earlier—a short pale green dress with a bustier top that shows more cleavage than I'm used to—Holly and April whistle.

"You look gorgeous," April says. "Wyatt is not going to know what to do with himself." She giggles.

"What she said," Holly agrees. "Makes me regret leaving tonight. Wow, that dress and your eyes." She fans her face, grinning. "We'll want details back in Landmark Mountain."

"Thank you. You both look amazing. And *nothing* is happening tonight," I insist, flushing.

I'm saying it as much for me as I am for them.

I might have considered what Wyatt would think of me in this dress, but a little space from him today has bolstered my resolve. It'd just be way too messy if we started something.

I should've been strong enough last night to not go down that path, but it's a new day.

Holly and April leave their packed suitcases near the door to pick up after dinner, and we walk out the door.

The elevator dings on our way down and then Wyatt, Sutton, and Callum step on with us. Wyatt zeroes in on me, his eyes sweeping leisurely down my body before coming back to meet my gaze.

"Ladies," he says, voice scratchy.

He swallows hard and steps into my space, facing me as we ride the rest of the way down. He's so close, smells divine, and his slightly scruffy face and messier-than-usual hair with his button-down shirt and dress pants are doing a number on me. His intense focus sends flickers of heat through me, and I'm unable to look away. When the door opens, he steps aside and motions for me to exit first.

Holly walks out next to me. "That was almost as good as an orgasm," she whispers.

I snort. "You obviously need to have more orgasms," I whisper back.

"You're not lying."

The couples are in the lobby and we walk to the sushi restaurant, Wyatt keeping his distance.

I wanted this, I remind myself.

But somehow, we end up side by side in the restaurant, and the jittery excitement in my chest tells the truth about what I really want.

The rest of the table is interacting, talking about the day, and Wyatt and I sit quietly on our end of the table.

"You look beautiful," he says.

"Thank you. You look pretty great too."

"Thank you." He clears his throat. "Are you enjoying your trip to Vegas?"

I glance at him and he gives me a forced smile, eventually lifting a shoulder.

"I realized I came on a little strong this morning. Trying to tone it down a bit tonight," he says.

I laugh, my nerves easing somewhat. "I didn't make it easy to know how to be this morning," I say quietly. "I'm sorry about that."

"You don't need to be sorry about anything."

I smile and take a sip of my cocktail. "I've enjoyed *everything* about my trip to Vegas."

His lips part and he leans in. "Tell me more."

I set my glass down and stare at it instead of him. "I don't want you to think I didn't...like...what happened between us." I glance at him then and my heart thuds in my chest, but I want to get this out. "I did. Very much."

He nods slightly, his tongue darting out to lick his lips. I stare at his mouth, remembering how it felt to kiss him, to feel his mouth, his tongue exploring my body.

"I just really love Landmark and this family, *your* family. I feel like I'm finally making a home there with Dakota." It comes out in a rush. "My job is great. My divorce is final, and I'm getting on my own two feet, gaining momentum." I bite my lower lip and take a deep breath, and his eyes flit from my eyes to my mouth, down to my chest and up again. "It'd be crazy to risk all of that for something we can't possibly know would work."

I'm quiet for a second and he studies me. When I don't say anything else, he gives me a tentative nod.

"Okay," he says.

"Okay?" I repeat.

He smiles. "I have a lot of thoughts on this," he says. "But I don't think you're ready to hear what I have to say. You asked me to be your friend, and I'll be that, regardless of how much I want to be more."

"Thank you," I say, relief flooding through me.

"Of course. Can I say one more thing though?"

"Yes," I whisper.

He leans in closer and my breath hitches in my chest.

"Some people will never experience what we shared last night," he says. His eyes skate over my face like he's memorizing me. "I certainly haven't ever experienced anything close to that before." The rasp in his voice makes me press my legs together. "I have no doubt we would work, Marlow. And I personally think it would be worth all the risk."

He smiles at me again and sits back in his seat. Huge platters of sushi are brought out and he turns his attention to the food, while I sit there, desire for him thrumming through me.

The next hour and a half, conversation flows freely between all of us as we eat and laugh and celebrate Theo and Sofie.

From there, we say bye to Holly, April, Sutton, and Callum as they head back to Landmark Mountain. The rest of us walk to watch the fountains in front of the Bellagio, Sofie and Theo, and Scarlett and Jamison wrapped around each other, while Wyatt and I keep two feet of space between us.

It's agonizing.

All I can think about is what if maybe, just maybe, Wyatt could be right about us?

But I don't make a move and neither does he.

We play a few slots and hit the roulette table, where I win five hundred dollars. I'm so excited, I turn and give Wyatt a huge hug, and his sexy grin is wide when I pull away.

"See? Worth the risk," he says.

I roll my eyes and he just takes my hand and kisses the palm, his eyes dancing.

A few hours later, Scarlett and Jamison leave the group first, and Sofie leans into me as the rest of us walk toward the elevators. "I've never seen you look so happy, Low." She puts her head on my shoulder.

"I am happy," I tell her.

"Does Wyatt have anything to do with this?" she whispers, smiling when she pulls back.

I flush and her eyes gleam with excitement. I quickly shake my head. "Don't get too excited yet. I just—" I shake my head again and laugh, making a face.

She puts her forehead on mine. "I won't get ahead of myself, even though the thought of you two getting together makes me *ecstatic*," she whispers. "But don't be afraid to just have a little fun. Okay?" She pulls back and looks me in the eye. "Take something for yourself for once. Don't over-think it."

"I have Dakota to think about," I remind her.

She levels me with a look. "You think I'm not thinking about my favorite little human too?" She leans in and whispers, "Get some of this tension out of you and you'll go back to her a much happier mama." She giggles and laughs at my expression when she backs away.

"We worked some of that tension out last night," I say through my teeth and she jerks back, mouth open.

She presses her hand to her mouth and when it drops, she's radiant. "I cannot believe you managed to keep that from me all day long. You are so busted." She giggles. "But what are you doing still standing here?" She looks over my shoulder at Wyatt, most likely. "Go get you some more."

"It's not that simple," I argue.

"I think it can be," she says simply.

She can't wipe the huge smile off her face as she turns and walks over to Theo, looping her arm through his.

They start walking to the elevator and she looks at me over her shoulder and motions for me to go get Wyatt.

I shoo her off and look around to see Wyatt turning toward me.

"Can I walk you to your room?" he asks.

"Is that code for sex?" I ask, emboldened by what Sofie said and the cocktails I've had tonight.

He smirks. "No, but it can be."

CHAPTER THIRTY-TWO

BLOWN

WYATT

Her cheeks get all pink and she's so damn cute, I can't take it.

She groans and moves past me toward the elevator. In one stride, I'm behind her and she sways slightly. When I put my hand on her hip, she sighs.

"If you were to put all your worries aside, what would you want right now, Marlow?" I ask.

The elevator door opens and we step inside. She moves

to one side of the elevator and I move to the other, facing her.

"If I didn't have to worry about tomorrow and things in Landmark Mountain?" Her voice is tentative at first and amps up the more she says. "And that maybe I'd be ruining our friendship and, therefore, all the other new friendships I've made with your family and friends?"

I exhale and nod.

Her voice is quiet, but steady. "I'd want to enjoy this night with you." Her shoulder lifts slightly.

"If we're together tonight, will it make you run later?" I ask.

"Well, since we're heading to my room, it's less likely." She tries not to smile.

I act like I'm having a lightbulb moment. "So that's where I messed up last night...you had an easy way out."

She rolls her eyes, but her shoulders are loosening.

"I'm just scared, Wyatt," she says.

"I am too. I've never felt this way about anyone, Marlow. Ever. Nothing that even comes close. Last night only solidified what I was already feeling."

"Are you sure we don't need to just get each other out of our systems?"

The elevator stops and I hold the door open as she steps out, my hand going to the small of her back as we walk down the hall.

"Do you want the truth?" I ask.

We stop in front of her door and she turns and looks up at me. My hand falls from her back and I resist the urge to touch her.

"Yes," she whispers.

"I think you're already so deeply embedded in my system that I don't see how I'll ever get you out." Her mouth parts and I put my hands on her waist, leaning in when I add, "And I don't want to."

"Wyatt," she whispers, her hands landing on my chest.

"If you don't feel the same about me, I'll do my best to deal with it," I tell her.

"That's what terrifies me the most," she says. "I think I *do* feel the same." Her eyes go wide. "This is crazy, Wyatt. We barely know each other."

I lean in until my forehead touches hers. "I think we know all that matters about one another for now, and I'm not going anywhere. We'll figure out the rest as we go. What do you think?"

"Yes," she says softly. And then she says it again, with more emphasis. *"Yes."*

I grin, and flustered, Marlow turns around and reaches in her tiny purse to find her room key, while I put my arms around her waist and nuzzle her neck. She laughs, fumbling to get the door open. Once we're inside, she turns to face me, her arms winding around my neck.

When my lips touch hers, a match is struck and the fire ignites, all-consuming. She leans up on her tiptoes, her fingers moving to undo the buttons on my shirt, and mine trying to figure out how to get her dress off. Our lips barely lose contact as we hurriedly undress.

When our clothes drop to the floor, only her lacy underwear and my boxer briefs between us, I pull back and look at her in the glow of the city lights.

I mutter a curse.

"You look like a fucking dream. You want this, Marlow?" I ask one more time. "I'm willing to take it as slow as you want. I can hold you all night if that's what you need. We can sit across the room from each other, preferably naked," I pause while she laughs, "and just talk.

Whatever it takes for you to still want me here in the morning."

"I want this," she says, her eyes shining bright. "I want *you*."

I hold up my hand and her palm meets mine. When our fingers thread together, relief whooshes through me, and when she steps closer, pressing her body against mine, another wave of desire takes over.

She surprises me by backing me against the wall and then getting on her knees, pulling my briefs off.

"Oh," I say as my erection hits my stomach and it's garbled when I say it again as she takes me in her mouth. "*Marlow.*" I hold onto her hair, watching her tongue swirl around my tip before her lips open wide and she takes me in as far as she can.

"You don't have to—" I start.

Her mouth comes off of me with a pop, and her hands wrap around me. She grips me tight, smiling when I can't help but thrust into her hand.

"I want this," she says, licking me from base to tip. "Did you know you have the most beautiful cock I've ever laid eyes on?"

"Uh. Fuck, I'm glad," I shudder.

"I regretted not telling you that last night." Her cheeks lift as she grins and goes back to intently sucking me, and I lose my mind.

I steady my heels against the wall and groan, fighting the urge to close my eyes and resisting because I don't want to miss watching this.

"You are perfect," my words are strangled.

The things she's doing, her mouth suctioning around me, the heat of her mouth, the way she's staring up at me, her hand fisted around the base of me while her mouth pumps up and down...it's the best fucking feeling. And hands down, the best fucking blow job I've ever had in my life.

I stand as still as I can and then thrust into her once, twice, on the verge of losing control.

"It's too good," I tell her. "Slide that lace to the side and touch yourself."

It's the first time her rhythm falters and she blinks up at me, but then she does as I ask.

"I love seeing how wet you are," I whisper.

She hums against me and I get harder in her mouth.

Her fingers move faster against her skin and her movements get frantic as we both race to the edge.

"Mmm...Marlow, I'm close." I try to pull back slightly, but she shakes her head, going even faster around me, faster against herself.

When her eyes squeeze shut and she bucks against her fingers, I let out a roar and explode inside of her. She swallows it all, some dripping out of the side of her mouth as she dazedly opens her eyes back up to look at me. I brush it off of her mouth with my thumb and she gradually slides her lips off of me and wraps them around my thumb, licking that clean too.

I whimper, my dick jumping at the sight.

"Fucking obscene," I say, grinning, and she laughs, eyes suddenly shy. "Oh, don't act shy now," I tease.

Her cheeks flush and she's so beautiful it makes me dizzy. I reach out and pull her to her feet and kiss her hard. She melts into me and I palm her ass, already wanting more of her.

"Was that good?" she asks when we come up for air. She palms my dick as if explaining what she means.

"Do you even wonder a little bit if I loved that?" I ask incredulously. "Mind *and* cock *blown*."

She laughs. "Good. I...hope it's not rude to say this, but..." She makes a face and I brace myself for whatever she's about to say. "That's the first time I've ever enjoyed doing that and I really...*really* loved it," she says.

I scrub my hand down my face. "I really...love your mouth."

She laughs and turns, taking my hand and looking at me over her shoulder.

"Want to see the amazing tub in this place?" she asks.

"If you're in it, absolutely."

CHAPTER THIRTY-THREE

DATES AND KNEES AND ENERGY

MARLOW

While the massive jacuzzi fills, Wyatt makes a quick trip to his room for his overnight bag, and hopefully condoms.

He yelps when he first steps into the scalding water, but he pipes down when he sees that I think it's the perfect temp. After almost an hour, we're still in the tub, adding more hot water when it gets too cool.

I forced him to sit across from me, which felt like torture

at first, but he's massaging my feet and teasing my inner thighs with his roaming feet as we talk.

I don't remember when I've had this much fun talking.

Our conversation has ranged from movie confessions—he wept during *Brother Bear* and I never saw it—to stories about the many elderly women in Landmark Mountain chasing Jamison's grandpa, Pappy.

"Well, he *is* the cutest," I admit. "I get the allure."

"Oh, so do I. The man is young at heart, has style, is funny and kind, and he still talks fondly about his wife, even though she's been gone for a few years now. What's not to love?"

We smile at each other and he lifts my ankle up and kisses it, sliding his hand up my smooth leg. I don't know if he realizes that he sighs as he does it, and I swoon a little more inside.

"What was your granddad like?" I ask.

"He was great. A bit of a workaholic, but he loved us and he loved Grinny. He had a hard job, filling that parental role when he should've been loving life as a grandpa. Grinny made up for wherever he lacked, and to his credit, he did his best with us. Were you close to your grandparents?"

"Yes, I was close to my paternal grandparents. I didn't really know my mom's parents—they died when I was little —but I would've lived with my dad's parents if I could've."

"I wish I could've met them."

"Me too," I say, my voice wistful. "And I wish they could've seen Dakota grow up. She's really missed out on the grandparent scene. My parents haven't been...great. I feel like Dakota is getting more of an example of what it's like to be around family in Landmark than she's ever had before."

He's quiet for a moment, and I change the subject so it doesn't get too heavy.

"What's the worst date you've ever had?" I ask.

"Eighth-grade graduation," he answers immediately. "Pilar Jenkins threw up all over my suit...while we were dancing."

"*No.*" I laugh.

"That's not the worst part," he says, cringing. "None of it got on her, only me, which was...okay, but she was so embarrassed about the whole thing that I pretended I'd been the one to throw up. And it probably would've died down, except she ran with it and told everyone we walked past on the way out of there what I'd done and was still talking about it a week later as she shot disgusted looks my way across the cafeteria."

"I hate Pilar Jenkins," I state emphatically.

"Me too." He gives me a guilty look. "I *was* kind of rude to her sophomore year though. Can you believe she asked me out after all that?"

"She *didn't.*"

"Yep, and I said, 'Sorry, I don't have another suit for you to ruin.'" It echoes in the bathroom as we both start laughing. "From that day until she left for college, she never spoke to me again."

I shake my head. "If that's the only rude thing you ever said to her after the eighth-grade horror date, that's pretty commendable. Does she still live in Landmark?"

"No, thank God. The last I heard, she's got four kids and lives in Wisconsin."

"I guess we should wish her well," I say, still laughing.

"What was your worst date?"

"This morning," I tease. "When this arrogant guy thought I'd be won over with his big dick energy."

His eyebrows lift and he rubs my foot over said energy. "Big dick, huh?"

"Hmm." I act unimpressed, but the way it's stayed alert throughout most of this bath time has been impressive and the way it's growing to its full stature now is even more so.

"How did that end up for you?" he asks.

I lift a shoulder. "With me on my knees."

A laugh bursts out of me, and his grin is primal as he puts his hands on either side of my thighs and tugs me until I'm straddling him.

"And your best date?" he asks, rubbing me over his hardness.

"This one night, I ended up in the tub with a guy and his big—"

He bites my bottom lip and tickles my side and I cackle, my head falling back. He kisses up my neck and I squirm over him, his hands sliding down to my ass and squeezing.

I put my hands on either side of his face, my lips brushing against his. "As incredible as this bath date has been, I think I'm ready for bed."

His kiss is light, sweet. "Sleepy?"

He wraps my legs around his waist and stands, and despite us both being wet and slippery, I feel completely safe in his arms.

"No, I'm not sleepy," I whisper in his ear and he pauses, his grin kicking up a few notches.

I grab a towel as we walk past them and put it around his shoulders. He walks into the bedroom and sets me in the middle of the bed. The towel slides from his shoulders and he dries me off as best he can.

"I'm just gonna get wet again anyway." I grab the towel and toss it over his shoulder and I can feel his smile as he buries his head in my neck, kissing down my skin.

"Marlow Agatha Walker, after last night, I didn't know I'd discover more favorite things about you today." He glances up at me as his tongue flicks my nipple. "These are still way up there," he says, giving the other side attention too. "But the things coming out of—*and in*—that pretty mouth, damn woman, they are giving me life."

I press my lips together and giggle. "I didn't know I had it in me," I admit.

"You're leaving so many openings with that one that I don't even know where to start," he teases.

"One hole at a time," I say and then clamp my hand over my mouth, shaking my head as I start laughing so hard I can't breathe.

He starts laughing too, and for the longest time, we just lay there laughing. When one of us slows down, the other starts laughing again even harder.

Something happens inside me, a weight I didn't realize I'd been carrying falls off of me. I feel younger, lighter, more carefree than...maybe ever. And it's weird, but I think the same thing happens to Wyatt. He looks so unbelievably happy, like he's a world away from Pine Community and the stresses there, or the unease of just this morning.

When we're finally quiet, the smiles still lingering on our lips, we face each other and our kisses are breathless and hopeful. I throw my fist in the air when he produces the strand of condoms and once one is securely on him, he sinks into me and we both breathe a sigh of bliss.

"Full disclosure," he says. "This has been the best date I've ever had too."

He rolls me on top of him and it doesn't take long for the urgency between us to build.

I can't believe I ever resisted this man.

CHAPTER THIRTY-FOUR

BLAST OFF

WYATT

The alarm goes off on my phone and Marlow moans next to me.

I fumble around trying to shut it off while still keeping her exactly where she is. Her hair fans over my chest, her thigh wrapped around mine, breast pressed against my side.

Best feeling ever.

I didn't imagine anything could beat our first night together, but last night proved me wrong. There were no inhibitions between us. I'm exhausted because I couldn't keep my hands...and other body parts...off of her all night long, but...fuck, I feel good this morning.

Euphoric.

Marlow's alarm goes off a few minutes after mine and she stretches against me. Of course, my dick already thought it was time to play, just being near her, but her soft skin arching into mine amps up the situation.

In the next breath, she's jumping up, not just out of my arms, but out of bed, her hair going every which way, as she power walks to the bathroom. I try to get a view of her ass, but she's moving too fast.

I lean up on my elbows, turning off the alarm for good. "What is happening right now?"

"What do you mean?" she calls from the bathroom, electric toothbrush buzzing.

"You shot out of this bed faster than...I'm too tired to think of a comparison."

The buzzing continues and when it finally shuts off, she comes back and stands in the doorway, smiling at me.

Naked.

My brain short-circuits as I take her in.

"Like a rocket," she says.

"What?"

"It's a thing Dakota and I do. I guess I'm fully in the habit now. Wow, good to know. I'll have to see if she did the same this morning...although she probably didn't set her alarm..." Her voice trails off.

"What?" I repeat.

She giggles, her cheeks pink, and her tits jiggle as she leans against the doorjamb.

God, she's gorgeous.

"We were having such a hard time getting up in

the mornings, and I saw this lady named Mel Robbins on Instagram—have you heard of her?" I stare at her and she keeps going. "She was talking about her concept 5-4-3-2-1, and you jump out of bed. Don't even give your body a chance to argue with your mind, just get up."

I stopped hearing her around the words *hard time getting up*, my eyes tracking the movement when she puts her hand on her hip. Her skin is so soft it feels like smooth fucking satin.

"You're not hearing a word I'm saying, are you?" Both hands on each hip now.

"Get over here."

She smirks. "I can't. I'm already up. That's the whole point of 5-4-3-2-1. And we have to be at breakfast in half an hour."

"5-4-3-2-1 your way right on over here. Plenty of time for me to ravage your body."

She turns and walks back into the bathroom. "Been there, done that," she calls.

That gets me up. I move in behind her, tickling her lightly but enough to make her squirm and laugh as my arms wrap around her. She looks so unbelievably happy when I look at her in the mirror.

"Been there, doing that over and over again, I hope," I murmur against her skin.

She swats me away. "Okay, Mr. One-Track Mind, hands to yourself. We have to get ready."

"If I held your hips steady, I bet you could still do your makeup."

She snorts. "Not the way you make my eyes cross."

"So you'd really rather get ready than cross your eyes, I see how it is." I reach around her and grab my toothbrush and she squeezes her fist around my dick, making the breath hiss out of me.

"There's nothing I'd rather do, trust me, but if we show up late together, they're gonna all know what we've been doing." She gives me two long pumps and I groan.

"Take a look at our faces," I tell her. "They're gonna know."

She looks in the mirror and laughs as her cheeks get even pinker. "It's like we have lightbulbs in our eyes."

I grin at her, nodding as I brush my teeth and then wincing with how good her hand feels. Multitasking.

"Make it quick," she says, leaning her elbows on the counter. Her hand drops off of me as the outline of her cheeks hug my dick.

I get my mouth rinsed faster than any time known to man and look around for a condom. She lifts one between her fingers that must've dropped out of my shaving kit.

"Thank fuck," I say as I slide it on and am inside her in the next second.

We both moan as I sink all the way in. I'm still for a few seconds, staring at her in awe in the mirror.

"You feel...so good," she shudders, "but this isn't making it quick."

"Mmm, you're right." I shift her hands on the counter so they're spread apart and lean her into the counter more so she's splayed out for me. I gaze down at her taking me in. "Oh, I wish you could see this."

She twitches around me and I don't know how it's possible after we've been at this all night, but I'm close. I slide out slowly and back in, watching us again and again, mesmerized. When she starts thrusting back, curving her torso so I'm hitting even deeper, she feels close too. Her legs start trembling and I hang on to her hips, our rhythm fast and sloppy, but so fucking effective.

"Wyatt," she cries.

"I know," I say, smoothing my hand over her ass before I pull her cheeks apart, angling to go even deeper.

Her whole body shudders and she grips the counter, her gasps and moans driving me faster. Our pace is urgent, frantic.

"You feel so fucking good," I groan.

And then she's fluttering around me, her walls clamping around me so hard I lose my vision for a few seconds.

"Wyattttt," she cries, and I'm right there with her.

"I-" I want to say something profound to express how extraordinary this moment feels, but my brain cells have blacked out.

When the tremors inside us both begin to still, I pull her back against my chest, my hands wrapping around her breasts, and we stare at each other dazedly in the mirror.

"Wow," she whispers.

I nod, still dumbstruck.

Still deep inside her.

Still dazed that we've moved from enemies to friends to lovers to frenemies to *lovers* in what feels like both an eternity and the span of a minute.

Her hand reaches back and squeezes my side. "Are you still with me?" she asks, her eyes lit with mischief.

With no small regret, I pull out of her and enjoy the pinch of loss on her face when she's free of me. I bend down and kiss her shoulder, smoothing back her hair. Her nipples are hard and I squeeze each tip between my fingers.

"Tonight I'm going slow. You'll be begging to come," I tell her.

I give her ass a smack and she jumps, startled. I take

care of the condom and move toward the shower, turning it on.

"Tonight?" she asks as I'm stepping in the water. "You're already planning a tonight? And begging?" She scoffs, but her expression is playful. "Someone's feeling themselves this morning."

She pins her hair up and joins me in the shower, grabbing her body wash before I've gotten fully wet.

"You'll see," I say, grinning at her as I lather my hair.

Her eyes wander over my body, glazed when they meet mine again.

We wash quickly and rinse, a thrum of heat still stirring between us. When we get out, I hand her a towel and dry off with my own, wrapping it around my waist when I'm done. She puts on her bra and panties, a cute pink matching getup with flowers all over that I like a lot. Not as much as seeing her naked, but a helluva lot.

While I get my clothes on, she expertly applies makeup. She doesn't need it, but damn, everything she does looks beautiful. I watch her from the doorway, enjoying every second. When her hair is the way she wants it, she hustles by me and I make it as difficult as possible just to feel her against me again.

"You're impossible," she says, squeezing past me.

"Irresistible, you mean."

A laugh bursts out of her, but she tries to play it off as she steps into her dress. And then, "Okay, that too."

I grin. "You're the irresistible one." I put my hands on her waist and kiss her cheek.

She waves her hand in front of her face when I pull back. "I need a fan to carry around and cool off when you're in the vicinity."

I slide my hands down to her ass, already established as

one of my most favorite places, and squeeze. "I like keeping you warmed up."

She pretends to be annoyed, but her smirk says otherwise.

"We've gotta go, but..." She puts her hand on my chest. "All fun and play aside...I'm not sure if I'm ready for Dakota to know we're...whatever we're...doing," she finishes awkwardly.

I nod. "Okay."

"Okay?" she echoes, her surprise evident.

"Yeah. I don't want to do anything you're uncomfortable with. There are options too though."

"Like what?"

"Like, what time does she go to bed and get up?"

She laughs and drags me toward the door, and we walk down the hall toward the elevator. "Eight and six thirty."

"You okay with me showing up at eight thirty? I have to be at work by seven in the morning, so I can leave by five thirty just to be on the safe side."

"You'd do that?" she asks.

"For as long as you want, absolutely."

We step into the elevator and she's quiet. I can't fully read this expression on her face now and it's starting to make me nervous, but then she looks at me as the elevator dings and gets off, singing the lyrics to "Dance the Night" by Dua Lipa.

And you better believe I follow.

CHAPTER THIRTY-FIVE

RUNAWAY HEART

MARLOW

Wyatt was right.

They knew the second they saw our faces.

Besides knowing smirks from the guys to Wyatt, the only thing I had to deal with was extra tight hugs from Sofie and Scarlett, both of them saying something like, "You better spill the second we're home!"

I shooed them away from me and laughed them off, trying to act like there was nothing to tell.

But now that we're on the helicopter and Wyatt and I can't keep our eyes open, I think any hope of playing that off went out the window. The noise, the excitement, the gorgeous scenery, and hanging out with our favorite people aren't enough to keep us awake.

"Wake up, sleepyheads," Scarlett sings sometime later.

I squint at her, not sure where I am. My body feels deliciously sore. I'm exhausted and when I look over at Wyatt, he stretches out and gives me a sleepy smile. The helicopter engine turns off and the quiet is jarring.

Theo glances at us and grins.

"Looks like a good time was had by all," he says. "Thanks again for making this weekend happen, you guys."

We all hug goodbye in the lobby of the resort, and Wyatt lingers with me. We walk out to the parking lot toward my SUV.

"You picking up Dakota or heading home for a while?" he asks.

"Yeah, I thought I'd go right over there."

He nods and I'm torn—I don't know what to do with myself. I hate to say bye, but I don't want to assume that he wants to hang out more today...or that he'd want to spend the afternoon with Dakota and me when he's obviously tired.

"Message me later if you want to hang out," he says, seeming reluctant to leave me too. "Or if eight thirty is too early..."

"You're welcome over anytime," I say quietly.

"Yeah?" His eyebrows lift hopefully.

I nod. "Yeah. You're kinda growing on me."

He tugs me against him, and my stomach does that swoop thing it does every time he touches me.

"Kinda?" he says.

"Kinda really."

He nods. "Okay. I can live with that." He grins and leans in, kissing me, both hands on either side of my face.

It's sweet and sexy, tame but so hot, and I want to pull him into my car and have my way with him.

His phone buzzes and he pulls away, making a face. "That's work. I made the mistake of saying when I'd be back." He kisses me again, and this time it's quick. "I'll check in with them and see what you're up to later."

I nod and he answers the phone as I get in my car and float away.

When I pull up to Grinny's, Grinny and Dakota are waving a huge wand with massive bubbles surrounding them.

"Mama," Dakota yells when I step outside.

She runs to me, her hair messy and the smile on her face so wide it makes my heart hurt in the best way.

"Hey, my Kota. Oof." She barrels into me and I bend to pick her up, hugging her hard. "I love you. So happy to see your face."

"I'm so happy to see your face too," she says. "Look, Grinny and I are making these bubbles."

"Amazing." I set her down and walk toward Grinny.

She meets me halfway, her smile almost as big as Dakota's, and we hug.

"Welcome back," Grinny says.

"Thank you."

She smiles at me again, this one intentional and...somehow, I can tell that she already knows about me and Wyatt. How is that possible?

"I wish we'd been there to welcome you back at the resort." She motions for me to follow her inside. "I heard there was quite the goodbye," she says over her shoulder, laughing at the shock on my face. "Secrets don't last in Landmark Mountain..."

The kiss in the parking lot.

"Wow. I guess I should've known that, but...that was record time," I say, feeling a little winded.

"What's a record time?" Dakota asks.

I squeeze her again and laugh, unsure of how to respond. It's way too soon to be telling my little girl I have a boyfriend when I'm not even sure that's what he is yet. And she still doesn't even know Cash and I are divorced, just that we're not living with him anymore.

Geez, you haven't complicated this at all, I snip at myself.

"Peg and Helen just said there was a fun goodbye with everyone at the resort," Grinny says, appeasing Dakota. "And record time means traveling fast, or like when you and Owen were running fast across the yard and Owen said *it's not a race...*"

"He said that because I kept beating him," Dakota says, her shoulders shaking as she laughs. She slaps her hand over her mouth.

Grinny throws her head back and laughs. "That's exactly right. You're the smartest little thing," she says. She looks at me. "Did you have a good time?"

"It was wonderful," I tell her. "I can't thank you enough for keeping Dakota. I didn't know how much I...needed that little trip."

Grinny squeezes my shoulder. "I'm so glad. We had the best time, didn't we, Dakota?"

Dakota nods. "Owen had to leave before me. But Grinny's a good player too."

Grinny laughs again. "Well, this old bag of bones isn't as much fun as Owen, but I'll do in a pinch, won't I?"

Dakota's face drops. "Where is the bag of bones?" She looks around Grinny and me, and then she turns to see if it's behind her.

Grinny shakes her head, wiping her eyes. "That's what I get for talking about myself like that," she says, still laughing. "There are no old bones here but mine, honey. And they're feeling like new today just getting a dose of you."

I stifle a yawn and Grinny smiles at me.

"You look like you could use a good nap. I expect I'll be taking one myself," she says.

"Not me," Dakota says proudly. "I don't need a nap."

"How about we watch a movie when we get home?" I ask, picking up her bag.

"Oo, yes. I like that. I haven't watched a movie in twenty years," she says.

Grinny holds out her arms. "Can I have one more Dakota hug?"

Dakota runs over to her and hugs her tight, her eyes squeezing shut.

"Tell Grinny thank you for everything," I urge her.

"Thank you for everything, Grinny," she says. "And for the waffles and berries and the bath toys...oh, and the meaty loaf. I very loved it."

My eyes get wide. Meatyloaf?

"You are so welcome, darling. I had such a fun time with you here. You come back any time, okay?" Grinny grins at her and then glances at me. "This little one ate two big helpings of my meatloaf. I think she liked it more than Owen and it's his favorite."

"I'll have to try yours sometime. My mom scarred me with hers, and I haven't had it since leaving home," I admit.

Grinny claps her hands together. "It's a date then. Next time you come over, we'll have my meatloaf."

"It's so good, Mama. You'll very love it."

I bop her nose and grin. "I bet I will."

We hug Grinny one more time and go home. I talk Dakota into unpacking her suitcase as best she can before we start a movie, and I throw our things in the laundry. Now that I'm home, the exhaustion is settling in more, and I put on a movie, cuddling up to my girl.

I fall asleep within minutes, dreaming of that guy with the green eyes, a dangerous smile, and all the right moves who also happened to run away with my heart.

CHAPTER THIRTY-SIX

FREE FLAVORS

WYATT

I wake up, groggy, picking up my phone to check the time and cursing under my breath.

I text Marlow.

> I went by the hospital for a couple of hours, came home, and sat down to check email…three and a half hours later, I'm just waking up.

MARLOW

I'd tease you about being an old man, but I
pretty much did the same thing. Dakota
watched two movies while I slept.

You kept me up all night long, woman.

MARLOW

Uh...take a good look in the mirror, you
and your BDE.

BDE...Best Dick Ever?

MARLOW

<eye roll emoji>

Biggest Delight...Experiment?

MARLOW

<eye roll emoji> <side smirk emoji>

I've got it.

Brilliant.

Doctor.

Erection.

MARLOW

Were you always this easy to entertain as a
child?

No, only with you. I miss you.

There's a pause for a few seconds. And then some dots
before they're all deleted and another pause.

What did you just delete?

MARLOW

That I miss you too.

> Why the hell would you delete that?

MARLOW

Because it's too soon to miss you!

I grin.

> When can I see Dakota again? I miss
> her too.

MARLOW

Have you always been this needy?

> Never. Only with you.

Again with the pause, dots, and poof, disappeared.

> What did you delete?

MARLOW

I like it.

Again with the cheesiest grin. Never mind that I'm all alone in my too-quiet condo. I think about the land I've got that I've never thought about very much. It always felt like a far-off, one-day kind of dream to build a home on my property. I've been consumed with med school and my work, enjoying the simplicity of my bare-bones condo near the hospital.

If I'd been told six months ago that a woman would come through here and knock me on my ass, making me dream about things I didn't think were for me, I would've laughed my head off and said there was no fucking way.

Joke's on me.

Marlow makes me want it all.

> **MARLOW**
>
> Did I scare you silent?

>> Oh, not even close, Little Rocket. Not even close.

> **MARLOW**
>
> Little Rocket, huh? I was hoping you didn't catch that. You were looking at me like words weren't registering when I said it.

>> It did take some time to sink in. Do you always talk a mile a minute when you've only had thirty minutes of sleep and the alarm goes off?

> **MARLOW**
>
> 5-4-3-2-1...it's a thing. And no. Only with you.

God, I love her.

I love her.

I swipe my hand down my face.

> **MARLOW**
>
> You can see Dakota anytime. She misses you too.

>> Now? Is now good?

> **MARLOW**
>
> Are you here?

>> No, but I wish I was. I can be there in ten.

MARLOW

Come on. She'll be awake for at least another forty minutes…I think. She's pretty tired from her weekend too.

I'll be there in eight. Unless you need me to pick up anything?

MARLOW

We're good. We'll even share our ice cream with you.

I cannot wait.

I brush my teeth and add a few more strips of condoms to my shaving kit. I pause in my closet and grab a dress shirt and pants, leaving them on the hangers, and I stuff pajama pants, a T-shirt, and work shoes in my backpack. The level of excitement in my chest is borderline troubling, but I'm too happy to be concerned.

I'm knocking on their door with a minute to spare and Marlow opens the door, smiling, Dakota peering around her legs.

"Wyatt!" Dakota yells, rushing at me with a hug.

"Sweets!" I yell back, hugging her hard.

"How did you know I wanted to see you so bad?" she asks.

"Because I wanted to see *you* so bad," I tell her. I push her hair away from her cheek and she beams up at me. "Ahh, I feel better already."

"Were you sick?" She frowns.

"No, I was just missing you," I tell her.

She leans her head against my side and takes my hand. I kiss my fingers and press them to Marlow's cheek as I'm tugged away. When I glance at her over my shoulder, she's still standing there, her expression sweet and vulnerable.

"Where are you taking me?" I ask Dakota.

She stops us in front of the refrigerator.

"We have free choices of ice cream."

"I love free ice cream. Yes, please."

Free," she says, lifting up three fingers. "One, two, free."

"Oh, yes." I nod. "Even better."

She opens the freezer dramatically, as it takes all her strength, and holds out her hand like a game show host. "See?"

"I do. Which kind are you having?"

"Strawberry."

"Solid choice. What about you?" I ask Marlow.

"I'm feeling the chocolate peanut butter pretzel tonight," she says.

I tilt my head. "I haven't had it, but it sounds delicious. Is that mint chip I see though? I have a hard time having anything else when that's around."

Marlow's lips poke out with her grin. "You look like a mint chip guy."

"Delicious and refreshing?"

Dakota giggles. "You don't look delicious and refreshing."

"No? Do I look green and chippy?" I tease.

"No." She shakes her head, laughing harder.

Marlow opens the cabinet as Dakota says, "Mama likes hers in a bowl. Do you want a bowl or a cone?"

"A cone!"

"Me too," Dakota says, eyebrows lifted in excitement.

She's absolutely the cutest little girl I've ever seen.

She runs to the other cabinet and stretches on her tiptoes to get out the waffle cones.

I pull all three cartons of ice cream out of the freezer and take the scoop out of Marlow's hand.

"How about you let me get that for you," I say.

"Oh...sure," she says, more bashful than I expected her to be after last night.

I wonder if it's weird for her to have me in her space...or if maybe she's still adjusting to living without Cash.

She's wearing leggings and a shirt that falls over her shoulder. I watch her as I scoop ice cream into the cone first for Dakota and then in the bowl for Marlow.

"Thank you," she murmurs after Dakota's loud, "Thank you, Wyatt!"

When I have mine, we move to the table and sit down.

Dakota tells us about her weekend with Grinny and Owen. How much fun she had and how they played with Hermioneep a lot and how many stories Owen read to her at bedtime.

"He can read *everything*," she says. "And you know what? I know how to read too now. Not like Owen, but I know c-a-t. Cat. And d-o-g. Dog."

Marlow looks at her with pride. "Nice. Did Owen teach you that?"

"Yep. Oh, and p-i-g. Pig." She grins.

"Look at you. Before you know it, you'll be reading everything too," I tell her.

Dakota notices the backpack by the door for the first time. "Are you doing a sleepover?" she asks.

My eyes shoot to Marlow's and she's blinking slowly, looking guilty as fuck.

"Uh...I like to bring my backpack sometimes," I stall.

"What do you bring?" she asks.

"Boring things like work papers and such."

God forgive me for this one small lie.

She sticks out her lower lip. "I wish you could do a sleepover. That way you'd be here when I wake up and we could have breakfast like me and Owen."

"That does sound fun. Maybe he can do that some-time," Marlow says. One of her eyebrows slants up at me and it's so damn sexy I swallow hard.

"Yeah," I say. "I'd love that."

Dakota grins a huge smile, strawberry ice cream peeking through her teeth.

Marlow's is more subtle, but the promise behind those eyes makes my heartbeat skip a beat.

Both of these girls are doing a number on my heart.

CHAPTER THIRTY-SEVEN

CLINICIAN SPEAK

MARLOW

"Wyatt, please," I whimper.

I didn't believe I'd resort to begging, but the man has brought me to the edge of an orgasm so many times, I'm desperate.

"This is cruel," I say louder.

His teeth nip the inside of my thigh and I arch into him, groaning when he chuckles against my skin.

"It hasn't even been ten minutes yet," he says, sliding up my body.

His lips are glossy from me, eyes mischievous, and his hair makes me want to jump his body right now...except he's making us TAKE OUR TIME.

"That can't be right. It takes me longer to get there than that, and I've gotten *there* at least five times before you stop and make me suffer," I whisper-shout so I don't wake up Dakota, but I'm still insistent on getting my point across.

His smirk is so sinful and sexy, I wrap my legs around his naked torso and lock him there.

"Where is this *there* you're referring to?" he teases, between kisses.

"Nirvana, the abyss, the—" I gasp as he slides his hardness over my slit. "Yes," I whisper, reassured that he's finally giving me what I want.

"I really like this side of you, Marlow Agatha."

Glide, thrust, glide.

"I regret every nice thing I said about you," I pant.

My breath cuts out when he does a glide, glide, glide, thrust. My head falls back, ready to fall, and he lifts off of me, sitting up.

I lean up and glare at him, and he grins, reaching out to pinch my nipple. When he holds up a condom, I want to cry with relief. I grab it out of his fingers when he's going too slow for my liking and enjoy the agonized groan he makes when I slide it on him. My eyebrows go up and he tries to frown, but he's still too deep in cocky mode to fully stop smiling.

"This hasn't been easy for me either," he says, when I do a glide, glide, glide myself along his thick, long length. "It's been *really hard*," he adds.

My eyes narrow and he tries to look contrite from using the pun. I can feel the heat of him through the condom.

"I'm burning for you. Can you tell?" he asks.

Again with the grin.

Right now it's hard to remember the scowly Wyatt I first saw.

I don't say anything, choosing instead to play with his balls as my other hand fists around him.

"Okay, you're not playing fair now," he says, his forehead dotting with sweat.

I smile and lean back, pulling him down on top of me. He kisses me, and I squirm against him, loving the friction.

He leans back, his hand grazing over my thigh before lifting my legs onto his shoulders. "I'm going in deep. Are you ready?"

"So ready," I tell him.

I'm so beyond wet that he goes in easier than usual. It's still a tight squeeze with his size, but he grips himself as he dips in and out, keeping that gliding motion over my clit in the mix too, and I swear I could swallow him whole.

Even when I'm stretched and ready, he keeps teasing me, and when I start clenching around him, he slides out.

"Nuh-uh, not yet," he whispers.

I'm sweaty and so is he, our skin glistening in the moonlight.

I whimper and he leans back in, kissing me hard, his tongue diving as deep in my mouth as I wish he'd do with the rest of his body. My hands sink into his hair and I tug it hard, as the intensity between us builds. He groans, jerking into me, and a feeling of power surges through me.

I've never wanted anyone like this.

Never been this bold, this greedy.

I lean up into him, the stretch with my legs on his shoulders making my stomach muscles cry out, but it's worth it. He thrusts into me, and I yelp, his kiss silencing me. When he said he was going in deep, he wasn't exaggerating.

"Thank you," I groan.

He plunges in even deeper and faster.

"Thank you, thank you," I chant.

I fall back against my pillow and he sits up, his hands on my ass gripping me tight as he drives into me.

"Oh," I say when he starts hitting a spot on me that I wasn't really sure existed or whether it was a myth. "Oh, that's—"

Wyatt's shoulders are flexing, his abs clenching, and his expression is pure focus as he watches us joining. His eyes meet mine. "I feel your G-spot swelling," he groans.

What?

"Is that doctor dirty talk?" I squeak out.

His teeth clamp his bottom lip and he doesn't break his tempo. "Do you like it?"

"What you're doing or the doctor dirty talk?"

"Your G-spot fucked," he answers. "Or both."

An orgasm catches me by surprise, literally coming so suddenly and so intensely, I see stars. I gush around him and he moans like he can feel it and loves it. My head shakes from side to side, eyes squeezed shut, and I don't think I breathe for a solid minute. When he starts coming with me, it brings on a second wave, and the feeling is so incredible, I almost cry.

A few minutes later, he slides out of me and falls onto his back, both of us breathing hard.

He reaches over and takes my hand, threading our fingers together, and I feel his eyes on me. I turn my head and he rolls to his side to face me.

"Are you okay?" he asks.

"I'm so good. That was..." I shake my head. "Are you...okay?"

He grins and pulls my hand up to his lips, kissing my knuckles. "I couldn't feel any better than I do right now."

I smile at him. "So...you busted a myth for me with that...episode."

He laughs when I say *episode*. "Yeah? How so?"

"I thought the G-spot might be a myth."

His eyebrows crinkle. *"Really."* He holds up our hands and angles them how he wants, then points toward an area like it's a display. "It's actually part of the urethral sponge, a fleshy cushion—"

I burst out laughing and he pauses.

"Too far?" He grimaces.

"I think I prefer the research trial runs to the clinical terms, Dr. Dirty."

"Noted."

"Although hearing you say 'G-spot fucked' did do something to me," I admit. "Just don't say fleshy cushion again when referring to..."

He nods, serious. I can picture him as a medical student taking notes during a lecture.

"There's a fine line, isn't there?" he says.

"Yes, definitely a fine line."

THE NEXT MORNING, we have sex in the shower. Again, haven't previously been a fan of sex in any water and especially the shower, but that's no longer true. Maybe because Cash never made sure I was ready before having sex. Or maybe because he didn't know what to do with his hands or dick except jab, jab, jab.

But the sounds of Wyatt's body slapping into mine alone makes me so hot, I'm ready to fire off within minutes. He's not making me take it slow this morning, thank goodness. He adjusts my body the way he wants it, and I oblige in every way. The man knows how to make a woman feel good.

I wonder if it's all those studies about the human body or if it's all his experience in the field.

Yeah, I don't like to think about that much.

"Where'd you go just now?" he says, out of breath. "Am I hurting you?"

"You feel so good, it has me thinking about all the other women who have enjoyed this before me."

"There's nobody but you, Marlow. Nobody but you."

He pulls my back up to meet his chest, his strokes inside slowing to a leisurely pace as he kisses my neck. We come like that, the slow build lingering long after our bodies are still.

He's gone before Dakota wakes up, just as he promised.

When I get to work, there's a blueberry muffin on my desk, and I wear a nonstop smile all day long.

I'm terrified over how easily he's worked his way into our lives, but for now, it feels too wonderful to fight it.

CHAPTER THIRTY-EIGHT

INTENTIONS

WYATT

The past two weeks have been the best of my life.

Marlow and I have fallen into a routine, and I can honestly say I've never been happier.

I leave her place each morning before Dakota gets up, or occasionally, I'll "show up" with Happy Cow treats or to take them to Sunny Side for breakfast, and the three of us hang out together after I get off work. Sometimes Dakota has eaten dinner already since the earliest I'm off most nights is seven, but when I'm not working, we eat together and go ride Sofie's horses. And every night, and most mornings if we haven't overslept, Marlow and I exhaust ourselves in bed.

The past three nights have been tied up with wedding prep. We've worked over at Theo and Sofie's place until it's time for Dakota to go to bed. Last night after the rehearsal dinner at The Gnarly Vine, I carried Dakota in from the car and helped tuck her in, and my heart turned somersaults when she opened her eyes and patted my face.

"Night-night, Wyatt. I love you," she said.

"I love you too, Sweets." My voice was thick and when I looked back, Marlow stood there watching us with glossy eyes.

This morning when I left their house for a second time after bringing back pastries, I was still thinking about her telling me she loved me and how it's funny that we said the words to each other before Marlow and me.

I've come so close to telling her, but something holds me back each time. I think part of me is still trying not to scare her off and to take it at her pace. It's all going at rapid speed, but definitely too soon to be talking this way.

But since I know how I feel, too soon or not, it's like a secret burning its way through my chest.

I pull up to Sutton's and get my suit and shaving kit out of the car. Marlow and Dakota are getting ready with the girls at Sofie's, and the guys are taking over Sutton's place so we can be out of the girls' way.

It's loud when I walk in. Music is playing through the speakers, and my brothers and Jamison are spread out around the kitchen and living room, having a beer. Jamison's brother and football god, Zac Ledger, is also here for the wedding from Boston, and their grandpa, Pappy who we've adopted as family now too. Owen is in his element having everyone over here, hair wet from the shower and running around in his briefs, his gappy grin as big as Christmas.

"Hey, Uncle Wy, you're the last one here. Dad said he was gonna send a search and rescue team out for you if you didn't get here in the next few minutes."

"Did I say that, or did I say I'd send them straight to Marlow Hennessy's place?" Sutton smirks that devil-may-care grin and I lay my suit over the back of a chair, ignoring him except to say, "Walker," under my breath.

"What's that you say?" Sutton, the shit stirrer asks.

"Marlow Walker," I say louder.

"Oh, is she going by Walker now? I hadn't heard." His grin deepens and he smooths his hand over his jaw. "Jamison was just telling us how he keeps seeing your car over there."

Jamison clasps the back of his neck and looks at me apologetically. "Sorry, man. I was just talking about how I went looking for you in the hotel after I'd seen your car in the parking lot, but then I realized Marlow's condo is—" He shakes his head. "Not my business."

"Might be your business if he's using your parking lot all night," Sutton says.

I shoot him a look and he laughs, holding up his hands.

"So things are good?" Theo says. He hasn't laughed as much as the rest of the guys; in fact, now that I look at him closer, he's actually tense.

"Things are great. Are you okay? You nervous?" I ask.

"What? Nervous? No, not at all. I can't marry Sofie fast enough. I...what are your intentions with Marlow?"

"My intentions? What are we doing right now?" I laugh.

"Well...she's Sofie's best friend, and it wasn't that long ago that the two of you weren't getting along. She's been through a lot and has a daughter to think about, so I just want to be sure you're thinking this through."

I take a deep breath and count to ten before saying anything. When I do, it's measured and through slightly gritted teeth.

"Since it's your wedding day, I'm going to give you a pass. If you think I'm taking any of this lightly with Marlow, think again. I care about her, probably way too fucking much given the timing of things, but I do nonetheless, and I'd never jump into something with someone who has a child to think about if I weren't serious."

The room has become silent and tense, and then Theo smiles. In two long strides, he's in front of me, wrapping his arms around me and pounding on my back.

"You love her," he says.

"Yeah, I do."

"Then I'm not gonna worry about her for another second," he says.

"You should probably be more worried about me than her." I laugh, shoulders relaxing. "Marlow and Dakota already have me wrapped around their little fingers."

"Happy for you, brother," Sutton says, pounding me on the back.

"Goddamn," Callum says, squeezing my shoulder.

"Congratulations," Zac says. "I'm glad we had this talk before the wedding. Autumn was going to see if you'd want to meet a friend of hers. I'll nix that plan."

"Good idea, thanks," I say, giving him a bro-shake. "Great to see you, man."

"You too."

"Scarlett's been dying to ask you about it," Jamison says.

"You've gotten a breather because of the wedding, but my guess is once we get through the ceremony, the focus will be on the two of you."

"Or *you* could distract her with something else," Pappy says, "like another wedding to plan."

Everyone laughs at Pappy, and Jamison puts his arms on his granddad's shoulders and shakes him gently. "And take away from Theo and Sofie? I think not."

"Mm-hmm," Pappy says. "You know my thoughts on marriage when you find the one you love. Don't waste another second. Marry them and begin your life together. Don't look back."

"We're not looking back and not wasting any seconds, I promise, Pappy," Jamison says. "I could say the same to you, you know. You'd make one of these women around here really happy if you'd give them a chance."

Pappy scoffs. "They're all so forward." He shakes his head. "Three nights this week, my phone rang after nine o'clock."

"Uh-oh." Jamison laughs. "The ultimate no-no for Pappy."

"Because when I was little, I had to go without breakfast and lunch for calling my buddy Joe after nine. I guess that made it stick with me." He chuckles. "It's not even taken into consideration these days. And I don't know...I don't know how I feel about a woman calling me when I've shown no signs of interest. I prefer a little more of a challenge."

"Maybe we should let it be known that that's your preference," Theo says, laughing.

"Nah, then it wouldn't be authentic. I'm good," Pappy says. "So, back to you and Marlow."

I laugh. "I see what you're doing. Are we getting ready

for a wedding or what? This day is about Theo and Sofie, not me."

"Or me, thank goodness," Pappy says.

A FEW HOURS LATER, I'm standing down by the lake behind Theo and Sofie's house, my heart in my throat when Marlow walks down the aisle looking like a vision.

And then Dakota tossing flower petals on the ground, her smile radiant—she steals everyone's heart all over again.

It takes consistent effort to focus on anyone but Marlow during the ceremony, even as Theo and Sofie exchange heartfelt vows. Marlow's hazel eyes look greener as she wipes the tears from her cheeks, her cheeks lifting with her smile. There's not a dry eye anywhere when Theo tells Sofie he'll love her until the end of time.

Before long, we're eating and toasting to Theo and Sofie's happiness, the sounds of laughter combined with the bird songs and frogs croaking traveling through the water and trees and twinkle lights. And then we're out on the wooden dance floor that we built for this occasion, arms raised and hips shaking as we all let loose.

By the third song, Dakota has danced hard enough to be out of breath. Her hair is falling out of her "princess updo" and her tiara is hanging precariously.

"Here, let me see if I can fix this crown, Princess Sweets." I put my hand on her shoulder while she keeps swaying.

I find the pin and hold it up triumphantly. Marlow grins and pushes back Dakota's hair and I pin the tiara in place, feeling more victorious over this small feat than when I help someone in the ER.

Dakota runs off to dance with Owen and his friends, and I put my hands on Marlow's waist.

"I got called out for having my car parked outside your condo every night," I admit, as we slow dance to a fast song.

"I got called out for the healthy glow I've been wearing for the past couple of weeks," she says, smiling up at me.

"Damn nosy birds," I mutter, smiling back at her.

"Who needs 'em?"

"What would you do if I kissed you right here in front of everyone?" I shift so we're even closer.

She laughs, looking so happy, and then she looks around at everyone dancing around us. Her mouth parts and she gasps and puts her hand over her mouth. "Oh my goodness, Wyatt, *look*."

I look in the direction she's facing and we stop moving. Grinny and Pappy are out on the dance floor, dancing.

"Is it my imagination or is he blushing?" I ask.

"It's hard to tell with only the twinkle lights out here, but...I think so," she whispers. "They look really sweet together. Do you think they'd ever—"

For a second, I think there might be a spark there, but seeing the grim expression on Grinny's face and then the way she lets go and nods at Pappy when the song ends, hurrying away...I shake my head.

"No...I don't think so. I think they're just friends."

"Hmm. Well, we know how that can turn out," she says softly.

CHAPTER THIRTY-NINE

OVER THE OVERS

Marlow

A couple weeks later, I hang up from Sofie's call and am still smiling.

She told me all about their honeymoon—well, not *all* about it, but a few of the highlights from their time in Alaska.

I get back to cleaning my place. Dakota's at a birthday party for another hour and Wyatt went to run a few errands. We've been spending so much time together, it feels strange to be alone this afternoon, but my overflowing laundry basket needed the attention. We're supposed to go over to Grinny's house later, and I need a cute, clean dress to wear.

I set the basket of clean laundry on the shelf above the washer and start folding, absentmindedly reaching up to close the door of the cabinet that holds detergent and extra toiletries. A tampon drops onto the shelf and I pick it up to put it back in the box above the cabinet, pausing to stare at the box.

My periods have been more irregular than usual with all the stress of the move and all that, but...how long has it been this time?

Oh God.

I break out into a sweat and rush to my phone to see if I put it in my tracker like I'm supposed to. Dammit. I haven't been keeping up with it like I should be, but I know it's been a while.

You're not pregnant, I tell myself, sliding my feet into my tennies and grabbing my keys.

There hasn't been a single time we've gone without condoms. Not because I haven't wanted to, but because I've needed to make an appointment with a gyno here and get my prescription for birth control renewed.

I don't want the whole town knowing I might be pregnant, but can I really wait for an Amazon delivery to find out? I don't think so. I won't rest until I know for sure. So, I run over to Cecil's since it's the closest. While I'm walking to the car, I see Wyatt walking out of the store with a few grocery bags and a handful of flower bouquets.

He stops walking when he sees me and makes a face. "Busted."

"What?" I yelp.

"You caught me," he says, waving the flowers. He frowns. "Are you okay? You went pale on me."

"Oh," I laugh weakly, "flowers. Yay."

He chuckles and comes closer, kissing me on the cheek. "I'll go put them in water and you can pretend to be surprised when you get home. You should have told me you needed to come here—I could've grabbed it."

"I...didn't know."

He studies me a second longer. "You sure you're okay?"

I nod and don't trust myself to say anything, which makes the whole conversation even more awkward.

"Okay then, I'll see you back at the house...if that's all right with you?" he asks.

"I'll be a little bit. Picking Dakota up from the party after this."

"Oh, that's right. Do you...need a little time just you guys? I can go grab my mail, get a few things ready for the week, and pick you up for dinner."

"Okay," I say softly.

He smiles, but I didn't miss the hurt that flashed over his face. It's gone in seconds, and he leans in and kisses me again, this time on the mouth. It's over before I want it to be, and he's walking toward his car saying he'll see me in a few hours.

Mar from Happy Cow is in the grocery store, chatting up Cecil, and I take way too long hiding in the card section with the box of tests tucked on the bottom shelf just in case anyone else walks by. When I see Mar making gradual movement toward the exit, I grab a box of tampons and a box of condoms just to add to the boxes and make it confusing.

As soon as she's out, I go to the checkout and when I set the things down and Cecil picks up each box excruciatingly slow, I realize what a stupid idea it was. Now it's like I have three embarrassing things instead of just one.

Cecil looks at me through his bushy eyebrows. "I once had a lady buy six hundred dollars' worth of paper products along with her pregnancy tests," he says, chuckling.

"Wow...intense." I make a face like *how ridiculous is that?* even though we both know I'm just as ridiculous, albeit on the thriftier side.

He hands me the change and puts the receipt in the bag.

"Good luck," he says.

I blink rapidly, the sudden onslaught of emotion taking me by surprise.

"Thank you."

I get to the condo, forgetting at first that it's almost time to pick up Dakota, but when I check my watch and see there's probably enough time to pull it off, I decide I'm too antsy to wait around any longer than I have to.

I hustle inside, pausing briefly to melt over the flowers Wyatt placed in a vase on the table. And then I'm in the bathroom, washing my hands and doing the test as fast as my shaky hands will allow me.

I set the timer for ten minutes and pace the floor, watching the clock. I need to leave within twelve minutes to get Dakota, and then I'm second-guessing that too. Maybe I should leave in five minutes...traffic was hectic earlier. It's officially tourist season in Landmark.

It hasn't even been three minutes when I rush back into the bathroom to check the test and gasp out loud when I see the two lines.

Noooooo.

I slide to the floor of the bathroom, head reeling.

I can't believe this.

I'm pregnant.

As wonderful as the past few weeks have been, I have no idea how Wyatt will respond to this news. I can't imagine it being positive.

I put my head in my hands and cry, shocked and embarrassed that this is happening again. Was the first time not enough to get the message across? I should've been on birth control along with the condoms...or better yet, I should've waited to get involved with Wyatt when, oh, I don't know, a few years had passed and I could've been more prepared for bringing another life into the world.

My alarm goes off, sending me skittering off the floor and hopping around to find my phone. I rush out the door and try my hardest not to cry all the way to Dakota's friend's house. When I get there, I pinch my cheeks and get my fakest pageant smile in place.

I'm numb on the ride home, listening to Dakota talk about the party and chiming in with the appropriate responses.

How will she feel about having a baby brother or sister? It's already not fair that her dad doesn't want anything to do with her—what's it going to do to her to have another baby in the house?

Tears roll down my face and I hurriedly wipe them off before we go into the house.

"Where's Wyatt?" she asks when we walk in. "Ooo, flowers! Pretty."

"He's coming to pick us up for dinner at Grinny's. We should get ready."

"Will Owen be there?"

"Grinny said he would be, yes."

She pauses, studying my face. "Did Daddy call?"

"Uh, no, he didn't."

"Did Grandma call?"

"No, she didn't either. Why?"

She comes over and leans her head on me, her arms going around my legs. "You look like you need a hug," she says softly, squeezing me tighter.

"Kota, you are the best thing that ever happened to me," I tell her, the tears starting all over. "I love you so much."

"Love you too, Mama." She looks up at me and her lips pucker. "Why are you sad?"

"I'm just overwhelmed."

"Over what?"

I laugh softly, smoothing her hair as she leans back into me. "Overwhelmed means I'm just feeling all the feelings. Everything seems big when you're overwhelmed. It can be good and bad to have so many emotions going at once."

She nods sagely, like she understands, and somehow, I think she really does. She's my little old soul.

"Is it because of Daddy?" she asks, frowning as she turns to look at me.

I wipe my face and will the tears to stop. "Not really... well, I guess in a way, it could be a little bit. Your dad and I aren't married anymore, and that's probably really confusing—"

"And that's why we don't live with him?"

"It's a little more complicated than that, but yes, we won't be living with him anymore. But even though we aren't married and living together, we both love you very much."

"When will we see Daddy?"

"I'm not sure, baby, but remember he loves you even when he's not here."

I wait to see if she'll say anything else about her dad.

The tears start falling again, this time for her, since Cash hasn't made an effort at all to have a relationship with her.

"Don't cry, Mama," Dakota's voice is shaky as she sniffles too.

"Okay, I'm shaking it off. Oh, I love my girl so much." I give her another hug. "Let's go have fun at Grinny's house," I say, wiping my face again.

She leans back and nods, looking up at me with a big smile. "I love Grinny's house."

"Me too." I lean down and kiss her forehead. "How about you hop in the tub real quick?"

"Are you sure I need one now?" she asks, crinkling up her nose.

"I guess we can wait until we get home. You'll just be tired then."

She grins and rushes off to her room, happy to get out of a bath a little while longer.

I spend extra time on my makeup, my mind obsessively looping, *You're having Wyatt's baby.*

I do my best to override the noise because I want nothing more than to stay in this happiness bubble with Wyatt a little longer.

Before he decides this it too much for him and bolts.

CHAPTER FORTY

OPEN MIND

WYATT

I thought maybe I was imagining something with Marlow earlier in the parking lot, but when she's still not herself on the ride to Grinny's, I know something's up.

"Are you okay?" I ask quietly.

She turns to me and smiles, but it doesn't quite reach her eyes. Dread churns in my stomach while I wait for her answer.

"I am," she says.

When we're in Grinny's driveway, I turn to face her. "You sure? You're being awfully quiet."

She lifts her shoulders and takes a deep breath, her smile feeling all wrong, and yet, she pats my arm and then lets her hand slide over mine. The gesture abates some of the apprehension and when she says, "I'm looking forward to this dinner," I feel even better.

"Me too."

"Me free," Dakota pipes up from the back. "Actually four...years old," she adds, giggling.

Marlow smiles and this time it does reach her eyes as she looks back at Dakota.

"We love the flowers," she says to me. "Dakota noticed them right away."

Dakota hums her agreement, and we get out of the car. When the three of us walk into Grinny's great room, all eyes turn on us. This is the first time we've all been together since the wedding. Dakota runs over to Owen and they take off outside, while Sutton looks at us and smirks.

"The restraint I'm using right now is painful," he says.

I level him with a look and he holds up his hands but makes a face.

"No teasing at all?" he asks, pouting.

"Shut it," I say.

Sofie and Scarlett laugh, and I glance at Marlow, relaxing when I see her smiling. Since we haven't talked to Dakota about us, I don't know how comfortable Marlow is with this, but since Dakota's not in here right now, maybe we're okay.

"It's down to us," Callum says, elbowing Sutton.

"Well, no one is surprised that your grumpy ass is still single," Sutton says, stretching. "But makes me think I need to get out of Landmark for a while. There must be something in the water," he teases.

I throw a piece of paper at him, which is completely ineffective, but he pretends to be wounded anyway.

"All kidding aside, I'm very happy for you two," he says.

Marlow frowns and tilts her head. "What are you talking about?"

The look on his face is priceless.

"Uh, I—" he stutters.

Marlow and I start laughing, and Sutton's shoulders relax.

He chuckles, pointing at her. "I deserved that."

"Well, I for one, could not be happier that the two of you are spending time together," Grinny says, coming over to hug us. "I wanted to say so at the wedding, but I didn't want to assume that you were together just because you danced together the whole evening..." She flushes and Sutton jumps on it.

"Speaking of...will Pappy be joining us this evening?" he says.

Scarlett and I both glare at him and he lifts a shoulder defensively.

Grinny frowns. "No, why would he be?" She looks at Jamison apologetically. "Not that he isn't welcome here..."

He smiles at her but doesn't say anything, and I wonder if he's okay with the thought of his grandpa being with someone other than his grandma.

It *was* weird to see Grinny with someone other than Granddad, even for those few minutes.

"I was happy to see you having a good time, Grinny," Sutton says, going over to hug her. "We all want to see you happy, and if you ever decide that you'd like someone in your life, we're not going to make it hard for you. Are we?" he says, looking around the room.

"No," we all chime in with various levels of enthusiasm.

Of course we want her happy, and there's no better man out there than Pappy, but that doesn't mean it wouldn't take some getting used to.

"Well, I *am* happy," she says emphatically. "And I have all of you in my life, so there's no need for me to have anyone else—I had my love story already with your grand-dad. Now it's your turn."

Callum clears his throat and we all turn, surprised when he opens his mouth to speak.

"Best to keep an open mind," he says. "That's what you've always told us."

Well damn.

It's quiet enough to hear a pin drop, and Grinny runs her hand down her arm like she's stunned speechless herself. But in the next second, she snaps out of it and slides her hands together.

"Who's ready to eat?"

It breaks the spell, and we start piling the food on our plates.

Marlow's quiet throughout dinner, but afterwards, Theo rolls out the chalkboard that we've played games on for years and we play Pictionary. Before long, she's laughing and joking like she always does.

"That's nothing close to a donkey," Scarlett cries, pointing at Callum's attempts.

"Ears," he says, pointing to the two long triangles on top of what looks like a skinny dog.

Scarlett grumbles and Callum tries to embellish his drawing before erasing the whole thing.

When we're done with the game, we walk into the room

where Dakota and Owen are watching a movie. Both of them are asleep, their heads touching.

"Aw, they're so cute," Marlow whispers.

Owen's eyes open and he blinks slowly.

"Hey, I think we're heading out," I tell him.

Marlow bends down to pick up Dakota, and I put my hand on her waist. "I can carry her."

She looks at me over her shoulder and after a moment, she nods, standing up straight. I bend down and pick Dakota up, telling her I've got her when her eyes open. They flutter closed again and I smile down at her, feeling a rush of love I didn't expect to have in my life.

God, I love this little girl. I almost say it out loud to Marlow, and then I'd add, *And I love her mom too,* but I'm not sure Marlow's ready to hear that...especially not today when she's seemed off.

It's probably not the time or place or way to tell her for the first time.

But there's no question in my mind.

We tell everyone bye and head out to the car. Marlow opens the door for me, and I put Dakota in the booster seat. And then before she can get in the car, I put my hands on either side of her door and lean down to kiss her.

Someone whistles at us and Marlow jumps. I lean back reluctantly, looking over her shoulder. When I see Sutton laughing as he drives past us, I shake my head.

"Yours is coming, brother," I yell at him. "Sorry 'bout that." My thumb brushes over Marlow's cheek. "You'd think for a judge, he'd know how to play it subtle, but he can't help himself."

"It's funny," she says. "Does he do this with every woman you bring around the family?"

"Yeah, I don't bring women around the family."

"Mm-hmm." She gives me a look.

I lift my shoulder. "I don't."

"Hmm. Just not the commitment kind?" she asks.

I frown. "I think I'm totally the commitment kind." *Or I wouldn't have camped out at your place all these nights.* Instead I add, "Just hadn't met the right girl yet." I nod toward Dakota sleeping in the back of my car. "The right *girls.*"

Marlow shivers and I run my hands down her arms. "Let's get you warmed up," I tell her.

I open her car door and she gets in, and I feel the distance from her again. Did I say the wrong thing?

On the way to her condo, we're both quiet and for the first time since I started staying over here during the night, I wonder if maybe I should go to my place tonight. Maybe she needs some space.

But I get Dakota inside, tucking her under the covers. Marlow bends down and kisses her goodnight and I follow her into the hall. We leave Dakota's door cracked and then Marlow puts her arms around my neck.

"I'm so sleepy, but I need you," she says, leaning on her tiptoes to kiss me.

"You've got me," I say against her mouth.

I put her legs around my waist and carry her to the bed where we get lost in each other all night long.

Just as I think she's falling asleep, she does something to set me on fire again. It's like she can't get enough, and it should make me ecstatic that she wants me like this—it does every single night normally—but tonight I can't shake the feeling that something's wrong.

CHAPTER FORTY-ONE

GREEN

MARLOW

I'm dragging the next day.

Fortunately, it's a Sunday so I don't have to be at work, but Wyatt's working today, and I feel bad for keeping him up so much of the night.

I felt desperate for him. I don't know any other way to describe it. I'm almost embarrassed by how much I craved him. It was like he knew that I needed extra...everything, and without asking any questions even though I felt them unsaid between us, he gave it to me.

I nap while Dakota watches a movie and could still sleep a few more hours, but I force myself to get up. Dakota and I go for a long walk, and when we get back, I start working on dinner. All day I've tried not to stay in my thoughts, but they're there, screaming at me.

The desire for normalcy and to keep things as they are is at war with my new reality. When Wyatt comes over after his shift and we're cleaning up the kitchen, Dakota already in bed, he turns to face me and I come so close to blurting it out then. But he pulls me against him, and I rest my head on his chest instead, letting the warmth of him fill me from the inside out.

"You distracted my thoughts all day," he whispers. "In the best way."

"I hope you weren't too tired to think straight."

"I'm tired now, but I was still on an adrenaline rush from loving you up all night." He laughs and my skin heats.

I'm thinking about how glad I am that he can't see my face right now when he tilts my chin up to look at him.

"You gonna tell me what's going on with you?" he asks.

My mouth parts and I just can't get the words out. I lift on my tiptoes and whisper against his mouth, "Soon."

He looks disappointed, but he nods. "Okay. I guess I can live with that." His forehead crinkles in the center of his eyebrows. "You can tell me anything. You know that, right?"

I nod and take a deep breath, bracing myself to just spit it out already, but his hands fall from my waist and he takes a step back.

"Okay." He kisses my forehead and turns away. "I think I'm going to head to my place. I've got a crazy week at work and I need to put some time in tonight to get ready for it."

I try to keep my face from falling, but I think I fail because he smiles, and it's so sweet, it breaks my heart a little more.

"You know we won't get any sleep if I stay," he says.

"I think I'm too tired tonight to do anything but sleep," I say, but he still walks into the living room and grabs his backpack.

I want to stop him. I really do.

But I let him go.

Something tells me he's operating under self-preservation as much as I am, but I still can't bring myself to tell him.

I can't stand the thought of seeing his feelings change for me.

Since history is repeating itself, that seems like the inevitable outcome of all this.

Of all times for my mom to call...and of all times for me to answer.

I regret it immediately when her first words to me are, "I saw Cash tonight. He looked good, but I think he's missing you."

"I doubt that, and I don't care either way."

She scoffs, and I can picture the scowl on her face. "The best thing you could do for that little girl of yours is to reunite with her daddy. I don't know what you were thinking moving across the country where he can't even see her when he wants."

"He didn't want to see her when she lived in the same house," I say as quietly and emphatically as I can, while also ensuring I don't wake Dakota up to hear this.

"You can't make me believe that nonsense. He said he misses y'all, and I told him to do something about it." Her tone is proud and I clench my fists to keep my rage in check.

"I've gotta go, Mom." I hang up before she can say anything and after a quick shower, I climb into bed, giving in to the exhaustion.

But sleep doesn't come.

I toss and turn, missing Wyatt so acutely, I see every hour on the clock pass.

The next morning, there's a blueberry muffin on my desk when I arrive, and I inhale it but then throw it up within ten minutes. The lighting over the bathroom mirror highlights the circles under my eyes and I splash water on my face, hoping that helps.

Of course, I see Wyatt on my way back to the desk. He frowns when he sees me, but he's in a hurry and doesn't stop.

"You were supposed to sleep last night," he says.

"I tried." I shrug, playing it light, and he makes a face.

"Ugh. So I was missing you for nothing?"

"Guess so."

I hear my name and turn, mouth dropping when I see my brother standing near my desk.

"What are you doing here?" I squeal, hurrying over to hug him.

He lifts me up and gives me the biggest bear hug.

"Surprise," he says.

When he lets me go, I turn to Wyatt and he's got a fierce expression on his face.

"My brother, Logan," I tell him.

The relief that washes over him makes me laugh and he grins sheepishly at me, walking over to shake Logan's hand.

"Wyatt Landmark," he says. "I should've recognized you from the picture...I'm seeing it now."

"My sister and I have been playing phone tag a lot, but

I've still managed to hear a few things about you here and there," Logan says, grinning. "Great to meet you."

"You too," Wyatt says.

"Phone tag would require you calling me back." I put my hand on my hip, my eyes narrowed on Logan. "So far, it's just been me calling you and you texting back occasionally."

He puts his hand on the back of his neck and nods, his chuckle gravelly. "I suck," he admits. "But in my defense, I've been on a boat for ninety-nine percent of the time the past few months." He puts his hand on my shoulder and gives me a little shake like he always has, but this time it makes my stomach turn upside down again.

I try to breathe through the nausea, thankful he stops the rough-housing, and he gives me a weird look.

We might not see each other much since we both took off as soon as we were old enough, and like he said, he spends most of his time on boats, chartering fishing excursions, but we can pick right up where we leave off every time, no matter what.

"Well, it's good to see you now," I manage to say.

"I've gotta get to a patient," Wyatt says. "Running behind this morning, but I'd love to get dinner while you're here. You staying long?"

"I was hoping maybe a week or two, if my sister will have me," Logan says.

"Are you kidding? I always want you to stay."

As soon as Wyatt walks away, I walk around to my seat, and Logan leans his forearms on the reception counter and stares at me.

"You wanna tell me what's up?"

I roll my eyes. "Not here, not now."

His eyes narrow on me, and he leans in closer. "The last

time you looked green like you do right now was when you told me I was about to be an uncle."

I glance around, worried someone might hear him, but the coast is clear.

"Holy shit," he says.

"You've got that right."

CHAPTER FORTY-TWO

HAIR AND OTHER WEIRD VIBES

WYATT

I've tried to give Marlow time with her brother, but when days go by and she still hasn't invited me over, I start taking it personally.

It was my idea to give them time and stay at my place while he's visiting. When she readily agreed to that plan, I completely understood and was fine about it.

But then I expected an invitation to dinner or, I don't

know, a quick meetup at Sunny Side or something...anything.

If she hadn't acted unlike herself before he ever got in town, I might not be taking it as seriously, but she did and she still is. At work, she's been distracted and hasn't met me for lunch. When I stop by her desk, she acts too busy to talk even when there aren't any patients around. We've texted every day after work and I send memes for Dakota, mostly to let Dakota know I'm thinking about her even when I'm not around.

"Fuck it. Enough of this." I pick up treats at Happy Cow and knock on Marlow's door around the time they're usually getting up on Saturday morning.

Marlow answers the door looking sleepy and gorgeous, her wild bedhead my favorite look on her.

"Hey," she croaks, her arms wrapping around herself rather than around me.

"Are you sick?" All annoyance fades as I take her in.

There are dark circles around her eyes, and she looks pale.

"I'm okay, just worn out. Haven't been sleeping great."

I step closer, intending to hug her, but she takes the pastry box from me, and just in time too, because I'm nearly knocked over by Dakota.

"Wyatt!" she yells, her little arms squeezing me as hard as she can.

"Hey, Sweets. Oh, that's the best hug. Thank you."

She takes both my hands and climbs up my legs, flipping upside down and then hugs me again.

"Wow. It's good to see you too." I grin at her and she beams.

"I missed you," she says. "Where ya been?" She takes a

better look at me and crinkles up her little nose. "What's all that hair doing on your face?"

I smooth a hand over my scruff as I laugh. "You don't like the hair?"

"I don't know," she answers.

"Well, that's fair. I don't love it myself, but some days I get lazy and don't want to shave." She takes my hand and does another flip. "Hey, I've missed you too," I tell her when she's upright again. "I've been trying to give you time with your uncle Logan. Have you had a great visit with him?"

"Yes," she says emphatically. "He's so funny. You've gotta talk to him. Uncle Logan," she yells, "come see my Wyatt."

God, this little girl. She wrecks me.

Logan walks out with wet hair and grins when he sees me. "Hey, man. Good to see you. Dakota hasn't shut up about you since I got here."

"We don't say *shut up*, Uncle Logan," Dakota sings.

"Dadgum, girl, I can't afford to stay around here much longer. You're cleaning my wallet out," Logan says, laughing.

I glance at Marlow who's smiling but quiet as she watches all of us interacting. The concern I had about her quadruples as I take her in. Something is definitely wrong.

"I wanted to see if you'd be interested in dinner tonight. Tiptop, on me. It's a beautiful restaurant I've wanted to take you and Dakota to for a while," I tell Marlow. "And I think you'd like it too, Logan. My friend Blake owns the place with his wife, and the view from on top of the mountain is spectacular. Food's great too."

Logan smiles agreeably, but he looks at Marlow, waiting for her to say something. When she doesn't, he says, "What if I watched the peanut here while you guys get out? I could take her out for pizza and we could go skating or something fun."

I look at Marlow and she frowns, shaking her head. "I don't want to miss out on being with you while you're in town. You're only here another couple of days."

"But I'm not going to stay gone as long next time," he says.

Marlow scoffs, but she doesn't look mad. "Yeah, you said that last time."

"Let's all go. It'll give me a chance to get to know you better, Logan, and I've missed seeing you and Dakota," I say to Marlow.

She pauses and then nods. "Okay. Can it be on the earlier side tonight? Would we be able to get in by four thirty or five?"

"That should work. I'll call Blake and see if he can fit us in."

"Any earlier and we'll be going senior citizen style," Logan teases. "How do you ever expect me to find a woman if we're dining with the elderly?"

It's the first laugh I've heard from Marlow in too many days, and it eases some of the tension in my shoulders.

"If I thought taking you any later would hook you a wife, I'd do it, but I don't think you stand a chance until you stay in one place longer than a week." She rolls her eyes, still laughing under her breath.

"I'm too young to get married," he says, waving her off.

"You're thirty!" Marlow argues.

"Thirty's the new seventeen," he says, but he can't keep a straight face when he says that.

"Disgusting." Marlow laughs. "I have a couple new single friends that I adore and I don't want you within two feet of them." She shakes her head and looks at me, her eyes still bright.

Do I imagine that they dim as she looks at me?

I want to take her in my arms and kiss the worry away, plead with her to talk to me, do whatever it takes to fix this...

But for now, I just smile at her and take a step toward the door. "I'll go for now. I'll text you the time after I talk to Blake and meet you back here about twenty minutes before. We can walk from here to catch the gondola."

She nods. "Great. Dakota's been wanting to ride that thing since we got here. Did you hear that, Kota?"

"We're riding the gondola? Yay!" Dakota dances around the room.

"You'll love it," I say. "Okay, I'll see you later."

Dakota runs over and throws her arms around me again. "You're leaving?"

"Yes, but I'll be back." I bop her nose and she grins.

"I wish you never left," she says. "I wish you stayed here always."

I bend down and kiss her forehead. "That would be amazing, wouldn't it? But you know what, Sweets? Even when I'm not with you, I'm thinking about you and wishing I could be."

When I straighten, I glance at Marlow, and her eyes are glossy. Instead of reassuring me that she wants me around, I have the sick feeling that she's about to tell me goodbye.

It's only a matter of time.

I get out of there, my heart rate beating too fast. I'm sweaty despite the chill in the air. I bend over at the knees before I get in my car and try to get a grip. Once I'm breathing steadier, I head over to my brother's and knock on the door. I glance at my watch when no one answers right away and head to the stables.

Sofie's out there, brushing Fiona.

"Hey," I call out, and she glances up.

"Hey," she says, smiling. "Theo went for a hike, but he'll probably be back within an hour or so."

"I was actually hoping to talk to you," I tell her.

She tilts her head and sets down the brush, moving out of the stall to face me. "Oh, okay. What's up?"

"I hope this isn't out of line...I just—I don't know who else to talk to about this. I've tried talking to her, but she's not really saying much right now, and her brother is in town...hey, I invited them to go to Tiptop tonight, if you and Theo want to join us...but I'm just—" I take a deep breath and she stares at me for a second before laughing.

"Whoa, I don't think I've seen you this frazzled...ever. The closest may have been when you were sending out applications for college because you were such a perfectionist, but...no, not even close." She puts her hand on her hip and studies me. "Take a breath. Start over. What's going on? By her and her brother, I'm assuming you're talking about Marlow and Logan?" She smiles as she says Marlow's name, and I do as she says and take a deep breath, willing myself to chill the fuck out.

"I'm sorry. I—" I run my hand through my hair and start pacing down the long space in the center of the stables. "I don't know how much Marlow has told you about me, about us. We've been quiet about it because of Dakota, but you've seen us—it's not like we're really working hard to keep it a secret either."

"I know she's happier than she's ever been," Sofie says.

I pause for a few seconds and then keep walking. "Have you talked to her this week?"

Sofie's eyes narrow as she looks up and chews the inside of her cheek. "She's been quieter than usual this week. And

I had to go pick up a few new rescues, so I haven't even gotten to see Logan yet myself. They're supposed to come to Grinny's tomorrow for Sunday dinner."

"Oh...that's good."

"You didn't know that?" She frowns.

"No, she's acting distant, and I've been trying to give her space to spend time with her brother, but something's going on. She was acting different before he got here, and I'm worried I'm losing her."

She shakes her head. "I don't think so. She's really into you, Wyatt," she says, smiling again.

"You think so? I thought she was, but...God, I've never been so whipped. I've never wanted anyone in my life like this, but she's all I can think about. And Dakota...I'm crazy about that little girl. If I could move in with them today or have them move in with me—hell, I'm ready to build on that land that I wasn't sure I'd ever build on just to be with them all the time."

"You love her," Sofie whispers, her eyes glistening.

"I love her so fucking much," I whisper back.

"Tell her. You have to tell her."

"What else? What are her favorite things? What makes her smile?"

"Well, you make her smile."

"Not right now I don't."

She makes a face. "I find that very hard to believe, Wyatt. But okay, let me think. She loves the simple things. Daisies, the drive-in...oh, she loves those chocolate truffles that come in the shiny foil...I think her favorites are the sea salt milk chocolate and the caramel milk chocolate. Honestly, you know what I think Marlow loves most? Time together." When I start shaking my head, she stops me. "I mean it. Cash was never home, Wyatt. He was working late and then out with his buddies. Not that she really loved spending time with him when he was around—they were not a good fit." She rolls her eyes and then walks toward me, putting her hand on my arm. "The fact that you went to Donuts for Dads with Dakota meant everything to Marlow. She loved when you spent the day riding the alpine slide. I think you could take a drive into the mountains and she'd be there for it as long as you were together."

"Before a week ago, I would've thought the same thing. I don't know what's happened to change it for her, but she's looking at me differently." I exhale a ragged breath and clear my throat. "I'm sorry to unload all this on you. Thank you for the ideas. I'll be working on them..." I run my hands through my hair for the millionth time and laugh. "Bet you never thought I'd be such a wreck over a woman, did you?"

She grins a wide smile and I can't help but smile back. She hugs me and laughs when she says, "No, I sure didn't, but I'm so happy about it, and I'm even happier that it's Marlow. I can't think of anyone I'd rather her be with than you."

"Thanks, Sof. Love you."

"I love you too. Now, quit moping and tell her how you feel."

I nod. "Okay."

I leave feeling slightly better. I've never told a woman I love her and the thought of doing it now, when I'm uncertain about where I stand with Marlow, feels daunting, but maybe Sofie's right.

Maybe she just needs to know how I feel.

CHAPTER FORTY-THREE

DENIAL WITH A CAPITAL D

MARLOW

"Look at you," Logan says when I walk into the living room wearing a cute sweater dress. "I don't think I've seen you in a dress since your pageant days."

"It took me a while, but I actually wear dresses a lot around here."

He smiles. "Landmark Mountain is a good fit for you. And I'd say Wyatt is too, from what I can tell. But you're making the poor man anxious."

I turn to face him, eyes wide. "You think he can tell something's going on?"

"Uh, if he has a brain, which I think he does, yes, he can totally tell. You barely said two words to him, and you've put off hanging out with him."

"I'm seeing him tonight."

"With your brother and daughter in what *sounds like* a romantic setting," he volleys back.

I sit down to put my boots on. "He said himself he wants to get to know you."

"And that's nice of him. Not sure how I'd feel about me if I were him, the way I'm cockblocking his every move."

"Ew, don't say cockblock."

His eyebrows go sky-high. "You gonna make me put money in the jar? I can't say cockblock now?"

"You can say it. Just not around me."

He scoffs. "You and your rules. If I were you, I'd want to know right away if he's up for this next phase of life with you or not." He looks around to see if Dakota is anywhere nearby and when she's not, he adds, "Then you know what you're dealing with."

"It's been so good between us. I have no idea what he'll do, and part of me doesn't want the perception I have of him to be ruined if he's not happy about it."

"I'd hoped you'd given up on denial when you divorced Cash," Logan says grimly.

I growl at him. "Quit being so damn right."

He laughs. "O-kay. You said it, not me."

"I'll tell him." Once my boots are on, I stand up. "What if I wait until I'm ten or twelve weeks and we know for sure everything is—"

He's shaking his head before I can finish. "And you continue suffering the way you are? You'll either make yourself sick or you'll drive him off. Come on, sis. Where is that girl who said the hell with this when she wanted out of pageants? The girl who got the fuck out of Dodge when she realized her husband was cheating?"

"You're right." I nod. *"You're right,"* I repeat. "I'll tell him soon, I promise. Tonight I want to just pretend it's not happening and have a good time. I know it's ridiculous, but..."

"It's not ridiculous. As long as you really can have a good time, I think it's fine to have a night out and not be obsessing about it the way I know you are. You also need to come clean to Sofie. She's always been able to talk sense into you."

"If she'd been in town and you hadn't been here right when I was finding out, I would've. But I also don't want to make it weird for her since he's her brother-in-law."

"Sofie would never be weird with you."

"You're right. Again."

He laughs. "Setting world records here today, telling me I'm right twice in one day."

I sigh and then smile when Dakota comes out of her room. I did her hair in two French braids, and she looks so cute.

There's a knock on the door and Dakota flies to the door.

"Can I open it, Mama?"

I lift her up to look out the peephole. "Is it Wyatt?"

"It is," she says excitedly.

I set her down. "Okay, go ahead."

She flings the door open, and Wyatt stands there looking like everything I've ever dreamed of in his green sweater that matches his eyes and his messier-than-usual hair. He's shaved the scruff, and his cheeks are pink from the fall evening.

"Hello," he says, looking at the two of us. "You both look beautiful."

"Thank you," I say. I nudge Dakota and she thanks him, shy all of a sudden. "You look great too."

He smiles. "Thank you."

"We're ready," Dakota says, reaching out to take his hand. "Right, Uncle Logan?"

"Right," he says, getting up from the couch. He rubs his arms. "Damn, I can't get used to how much cooler it is up here." He grabs his jacket and follows us out the door.

We start walking toward the gondola station, tourists and locals milling around the shops on Heritage Lane.

"It's so busy around here," I say to avoid any awkward pauses.

"Within the next few days, you'll probably need an extra half hour before work to exit the resort parking lot and drive through town," Wyatt says.

"It's that bad?" I make a face.

"It can be."

Dakota asks Wyatt about the gondola ride, and he tells her about that until we're approaching the station. We get tickets and stand in the short line, waiting to get on.

"Hey, Wyatt," the man operating the gondola calls. "Long time, no see."

"Hey, Benny. Good to see you."

When the doors open, we step inside, along with as many others as can fit, and we take a seat by the windows.

"We're going to the top of the mountain?" Dakota asks again.

"The very top," Wyatt says, nodding.

"I think...what if I'm scared to go to the top?" she asks, glancing out the window nervously.

"If you get scared, just look at me or the two of them"—he points at Logan and me—"and you'll feel better." He puts his hand on her shoulder, and she nestles into the crook of his arm for a second and sighs, like she's right where she wants to be.

A wistful sigh comes out of me too, wishing I could be surrounded by his strong shoulders and toasty goodness. So instead of overthinking it, I lean into him, and he glances at me, surprised. His other arm goes around me and I tuck in close.

"Aren't y'all cozy?" Logan says, smirking at me.

I roll my eyes but grin at him, and when I look over to see Wyatt up close and smiling back at me, everything inside me warms.

"It's good to see that smile on you," he says softly. "I've been worried about you."

"I'm sorry I've made you worry."

"As long as you're okay, I will be too."

I swallow hard. "I will be, I think."

Concern flickers in his eyes, but he nods. "And you'll fill me in on what's going on sometime?"

"Yes," I whisper.

He nods again. "I'll be right here until you do."

Guilt consumes me, and if we weren't on a crowded gondola and I wasn't terrified about his response, I'd lean over and whisper it in his ear right now.

I can't keep putting off telling him the truth.

CHAPTER FORTY-FOUR

WYATT

Dinner goes well.

I like Logan a lot, and it's fun watching him and Marlow together. Blake and Camilla are both in the restaurant tonight, and it's apparent within a few minutes of talking to her that they are sold on Marlow. And Dakota, for that matter.

When I walk to the men's room before dessert, I stop by the bar.

"You think the two of you could make it a little more obvious that you like Marlow for me?" I ask them, leaning on the bar.

Camilla laughs and bumps Blake's hip. "Should we say it outright the next time we're at the table?"

"You already have with your expressions." I do a reenactment of them walking by the table with wide eyes and tucked in shoulder, and Camilla cackles.

"I did not do that," she says.

"That was Blake. This is you." I point at the stool in front of me. "Pretend that's Marlow." I give Camilla a dry look and start waving my hands and mouthing, *oh my God.*

"Pfft," Camilla says. "I don't act like that." She smirks.

"We can tone it down a bit if you want us to," Blake says. "I can tell her you've reserved the entire restaurant for the two of you and your special news...think we can get an engagement party on the books?" he asks Camilla.

"Don't you dare," I say under my breath, sweating now. He's capable of doing something like that, and normally, I'd think Marlow could take it, but tonight's not the night.

He holds up his hands. "Okay, okay." He leans in. "I'm feeling love in the air, and you're not getting any younger." He winks and puts his arm around Camilla. "Best thing I ever did was marry this girl right here."

"I know. And it's not that I'm not thinking about it," I admit. "But the last thing I want to do is scare her off." I point at him and then Camilla. "Behave."

Camilla salutes and Blake just grins, but I think I got the message across.

Dessert passes without any theatrical visits from the two of them, and we're leaning back in our seats, talking about how delicious everything has been, when Marlow suddenly stiffens.

She clutches the table and then says, "*Oh*," as she clutches her hand over her mouth and bolts.

"Where's Mama going?" Dakota asks.

We turn and she's already out of sight.

"She probably just needed to use the restroom," Logan tells her.

Dakota nods. "Sometimes I have to go really bad like that too," she says.

"I'll go see about her." I stand up and smile at Dakota. "Maybe you can talk your uncle into taking you out to see the lights." I point in the direction of the deck with the best view. "It's really pretty from the overlook," I tell Logan.

He nods and they get up and walk outside while I go stand outside the bathroom. When she doesn't come out for a few minutes, I knock on the door and stick my head in. She's sitting on a long velvet-tufted bench, elbows on her knees and head in her hands.

"Marlow?"

Her head pops up at the sound of my voice, and that's when I see how hard she's crying.

"*Marlow*, what's wrong?" I rush toward her, sitting down on the bench next to her and putting my arms around her.

She turns her face into my neck and cries so hard, she gasps for air after a few seconds. She smells like peppermint candy so strong, I think she might have a piece in her mouth.

"Breathe, baby," I whisper. "Please...tell me how I can help."

She tries to catch her breath, and I pull back, wiping her tears away, only for more to spill down her cheeks.

"You're breaking my heart," I choke out. "We can work through whatever it is, okay? Just talk to me."

"I'm so sorry," she says between her sobs.

I'm terrified for her, for myself, for whatever she has to tell me.

"Just tell me," I say. "Are you sick?"

"N-no," she gasps.

"Are you breaking up with me?"

Her brows crease and she laughs but then cries harder, eventually crunching on the peppermint. "No, I'm scared you're going to want to break up with *me*."

"I can't imagine why."

"Because I'm pregnant." Her breath hitches after she's said it and the words hang in the air, suffocating my airwaves, as she stares to get my reaction.

Her expression is devastating.

"I...I thought you hadn't been with Cash in at least a year," I say hoarsely.

Her mouth drops. "I haven't." She waits a beat and when I don't say anything, she puts her hand on my elbow. "Wyatt, the baby is yours."

My hands are still on her face, and I lean back to get her in better focus.

"What?" My voice shakes.

"I haven't been with anyone but you. It's *your* baby." She bites her bottom lip and it trembles when she frees it from her teeth.

"We're having a baby." The words sound foreign when I say them.

She nods reluctantly, a few more tears dripping over my thumbs.

A laugh bursts out of me, and I say it again. "We're having a *baby*?"

She gasps and it sounds more like a sob. She nods again.

I gulp and lean in, kissing her face, before suddenly

pulling back again. "Wait, why would I be anything but ecstatic over this?" I ask.

"You're happy?" she squeaks. Her eyes squeeze shut and she lifts her hand up to her nose. "I'm sorry I can't stop crying."

"You're not happy about it?"

"It's...more that...I'm freaked out about it. I was terrified of telling you, of what you'd think...of how I'm just repeating the same—" Her face breaks and she leans her forehead on my chest. She's there for a few minutes while I try my best to console her.

A baby. I can't believe it.

"I will never think of Dakota or this baby as a mistake," she finally gets out. "But I was trying to get our lives together here, make a new start, and the timing feels...not great. It's a pretty big speed bump, to put it mildly. I'd understand completely if you didn't want to be part of the ride."

"I can't believe you'd think I wouldn't want to be part of all of this," I say, tilting her chin up to look at me.

She's never looked more beautiful to me than she does right now, her watery eyes, red nose, and puffy lips tugging at my heart.

"It's so soon, and we haven't even told Dakota we're a couple yet, or—" She shakes her head as her voice tapers off.

I lean in and kiss her. Hard. When we finally come up for air, the words rush out of me. "Thank God you're not sick. My thoughts were going to the worst place. You scared me to fucking death, Little Rocket. Fuck. *A baby.* I can't believe it. I can't think of anything better, except that *I love you*, Marlow. Before ever hearing this news tonight or-or knowing whether you feel the same for me or not, I know without a doubt that I love you so goddamn much."

Her breath hitches and she takes a shuddery breath.

"I love you too," she whispers.

"And if a baby managed to be conceived through all the obstacles we've put in its way, it's a fucking fighter and meant to be...to hell with the timing."

Two ladies walk in and pause when they see us sitting here.

"We've gotta tell Dakota before I can start announcing it to everyone, including these strangers, right?" I double-check with Marlow before broadcasting the news.

"Yes, please," she says, laughing.

"Sorry, I'll be leaving now," I tell the women, standing up, and they laugh nervously, holding onto each other's arms like I might harm them.

I look at Marlow. "Do you need a little more time in here?"

She stands up and takes my hand. "I think I'm ready... for anything," she adds.

We walk out of the restroom and I hug her once we're in the hall.

"So you haven't been feeling great?" I ask.

She shakes her head. "Mostly just exhausted, but tonight, I think the nerves got me...and something I smelled on one of the plates being carried to another table."

I wince and then am grinning in the next second. "This is gonna be so fun. I mean, sorry"—I put my hand on my forehead—"not you getting sick or any of that, but...everything else."

"I didn't know you wanted a baby so bad," she says.

"I didn't. Not until you said you were pregnant. And then the way you looked so guilty—I thought you must've lied to me about not being with Cash...but that didn't really deter me." I shrug slightly, lowering my head and taking her hand in mine. "I already wanted to help you raise Dakota before I knew about this baby," I say quietly.

She puts her hand over her mouth and starts sobbing again.

"I might be an emotional mess for the duration of this pregnancy." Her breath hiccups, and she wraps her arms around my waist, laying her head on my chest. "Especially if you're going to say the most incredible things like that."

I hold her tight and eventually she leans back and looks up at me.

"I'm sorry I ever doubted that you would be anything less than the amazing man you are," she says.

"I'm far from perfect, but I love you, and I want us to build a life...together. I should have been saying how I felt before now, so there was never any doubt in your mind. I'll do better."

She laughs. "You can't possibly do any better, Wyatt Landmark."

"Watch me," I whisper against her lips, kissing her until she sways into me like I'm her anchor.

CHAPTER FORTY-FIVE

SLOGANS TO LIVE BY

MARLOW

Logan and Dakota aren't at the table when we walk into the restaurant.

"They're outside." Wyatt points them out, and they look so cute, Logan holding Dakota so she can see better.

I wish Logan lived close or even that he would just visit more often, but I know better than to expect anything—he's a wanderer through and through. It used to bother me, how okay he seemed to leave me behind, but being in Landmark and building a community of my own, I understand my brother a little better. He's most at home on the water, doing what he loves, and he always makes time for us when he's on land for any length of time.

Before we reach them, I grab Wyatt's arm.

"Are you okay if we tell Dakota about us tonight? Not the baby yet, but about us," I say quietly.

He puts his hand over mine and lifts his head to the sky. "Thank *God*," he whispers. And then louder, "*Yes*."

When he looks at me, his eyes are dancing. His face is radiant despite the only light being the lamps flickering around the deck and the lights of Landmark Mountain below us.

"I didn't know how much longer I could attempt to keep my hands to myself," he says.

I laugh. "You haven't really done that at all."

He pretends to be outraged. "Have too! We hardly ever hold hands. I have to resort to friendly shoulder pats or an occasional lower back cop-a-feel."

We're both laughing now and he puts his arms around me, hugging me against him.

"You told me you loved me tonight," he says softly. "*And* that you're having my baby," he croons in my ear. "The urge to be all over you is strong."

I shiver and he holds me closer, rubbing my arms.

"Cold?"

I shake my head against him. "No, it's just what you do to me."

His chuckle is devious and I pull back, holding my hands up.

"Cool it with the BDE," I practically pant with lust. "It's making me want to haul you back in that restroom and tell those women to take a hike."

"That's a perfect idea." His voice is hoarse as his hands span around my waist.

I love everything about the way he makes me feel.

He loves me. He wants to have this baby with me! I can hardly get over it.

I wish I hadn't wasted a single second panicking about this.

It's gonna be okay.

With Wyatt, everything will be okay.

"Mama, look!" Dakota calls.

I look over and she's waving at us.

"It's so beautiful," she says.

From the time she could first say it, she's always pronounced it *bootiful*, and I will be so sad when she corrects herself.

"Wow, it sure is," I say.

"Do you feel better?" she asks.

"So much better. Thank you, sweet girl," I tell her.

"Remember when I almost went potty in my pants and you picked me up and we ran so very fast?" She runs out of air, takes a deep breath, and keeps going. "And there was that yucky place with the—"she makes a disgusted face—"ewww-y floor, and you said—"

I open my mouth to interrupt because I'm not sure where this story is going.

"*Don't hold it so long next time*," she finishes. "That's what you said. Oh, and you said, 'When you put off the poop, you gotta scoot.'" She covers her mouth and giggles when Logan and Wyatt lose it.

"It's really good to know how well you listen." I nod, trying to keep it together. "I do remember that. You didn't want to go potty before we left the house, so we had to stop and go in that gross gas station."

She shudders again and I'm making an icked-out face right along with her.

"Let's not think about that place right now, okay?" I reach out and run my hand over her cheek.

Wyatt hasn't stopped laughing during this entire exchange.

"I feel like I'm out on the boat with the crew instead of outside this fancy restaurant, with all this potty talk going on," Logan says drily. "*When you put off the poop, you've gotta scoot.* That is valuable information right there. Such great slogans to live by, Low."

I roll my eyes at him but can't stop laughing.

"Can we put that on a T-shirt?" Wyatt wheezes out.

"Absolutely not." I jab him in the side and he yelps, ticklish, which strikes Dakota so funny. "Let's get out of here before someone complains about the disruptive potty talkers."

Dakota's eyes widen and she looks around. "Are we in trouble?"

"No, I was just kidding," I tell her, wiping the tears from my face from laughing so hard.

Goodness, my heart has gotten an emotional whiplash today.

She still looks worried, so I put my hand on hers and squeeze it.

"I promise we're not in trouble," I say.

My little tenderhearted girl. I want her to always stay like this, and it pains me to think of whatever hurts she's going to face. But if I've learned anything tonight, it's that the people we love can make everything better, just by loving us back.

"I love you so much, Kota." I lean over and kiss her cheek.

"Love you too, Mama."

"You want to walk back to the gondola or want me to keep carrying you?" Logan asks her.

"Carry me," she says, her head touching his.

"Can Wyatt and I tell you something before we go? Just in case you get sleepy on the ride down the mountain..."

"I'm not sleepy," she says, perking up.

"*Mm-hmm*," I say under my breath.

"What is it?" she asks. "Are we going on the alpine slide again?"

"Sure, yeah, we can do that again sometime," Wyatt says. "If it's okay with your mom..."

I grin up at him.

"You are so getting all the brownie points tonight," I say, as Logan coughs, "Brown-noser," into his fist at the same time.

"Yay," she cheers.

"I'll make this short and sweet since all of us are distracted." I laugh. "Wyatt is going to be spending a lot more time with us."

"Yayyy," she cheers louder.

"He's Mama's boyfriend," I add, and her little head bounces side to side.

"And what else?" she asks happily, clapping.

"Uh...that's it for now." My voice trails off, and I look up at Wyatt to see him grinning at Dakota.

I swoon a little.

Okay, a lot.

"I already knowed he was our boyfriend," she says.

"You did?" Wyatt laughs. His eyes meet mine for a second, all lit up. "How did you know?"

"Because you bring us flowers and our favorite treats,

and you call me Sweets and sometimes you call Mama Little Rocket..."

Wyatt nods thoughtfully. "Yep, that pretty much sums it up."

Logan chuckles. "Sounds like she's got your number, bro."

Wyatt laughs.

Dakota shivers against Logan and he tries to warm her up, as we start walking toward the gondola station.

"Brr," Dakota says. "Is this winter?"

"Oh, Sweets. We're only getting started. This is technically still fall, but around here the snow comes anyway. Snow is in the air. I can feel it."

"Really?" I stare at him, shocked. "Already?"

"Oh yeah. We're into November. Sometimes it's already snowed long before now."

"I love snow!" Dakota says. "Is it snowing tonight?"

"When were you around snow?" Logan asks.

"She hasn't been yet," I tell him, laughing. "She just already knows she loves it...my eternal optimist."

"It's nice to have one in the family," Logan says, chuckling.

The sound of our feet crunching the fallen leaves is the only noise for a minute or two.

And then Logan clears his throat. "Speaking of nice to have in the family," he says, all teasing aside now. "Thanks, man, for making my girls so happy."

It's too dark now to see Logan's expression, but I suspect the lack of visibility is what's given him more nerve to say this. He doesn't usually talk like this with people he barely knows, and I'm grateful for the effort he's making. And not that I needed it, but it validates my feelings for Wyatt and his for me, knowing that my brother was able to see it in so little time.

"I've heard nothing but amazing things about you from both Marlow and Dakota," he continues, "and from what I can tell, you actually deliver."

We get to the gondola station and are able to walk right onto the gondola, the sudden light shockingly bright.

"That means a lot to me," Wyatt says gruffly.

His face is so earnest, it makes me love him even more.

"I love them," he tells Logan. "And I promise you, I'm going to do right by them."

"See that you do," Logan says, but his words are softened by his huge smile.

CHAPTER FORTY-SIX

HEART COLLISION

WYATT

Dakota's asleep by the time we get to the condo, her head lolling and arms limp over Logan's shoulders.

He puts her in bed and whispers that he's heading out for a while, and Marlow and I tuck her in. Her eyes open when I bend down to kiss her forehead.

"Will you be here in the morning?" Her little voice is already groggy from sleep.

I look over at Marlow and she nods, her cheeks lifting

with her smile. The difference in her from the past few days —and even just a little earlier this evening—till now is *night and day*.

She looks so happy.

It kills me to think how worried she was about my reaction to her pregnancy.

"Yes, I will," I tell Dakota. "Sleep well, and I'll see you when you get up."

Dakota's eyes close, but she's still smiling, and I shake my head, glancing at Marlow.

"She could ask me to do *anything* for her right now, and I would do it," I whisper.

Marlow giggles and squeezes my arm as she puts her head on my shoulder. "She's got you so wrapped," she says.

"Guilty."

"And I freaking *love* it."

I poke her in the side where she got me earlier, and she puts her hand over her mouth when she yelps. She points at Dakota, eyes wide, and then points at me, trying to ward me off.

And then she turns and takes off down the hall to her room, and I'm on her heels, tickling her when she's within reach. I close her bedroom door behind us and turn her to face me, and she's red from holding in her laughter.

"Do you have any slogans for letting out your laughter?" I tease.

"Shut it," she says, laughing. "Just wait until our kids throw all your crazy words back at you." She gasps slightly, and her eyes widen. "I mean, I'm not trying to assume that we'll—"

"Marlow?" I pull her waist toward me and she lands against me with a thump.

"Yes?"

"I want all of this with you. All of it," I repeat. "I'm going to spell it out so you're clear and can assume your little heart out."

She flushes, but she's completely engrossed in what I'm saying.

"Tell me if I'm scaring you off, and I'll slow down, but here's what I'm thinking. You ready?"

She nods.

"Okay, I see you, me, Dakota, our baby…" I lift a shoulder. "Maybe another couple of kids if we're able—we can see how we're feeling as we go," I add when she laughs. "I finally take *all* my vacation time every year because I want all the moments I can get with you and our family. And we spend the rest of our lives riling each other up and cooling each other down. We wake up tired but happy and ready for a new adventure. Even the same-old, same-old feels like an adventure because we love what we do and we love being together."

Her eyes well with tears and I lean down to kiss her before I keep going.

"After dinner, we take a walk or go swim in our pool…or Theo's lake, and after the kids' baths, we read books to them until they're sleepy. We dance in the kitchen after they're tucked in, and we make love wherever we can get away with not waking up the whole house. I fall asleep thinking about how pretty you are and how lucky I am to be loved by you, and when we wake up the next morning, we get to do it all over again."

Tears spill on her cheeks and she sighs, her hair brushing against my hand.

"You really envision a life with me like that?" she whispers.

"I do. Before tonight, I had only dreamed about this

kind of life with you and Dakota, and to be clear, the two of you are all I ever need. But you've expanded the vision with this baby news. You've given me so much more to be excited about." I can't help but laugh softly even when her face crinkles in another sob. "I love you, Marlow."

Now that I've said it, I can't say it enough.

"I love you so much." She leans on her tiptoes and covers my face with kisses, and we're laughing and crying and so fucking over the moon.

"*PLEASE* DON'T EVER STAY AWAY from me so long again," I say against her neck, my pumps getting more urgent.

I'm bare inside her, and the sensations are otherworldly. I'm not going to last long.

She whimpers and pulls me down to kiss her as she falls apart. I inhale her cries, wincing through that fine line between torture and ecstasy. Her walls clamp around my dick so tight I can't breathe, and I fight to prolong this as long as possible.

"Ne-ver. A-gain." My thrusts emphasize my words, and her head thrashes from side to side.

If I thought I could get away with it, I'd enforce a no-night-apart rule, one that I'd gladly never break. But I just got her back, I'm not enforcing anything right now, but how much she needs me filling her up.

"Come with me," she cries.

Her hips buck as she gets another burst of energy and dammit, I can't fight it another second.

"*Fuck.*" The word thunders out of me, and in the back of my mind I hope it doesn't wake Dakota up. Logan went to The Gnarly Vine for a nightcap, so we're good there. But I can't even bring myself to care all that much if we're heard at this moment.

The rush is so euphoric, I feel suspended somewhere over my body.

The intensity of emotion and passion are almost more than I can take, and I bury my face in her neck, never wanting to come up for air.

When my senses return to me somewhat, I lean up, brushing her hair back. "Am I putting too much weight on you?" I ask.

"No." She smiles.

"How's the nausea?"

"I'm fine, really," she says. "Compared to earlier and the past few nights, I'm so much better."

"Have you been checked at the hospital at all?"

"No, but now that you know, I'll be more comfortable to do all that. It'd probably be best if we told your family before then though, the way the rumors might fly if word gets out."

I nod and slowly slide out of her. She gasps when I'm all the way out, and I miss her already.

"But you have no doubt?" I ask.

She shakes her head. "No doubt. I did three tests and they were all positive right away." She works her teeth over her bottom lip and I rub my thumb over both lips, wanting to inhale her.

"I ordered prenatal vitamins online so I wouldn't have to go back to Cecil's. That's what I was doing there the day I ran into you—buying tests."

I lean my forehead against hers. "I'm only going to say this tonight because I'm not holding any of this against you, I swear. As much as I wish you'd told me as soon as you suspected, I wish even more that I'd tried harder to get out of you what was going on."

I pull back and lean on my side to face her, my hand propped on my head. "I hated that sudden divide between us. It ate away at me, and I didn't know what I'd done or what I could do to bring you back to me. It felt hopeless."

My fingers trace her eyebrows and over her cheekbone, across those lips I can't resist. All of her so achingly beautiful.

Her eyes flutter shut and she opens them slowly, her lids heavy.

"Please don't shut me out, Marlow. I can take a lot, but that..." I shake my head.

She blinks and nods. "I won't," she says. "I promise."

"And if you start, I'll push for answers and get annoying until you talk to me," I add.

"Okay," she says. "But I'll try not to let it ever get to that point, all right? We'll both be open with one another and trust that we've got each other's backs?" Her face breaks and a tear drips down her cheek.

"Why does that make you cry? It feels like my goddamned chest is caving in when you cry," I admit.

"I'm sorry." She laughs and shakes her head, rolling her eyes. "Sofie warned me that the tears came flooding out of her when she got back here and felt all this...joy." Her voice cracks when she says *joy*, and she laughs harder. "Oh my goodness," she groans, and I love the way her Southern accent gets stronger when she's vulnerable. "I think pregnancy might already be having a heyday with my hormones too."

"Sorry, Little Rocket. I can't begin to know what all the pregnancy hormones must feel like. Are you sure these are happy tears?" My eyes sweep over her features, taking her in. And then it hits me. "Oh shit."

"What?"

"I've never even stopped to ask if you *want* this baby. Or if there was more than me finding out or your concerns about the timing making you so sad."

She exhales a long whoosh of air and takes a deep breath, her eyes serene when they meet mine again.

"Even in the middle of freaking out about all the things, I've only ever wanted this baby," she says, her hand sliding down my cheek.

Relief floods through me, but I kiss her palm, waiting for the rest.

"The thought of being in a relationship with someone who has my back—it's all I've ever wanted. It's why I pulled up roots and moved here to be near Sofie. She's the only one who's ever had my back. And feeling your support about this...about everything...it makes me feel like I can do *anything*. Be exactly who I've always wanted to be."

Her voice breaks again and she puts her fist near her nose. She turns to face me, and clasps my hands in hers.

"I hope my saying that doesn't make you feel pressured to stay with me if you change your mind about all this," she whispers.

My head falls back and I laugh, putting my hands on her back and hugging her body against mine.

"Just try to get rid of me, Little Rocket. Now that I know where we stand, nothing's changing my mind."

CHAPTER FORTY-SEVEN

BAE

MARLOW

I wake up to Wyatt's face between my legs, and me already on the cusp of an orgasm.

I whisper his name, my eyes barely able to focus on him, with the things he's doing with his tongue and fingers.

Sunlight is streaming through the shades and I put my pillow over my face and moan into it as the waves hit me hard. Even in my fog, I hear the sound of feet pitter-pattering down the hall, and I throw the pillow off of me and pull Wyatt's hair.

He looks up at me, stunned, and grinning, his lips shiny.

I bend down and pick up his shirt and hurriedly put it on, tossing his briefs to him.

"Dakota's up," I whisper-shout.

"Oh. *Ohhh.* Shit." He stands up and stumbles, trying to get his briefs on.

Sadly, I eye his hard length bobbing against his stomach as he covers it up.

"How'd you hear that?" he whispers. "You were supposed to be in the great beyond."

I snort. "It's this weird phenomenon moms get called *eagle ears*. Maybe you'll acquire it too. We'll see. Turns out I can experience the great beyond *and* hear my child—"

The door flings open, and Dakota lifts both arms wide.

"Wyatt," she cheers. "You *are* here just like you said!"

My heart tumbles over itself as she excitedly climbs on top of the bed and pats his face in wonder.

I know the feeling, baby girl, I still can't quite get over the fact that he means what he says either.

"Mornin', Sweets. How are you on this fine morning?" He pats the covers down and she plops down right between us, looking as content as I've ever seen her.

"Good," she says, smiling at me. "Mama, does this mean Wyatt can come to *all* the Donuts for Dads at school?"

I glance at Wyatt, who swallows hard and looks somewhat pained. My eyes narrow.

"Are you holding your breath?" I ask incredulously as his eyes start to bug out and his skin turns red. I sit up and jostle his shoulder. Dakota does it with me. "What are you doing? *Breathe!*"

He looks at me and shakes his head and then takes a huge gasp of air.

This is it, I think. *Here comes the panic.*

"Hell to the yes, I want to be at all the Donuts for Dads," the words shoot out of him.

Dakota's so taken aback she doesn't even cash in on the curse jar loot she could be scoring.

"The only reason I'd miss is if you were sick or I was sick or the bayyyy...belua...bay..." He looks at me for help, but I've got nothing. "Babelicious, you know, uh, your babelicious mom, or uh, if anyone else around here was sick...whoever."

Talk about a little rocket, those words are zipping and zapping right out of his mouth.

Loudly.

"And even if your dad comes to Donuts for Dads too, I'll still be there if you want me." He doesn't take a long enough breath before he continues, so it's raspy and like a deflating balloon. "And I want to live in the same house as you guys and be there when you wake up and when you fall asleep... sometimes I might have to work, but most of the time, I should—" Another heaving breath. "We'll figure it out and I want to mar—uh, your mom and I...I want to—"

Dakota turns to stare at me, and we have a silent conversation with our eyes.

What is happening right now—is he okay?

I don't know, baby girl.

And I turn my attention back to Wyatt and the same thing happens.

Stop me. Save me from myself, his eyes are saying.

And all I've got back is: *Damn, all that truth last night was like a gateway drug, diving into deep uncharted territory. We were bound to feel the effects.*

Hysteria is in the air.

I'm going to either laugh or cry, but it's going to be extreme either way.

What comes out of me is a snorty cry, but Wyatt's the one who clamps his hand over his mouth. He says something under his fist that we can't hear, hops up, and rushes to the bathroom, croaking out, "I cannot keep secrets!"

Dakota's mouth falls open and her eyes are round. "Wyatt gots thecreth?

I try to tamp down the laugh welling up, hearing the lisp and baby talk coming back out in full form.

"*Mama*," she says. "We should not laugh at him." She looks back toward the bathroom and leans closer to me. "Should we check on him?"

"Let's give him a minute," I tell her.

She keeps shooting concerned glances toward the bathroom. "I'm really glad he's coming to Donuts for Dad, unless *thicknetheth*."

Hearing her say *sicknesses* with that thick lisp, I can't keep it in another second. She's been talking so grown up lately, I've missed hearing that lisp so much. I laugh until I cry, my head falling back against the headboard. I wipe my face, trying to catch my breath.

"We'll just have to stay healthy then, won't we?" I say through my laughing tears.

"Do you think he'll be able to go to Grinny's?" Dakota whispers.

"Yes, I think he'll be just fine, my love. Why don't you go peek in there and see if Uncle Logan is awake? Don't wake him up, but check it out..."

She nods, happy to be on a mission, and skirts down the hall.

I knock on the bathroom door and hear a muffled, "Come in."

When I crack open the door, he's sitting on the edge of the tub, elbows on his knees. I ogle his naked chest, his long, tapered fingers resting on his thick, muscled thighs. He glances up sheepishly, and the tips of his ears turn red.

It makes me smile.

"You all right, BDE?"

He runs his hands through his hair and it goes every which way, underlining how out of sorts he is.

"I—" He leaves it hanging for a while and shakes his head. "I don't know what happened to me in there." He makes a sound with his mouth, diving his hand from up high to smack into his other hand like a big explosion.

I press my lips together. "It wasn't that bad," I say.

His head still lowered, his eyes lift to mine for a brief second. "Even Dakota looked at me like I'd lost my mind."

"I think the shock of everything may have caught up with you."

He snorts.

"And you're not used to getting interrupted in the heat of passion and having to think fast when all the blood has rushed to your dick."

His eyebrows lift, but he doesn't deny it.

"I have an idea."

He holds his hand out and drops it. "I'm all ears."

"I'll ask Logan to watch Dakota and we can go to the hospital."

His eyes meet mine again, the concern there now.

"I'm feeling fine. But I'd say the chances are high that you'll never last at Grinny's later. Our news and whatever else you're feeling, *bayyyybelicious*, just might fly right out of your mouth." I start laughing and he doesn't, but one side of his lips twitches. "So, how about you do my lab work or whatever will give us a ballpark idea of how far along I am, since that's what everyone will ask, and we'll tell them at Grinny's later?"

His head tilts as he looks up. "You don't know the first day of your last period?"

"Uh...no."

"We can get a tracker app for your phone. It's good information to have."

"Okay, good doctor."

"You still wouldn't be through your first trimester..."

"No, but—"

He shakes his head, rubbing his hand over his jaw. "I'll get my act together. I'm a fucking doctor. I keep a stoic face all the time. I can do this."

I laugh again and make a face when he scowls at me.

"Here's the thing." I hold up my hand when he starts to argue with me. "If something awful were to happen, I'd want your family to know about it anyway, so we could acknowledge that this baby was important to us, no matter what...you know?"

His Adam's apple bobs as he swallows and nods. "Yeah, I get that," he says softly.

"Okay. Think you can do all the things, Dr. McGorg?"

"Put me to work, Little Rocket. I'm sorry I lost my shit earlier."

"It was...*something*." I whistle. "But it only made me love you more," I add. "Aw, there it is." I point at his smile. "Took that long enough to show up. Geez."

"Why are you all fine this morning and I'm the one who's a mess?"

I shrug. "I was a mess for too many consecutive days and got it out last night, and I woke up this morning to the great beyond." I walk over to him and place his hands on my hips, leaning down to kiss him on the nose.

"Mmm, that was good."

"*So* good. Think you're okay to go out there or do I need to get them out of the house before you come out?" I ask.

"I...don't know," he admits.

"Okay, I'll see what I can do. But if they don't leave for some reason and you feel the gab pouring out of your mouth faster than you can contain it, count to ten and just smile." I snap my fingers. "Or, I know—give me a look and I'll kiss you."

"You're having way too much fun with this."

CHAPTER FORTY-EIGHT

PUT IT ON THE LIST

WYATT

Everything in me calms when we're at the hospital and I'm back in my element doing what I know.

Of course, the fact that the patient is the love of my life and she's having my baby carries a weight that isn't exactly familiar, but I'm thorough and unflappable.

The complete opposite of the shit show I was at Marlow's.

I've never been great at keeping secrets.

The family stopped telling me what they'd bought for everyone else as Christmas gifts because even when I got better about keeping it to myself, if anyone tried to trick or coax the answers out of me, I was toast.

I thought I'd gotten past that, but apparently fucking not.

"I cannot *believe* I didn't even feel the poke," Marlow says a second time. She pulls off the cotton swab and tape and marvels that there's no sign of the needle. "Can you always do my blood work?"

"If you want me to, absolutely. I'd rather be the one to do it than let anyone else touch you. Rumor has it I'm the best doctor in the hospital."

"There's that cocky doctor I remember so well," she says, laughing.

"I make sure I'm available to do it when any family members come through here," I tell her.

"Aw, that's sweet. Yes, please. I want you to do mine." She lays back and watches as I prepare everything for her ultrasound.

Fortunately, it's quiet around here and Emma didn't ask any questions when I told her I needed to run a few tests on Marlow. Even though we're doing things backwards, I make sure we have her insurance on file and fill out the necessary paperwork to dot the I's and cross the T's. Waiting to do an ultrasound when she's farther along would be better to see more, but if it puts our minds at ease, we'll do as many ultrasounds as necessary. I think we'd both be more comfortable knowing how far along she is.

Once everything is ready, I reach over and brush her hair back, suddenly nervous. "Depending on how far along you are, we might not see much today. We'd see more if we did a transvaginal ultrasound, but I'd rather not do that just yet. Just...try not to worry if we don't see much."

She nods, her fingers twisting. "I'll try."

I put on a new pair of gloves and smile at her. "This shouldn't be too cold," I say as I put the warm gel on her stomach and then press the transducer over her skin.

I've rarely done ultrasounds, so it takes me a little longer, but I pause and grin, as I measure the diameter of the sac. My hands shake slightly as I stare in wonder at the screen.

Oh my God, I'm going to be a father.

I clear my throat. "Wow. All of this feels different knowing it's ours."

I exhale and look over at Marlow through blurred eyes. I think hers might be the same way. I take another deep breath and turn back to the screen.

"This is the yolk sac and it's about ten millimeters. Based on everything I'm seeing here, I'd say you're around six weeks."

"Six weeks," she whispers. "So...would that be..."

"A summer baby."

We share a grin before looking back at the screen.

"I'm only seeing one sac, so no twins for us this time."

She laughs. "I can't imagine two at once, so that's probably good."

I make several scans and then point at the screen. "It's too soon to see, but this is the first stage of the embryo. In a couple weeks, we can try to listen for the heartbeat...if I can wait that long." I laugh.

"Does everything seem...okay?" she asks.

"Yes. So far, Baby Sweet Pea is looking good."

"Baby Sweet Pea, huh?" She grins.

"Would you rather have a different name?"

"Baby Sweet Pea is good. It's a nice gender-neutral term of endearment. I approve." She exhales and stares up at me. "This is really happening, isn't it?"

I set the wand aside and clean the gel off of her stomach, leaning down to kiss her while I'm at it.

"It really is," I whisper, getting lost in her eyes.

I take off my gloves and kiss her again, stopping before I try to have my way with her on this table.

She takes my outstretched hand and sits up, looking dazed.

"You feeling all right?" I ask.

"I feel...incredible," she says. "And really stupid for waiting to tell you. Are you okay? Do you feel better now?"

I take a deep breath and let it out slowly. "So much better, and listen, I'll be okay at Grinny's. I'll literally run out of the house and put some miles in if I lose it like I did earlier."

She laughs and stands up, putting her hands on my chest. "And let us all miss out on one of your panic rambles? Not a chance."

I make a face at her. "That was a one-off."

"Oh, okay," she teases.

"I'm serious. If you decide you're not ready to tell them yet, we can wait. Thanksgiving is coming up and maybe we'll have heard the heartbeat by then."

"I'd like to tell them today. I loved telling Dakota about us. It feels wrong to keep secrets from her. It's been the two of us for so long, I don't want to do anything that makes her feel left out. I think we should tell her right before we tell your family."

"Okay. Would you like it to be just the two of you?"

Her thumb rubs against my stubble and she smiles.

"You're really sweet, you know that? No, let's do it together."

My heart does that free-fall thing it does when she looks at me like this.

I lean my forehead on hers. "Together. Okay, Marlow Walker."

WHEN WE GET BACK to the condo, Logan leaves to run an errand, saying he'll meet us at Grinny's.

Dakota's playing with her Legos, and Marlow gives me the look before calling Dakota over to her. I walk to the couch and sit down and Marlow joins me, patting the space between us when Dakota runs over.

"What is it, Mama?" she asks as she sits on her knees facing us.

Marlow reaches out to tuck a curl out of Dakota's eyes. "I sure do love you, Kota," she says, her voice shaking slightly.

"I love you too."

"I love being your mama more than anything." She sniffles and I squeeze her shoulder. God, I love her and the way she loves this little girl.

"You're the best mama," Dakota says sweetly. "And you're the best Wyatt," she says, not wanting to leave me out.

I pick up her little hand and kiss it and smile when she giggles.

"Wyatt and I have some really exciting news to tell you," Marlow says.

"Oh, are we going on the alpine slide today?" she asks, eyes wide and excited.

"I didn't realize that alpine slide was such a hit." I laugh. "We've gotta get this girl back out there," I tell Marlow.

"I know it," she says, grinning at Dakota. "But today we're going to Grinny's, remember? And what we have to tell you can't wait another second."

Dakota claps her hands.

"It's going to be a while...lots of months, and my belly is going to grow and grow and grow..." Marlow laughs with how big Dakota's eyes get. "And *then*...you'll be a big sister!"

Dakota's mouth drops. "I will? Me?"

"Yes." Marlow nods. "We're having a baby!"

Dakota does a little dance and then she pauses midway through and looks at me, her brows furrowed.

"Does that mean Daddy's coming back?" she asks. Her backside rests on her feet like she's suddenly drained.

"Daddy?" Marlow echoes. "No, Cash—Daddy's not coming back. Maybe he will visit sometime? I'm not sure, but..."

"Samantha says that babies come from moms and dads, and I don't want Daddy...I-I want Wyatt to be with us..." She takes a deep breath and her face crumbles as she starts to cry.

Marlow and I look at each other, her expression as distraught as I feel.

"We're staying right here, and Wyatt is too," Marlow says, reaching out to hug Dakota to her.

"I'm not going anywhere," I tell her.

Marlow wipes Dakota's tears and smiles at her. "We're having a baby with Wyatt. He's the baby's daddy and he's going to be taking care of this baby with us..."

"He is?" Dakota sniffles.

"And taking care of you too," I add. "You and your mama. We'll all take care of each other."

"I like that," Dakota says, nodding, as she blinks back more tears. "I think...could we pretend you're my daddy too?"

Can my heart be ripped apart and bursting with love all at once?

I hold my arms out and Dakota moves into them as I hug her tight. My eyes meet Marlow's, my position precarious as I don't want to overstep, and yet, I have to make it clear to Dakota how important she is to me.

It's something Marlow and I will have to work through. I'd start the process to adopt her today if I thought Marlow and Dakota wanted that, but now's not the time to bring it up.

I say all I know to say.

"Sweets, I already love you like you're mine, and I will when that baby comes too. I'll be whatever you want me to be because I'm your Wyatt forever and ever. Okay?"

She leans back and pats my cheeks. "Okay," she says softly. "My Daddy Wyatt."

Whew. That gets me right in the gut. I swipe the tears from her face.

"Your Daddy Wyatt. I like that," I say hoarsely.

Marlow sniffles next to us.

Dakota grins at me, and her face suddenly brightens even more.

"Do you think she'll like Hermioneep?" she asks.

"I think she *or he* probably will." Marlow laughs, wiping the tears from her face too.

"He?" Dakota repeats. "It's a boy?"

"We don't know yet," I say.

She shakes her head. "No, it's not a boy. Can we name her Chester?"

Marlow and I try to hold back the laugh.

"Uh, Chester...well, we'll put it on the list and think about a bunch of names while we wait." Marlow's voice cracks at the end, still struggling not to laugh.

"Will she sleep with me in my bed?" Dakota asks.

"He or she will have their own bed," Marlow says. "But you might have to share rooms for a while..." Her voice trails off as she looks around.

It's time I talk to a contractor. I should've looked into it when I first started feeling this way about Marlow. Maybe Magnus could take on building a house now that the renovations on the resort are more under control. Or maybe he can recommend someone who could.

Time is going to fly between now and our baby coming.

Holy shit. I still can't get my head wrapped around the fact that I'm going to be a dad.

CHAPTER FORTY-NINE

PROGRESSION

MARLOW

"Get ready to have the entire Landmark family all up in your business for the next seven and a half months," Wyatt says before we walk into Grinny's house.

Dakota is bouncing on the tips of her toes, her excitement fully present now that she knows she's getting a baby and keeping Wyatt too. She broke my heart asking if she could pretend Wyatt is her daddy.

There are no signs of sadness in her now, and I can only

hope that the hurt she has about Cash dissipates the more she experiences Wyatt's love.

It's hard as a mom to know if the mistakes I've made will catch up to my daughter or if she'll be one who bounces back and defies all odds. I like to think she will. In a way, I've defied the odds after being raised by a narcissistic mother and not feeling loved.

Yes, I'm pregnant again and not married.

But if history were fully repeating itself, I'd take out my sadness on my little girl like my mom did. I'd try to live out my desires through Dakota without caring about what she wants, and I wouldn't be creating a full, meaningful life for myself and my daughter.

I smile up at Wyatt. "I can handle all the Landmark family love." I take his hand. "In fact, I'm counting on it."

His eyes are so full of love when he smiles at me. I don't know how I didn't see it sooner.

Logan walks up. "Hey, I was hoping I wasn't late."

"Right on time," Wyatt says. "Okay, here we go. I'll wait for your cue, Little Rocket, whether we're sharing our baby news today or not."

Dakota beams and bounces right through the door when Wyatt opens it. We walk back to the great room where everyone's gathered.

"Hey," Wyatt says. "For anyone who hasn't met Marlow's brother yet, this is Logan."

Logan reaches out to shake Callum and Sutton's hands and hugs Sofie hard when she rushes toward him.

"Just in time," Grinny says. "Grab a plate. We're just helping ourselves at the island. I didn't do much."

"Not much at all," Wyatt says, leaning over to kiss her cheek. "Just the biggest lasagna I've ever seen, two salads, and enough garlic bread to feed the town."

She laughs and swats his chest.

I walk over to hug Sofie and am about to whisper my news in her ear when Sutton yells, "Hey, Pappy! Glad you could make it!"

I glance at Grinny and she's frowning at Sutton and then Pappy like she's confused.

"Uh-oh," Sofie whispers. "Grinny doesn't look pleased."

"Well, hello there," Grinny says to Pappy.

Pappy's cheeks flush. "You seem surprised to see me. Did I get the day wrong? Sutton said you invited me over for dinner."

Sutton gives Grinny an innocent look.

"Of course! You are always welcome here," she says to Pappy and his shoulders relax a little. "I'm surprised you can still fit us in your schedule with how popular you've gotten around here," she teases, and Pappy flushes redder.

"I've always got time for this family," he says.

"Dakota, do you need to use the bathroom?" Sofie asks.

I look over and she's no longer bouncing, now Dakota is jumping up and down, eyes wide. My eyes narrow as she shakes her head.

"What's going on, babe? Can you stand still? Catch your breath," I say.

Wyatt chuckles as he watches her jump a few more times and then she stops and holds both hands in the air.

"We're having a baby," she yells at the top of her lungs. "My Wyatt and my mama and me!"

The whole room stops abruptly, chatter ceasing, and their eyes follow the same progression: They look at her, then me, then Wyatt, and then my stomach.

Sofie clutches my arm and I turn to her and smile as she gasps.

Dakota presses her hand over her mouth and nods fast.

Wyatt chuckles, holding out his hand to me. I take his hand and Sofie's and hold on tight to both of them.

"What she said," I say weakly.

Everyone starts talking at once. Sofie hugs me first and then everyone's surrounding us, hugging and congratulating us. My stomach gets patted a few times, and I remember how much I hated that when I was pregnant before. Strangers felt like they could just reach out and rub my belly, and my mom would tap it with her knuckles, saying how fat I'd gotten. But coming from this family who has done nothing but welcome me in, I love it so much. The joy and excitement over a new family member being brought into the world is infectious.

When the commotion slows down after a while, I wipe the happy tears from my face and feel like I can take the first full breath I've taken since I found out I was pregnant.

I won't be doing this alone.

"Let's let the poor girl eat," Grinny says, her hand on my elbow as she leads me straight to the food. "How have you been feeling?"

"Okay. I've had a few queasy times, but mostly a lot of anxiety at first. I was so nervous about telling Wyatt, but he's been...wonderful."

His eyes are shining as he smiles at me.

"Well, I couldn't be happier," Grinny says. "This is the best news."

"It's about time we have a baby around here," Sutton says. He puts his arm around Wyatt. "Have to say I'm surprised it's coming from you though. I thought Theo and Sofie would be the ones throwing out the birth control first."

"Yep. Same." Callum nods.

"I was actually counting on them too," Wyatt says, grinning at Theo. "But my swimmers *defied* protection." He puffs his chest out and then cracks up.

"Oh, we've got a virile one here," Pappy says, pounding Wyatt on the back.

That makes everyone laugh and the brothers take Wyatt's swimmers and run with that joke, getting louder and louder, while Scarlett and Sofie fill their plates next to me.

"I cannot believe you managed to keep this secret from me," Sofie says.

"Only because you were out of town and Logan was visiting...and I was rocking in the corner, panicking." I laugh and Sofie makes a face and leans her head on my shoulder.

"Don't do that again, the whole panic alone thing," Sofie says. "Need I remind you how fast I came running and got you here?"

"I will never ever forget the way you did that, Sof," I tell her. I shake my head and blink fast. "And you were right about all the tears too."

She laughs. "Just go with it. At least you're a pretty crier. I turn red all over and you just get prettier..."

I snort and Dakota squeezes between me and Sofie to point out the food she wants.

"I'm so happy for you, Dakota," Scarlett says. "You'll be the best big sister ever."

Dakota nods. "I'm gonna take her everywhere I go."

"Her..." Sofie says, grinning. "Are we thinking it's a girl?"

"Yes," Dakota says.

I laugh. "She's saying it is, and I really don't know yet."

"Well, I cannot wait to find out," Scarlett says. "And we can do such a fun party for you guys once we know. I can't wait to spoil it rotten."

"Wyatt's calling it Baby Sweet Pea," I say, looking back at him.

He's laughing so hard his face is red and his eyes are watery, and I'm blown away by how much I love him.

"Sweets and Baby Sweet Pea," Dakota says, giggling.

I grin at her. "Thanks for sharing our news, Kota. It was fun seeing how everyone reacted, wasn't it?"

"Yeah," she says happily. "I love it here, Mama."

"I do too. So much." I bump her with my hip when she tries to grab an olive with her fingers. "Hey, fingers out of the food. Did you wash your hands?"

Her eyes go wide and she turns and bolts to the sink.

Scarlett and I set our plates on the table and she smiles warmly at me then nods toward Wyatt. "I've never seen Wyatt this happy," she says. "Ever. You and Dakota did that, and I can't thank you enough." She leans in. "Plus, you're *cool*. I thought my brother was going to end up a lonely workaholic doctor, and practically overnight, you've domesticated him. He's not only head over heels for you, but he's *chill*. Look at him. His shoulders aren't up to here with all the tension." She lifts her hands up by her ears. "You let me know if you want any help planning a wedding and I'll be all over it."

"Oh, we're not talking about weddings yet at all."

I look back at Wyatt and imagine life married to him. For someone who thought she'd never want to be married again, the thought of marrying *him* sure is enticing.

"Mm-hmm," Scarlett says, smirking. "I give that approximately five seconds."

EPILOGUE

WYATT

Two Weeks Later...

I HAVEN'T BEEN able to sit still for the past hour. We're all at The Gnarly Vine waiting for Marlow and Dakota to arrive.

Because of what happened to me the last time I tried to

keep a secret, I asked Sofie to take Marlow and Dakota on a little girls' trip for the day while I got everything in order.

"You're making me so nervous," Theo says, putting his hand on my back. "Why don't you have a drink? Sit down for a minute, try to relax."

"I want to be levelheaded when they get here."

"You're the most levelheaded person I know. I think you'll be fine," he says.

"Let the man pace. Maybe it'll be out of his system by the time Marlow gets here," Sutton says.

"Doubt it," Callum says, smirking at me.

I sigh and look at my watch. "They should've been here by now."

"They will be—" Theo says as Scarlett yells, "They're pulling in!"

"I feel sick." I hold onto the bar.

Callum slides a glass of clear liquid down the bar toward me. "Drink it."

I pick it up and take a long drink, my nostrils burning. When I set it down, I look at Callum.

"Thanks."

He nods. "Go get her."

"All right."

When Marlow walks in holding Dakota's hand, the music starts playing "Isn't She Lovely" by Stevie Wonder. Marlow smiles, and I watch as her eyes search the room for me. Her brows furrow slightly when she realizes the only ones in the restaurant are Logan, my family, and a few close friends like April and Holly, and Blake and Camilla.

I step out so she can see me and her shoulders relax, her smile going even brighter.

"You look beautiful." I lean down and kiss her cheek.

"Thank you. So do you," she says, smiling. "Really beautiful."

"Thank you." I grin and glance down at Dakota. "And look at you. You look so pretty tonight."

Dakota sways back and forth bashfully. "Thank you," she says. "Is this a party?"

"It is."

"What for?" she whispers.

"To celebrate us becoming a family," I lean down to whisper in her ear.

She's beaming when I straighten.

I give Callum his cue to turn down the music, but he's on the phone and scowling. He says something to Sutton and then walks over.

"Sorry to bail," he says. "Pierre says his niece is stuck on my property and he's out of town this weekend. I gotta check it out."

"It's okay, man. Do what you need to do. Let us know if you need help." I grip his arm and we hug briefly. "Thanks for everything today. You made this happen."

"Happy for you," he says.

He winks at Dakota and grins at Marlow before he walks away.

Sutton mouths, "Ready?" and when I nod, he turns down the music.

I reach into my pocket and pull out a little white box, and I get down on one knee in front of Dakota. Marlow gasps and Dakota stares at me, surprised that I'm down on her level in a suit. I look at her as I open the box and her eyes widen as she sees the pretty ring.

"Is that for *me*?" she asks.

"It is, but I have a couple of questions for you first."

"Okay," she says softly.

"Sweets, will you be my Dakota forever?"

Her mouth parts and she nods, her eyes still huge. "Yes."

"And would you give me permission to marry your mama?" I lean in closer and whisper loudly, "*If* she says yes..."

"Yes, please," she says, and then she looks up at Marlow. "I hope you say yes."

Everyone laughs, including Marlow, although she's also sniffling and wiping the tears from her cheeks.

"I think she will," Dakota says, turning back to me matter-of-factly.

I grin and she starts bouncing with excitement when I take the ring out of the box and hold her hand up, sliding it on her finger.

"I very love it," Dakota breathes out. She turns her hand toward Marlow and shows her. "I very love it," she says louder, laughing.

Everyone laughs along with her. She's captured the hearts of everyone in this room, just like her mama.

I put the box in my pocket and get out the larger box.

Everyone says, "Oooooo."

When I face Marlow, she's radiant. Her cheeks are flushed, her eyes more green than hazel, and her lips a ruby red—when she cries, it's like her features go into hyperfocus and everything sharpens.

"What are you doing, Wyatt?" she asks.

I'd be nervous if she wasn't smiling.

"I know we're a whirlwind. We have been from the start. But you said something last night that made me think maybe you'd be okay with this," I tell her.

"I did?"

"You said that I make everything better and that you'd be happy anywhere as long as we're together…"

She nods, her breath hitching. "Yes," she whispers. "I meant that."

"And since Dakota gave me her permission," everyone laughs again, "and because I have been in love with you from the first time you argued with me," more laughs, "it can be tonight or a year from now, but I hope you'll become my wife. Please, will you marry me?"

Her smile is shaky as she says, "Yes."

I slide the ring on her finger and she doesn't even glance at it as she pulls me to my feet.

"Yes?" I echo.

"*Yes.*"

"Yayyyy," Dakota yells.

Everyone cheers, and I put my hands on Marlow's waist and claim her mouth. I don't kiss her nearly as long as I want to, because as soon as our lips connect, it's explosive. Every part of me aches for her, and for a moment, I regret inviting the whole family here to witness this.

"I didn't think this part through," I say against her lips. "How soon do you think we can get out of here?"

"It's a party," she says, laughing. "I think we have to at least dance."

"Instead of a dance, why don't you follow me?"

"Uh, I don't think we can sneak away to have sex," she whispers.

"Damn. Okay." I laugh and give her the quickest kiss.

Still makes me want to bolt with her, find a quiet place, and show her how much I love her.

That'll have to wait.

"Everyone outside," I yell, and there's a loud cheer as I lead the way out the side door.

In the back of The Gnarly Vine, Jack agreed to my plan, as long as I paid for all the heaters. There are pillows and blankets spread out over the wood pallets we brought out and just enough light so we can see where we're going. There's snow on the ground, but the heaters are doing their job.

"How about that one?" I point to the blankets lined with daisies and lanterns.

"It's so pretty. I can't believe you did all this," she says, her voice cracking. "I love daisies." She laughs. "Especially with snow everywhere."

We sit on the cushions, and I bring the blankets over us. "Are you warm enough?"

"Yes, those heaters are amazing. What are we doing?" She glances around and sees Scarlett and Jamison lying next to us on the pallet a few feet over.

Sofie and Theo are on the other side of us. Owen and Dakota are laughing with Grinny on their own cushions.

The projector starts and *The Notebook* starts playing on the screen.

"No way," Marlow says.

"I heard you love drive-ins, but I couldn't open one on such short notice, so this will have to do."

She pulls me in for a long kiss and Sutton calls out, "No kissing in the front."

I wave him off and keep kissing her.

"Did you really propose to me tonight?" she asks a few minutes later. "After only knowing me for a few months?"

"I did. If I could do it over again, I'd ask you the night we met."

She laughs and kisses me again. "You are rewriting history. You weren't even close to this lovesick the night we met."

"Can we get married tomorrow?"

"No." She giggles. "But I'll think about it," she adds. "You are something else, Wyatt Landmark."

"Something you want to spend the rest of your life with?" I ask.

"Yes, *please.*"

WOULD *you like more of Wyatt and Marlow?*
https://dl.bookfunnel.com/a3nzm4nsoh!

NEED MORE of the lovable grump, Callum? He's about to get knocked sideways by Ruby in Falling:
https://geni.us/FallingLM!

FIND OUT WHAT'S NEXT

Linktree @willowaster
Newsletter http://willowaster.com/newsletter

All your fun Landmark Mountain merch can be found here: https://willow-aster-store.creator-spring.com/

ACKNOWLEDGMENTS

Thank you to all of you who helped get *Irresistible* out into the world!

The common thread here will be gratitude and love, so get ready.

Nate, Greyley & Kira, and Indigo, I love you so much. Your love and encouragement, all the meals and movies and fun —I live for our time together. Kess, this goes for you too. We don't have to know what to call each other for me to claim you as one of mine now too. :)

Greyley, Kira, and Kess, thank you for all the artwork you're contributing to this series. With each book, I love seeing the way you're bringing Landmark Mountain to life more and more. (If you're reading this and haven't seen my shop, it's worth checking out!)

Laura, there are not enough words. I just love you so much and am grateful every single day for you. Catherine, your love and steady encouragement are so special to me. I love you and I love our love chain.

Christine, thanks for the love, the support, and the cheering me on always. I love you!

Natalie, thanks for saving me this year! I've loved every second with you. I love you!

Nina, you belong at the top of the list and right in the center of it all too! I'm so grateful for you! I love your guts. Thanks for making my books better and for ALL you do for me!

To the entire VPR team, I am so grateful for all of you. Kim, Sarah, Christine, Meagan, Amy, Valentine, Charlie! ALL OF YOU! :) I love you guys so much! And an especially huge thanks to Meags for all the input with this book!

Emily, I am CRAZY about you and your covers are awesome too.

For those who encourage me in my daily life with so much love and support: Troi, Christine Maree, Tosha, Courtney, Claire, Tarryn, Terrijo, Kalie, Savita, and so many more... Erin, thank you for the sprints and encouragement!

The family and friends I haven't mentioned specifically, I'm still so grateful for all of you. Dad, I love you. I hope you're not still reading my books, but if you are, I love you so very much. :)

To anyone who has read my books, reviewed, shared, sent me messages, or had me on your IG lives and podcasts—THANK YOU SO MUCH!

ALSO BY WILLOW ASTER

Ruin

Pride

The End of Men Series with Tarryn Fisher

Folsom

Jackal

The G.D. Taylors Series with Laura Pavlov

Wanted Wed or Alive

The Bold and the Bullheaded

Another Motherfaker

Don't Cry Over Spilled MILF

Friends with Benefactors

FOLLOW ME